I0610993

# The Angels' Share
## By

## S.G.Norris

Copyright © 2020 S.G.Norris

ISBN 978-1-5272-7571-3

The moral rights of the author have been asserted.

All rights reserved. No part of this publication may be reproduced, distributed, or transmitted in any form or by any means, including photocopying, recording, or other electronic or mechanical methods, without the prior written permission of the publisher, except in the case of brief quotations embodied in critical reviews and certain other non-commercial uses permitted by copyright law. For permission requests, write to the publisher, addressed "Attention: Permissions Coordinator," at the email address below.

Cover designed by Bookstyle using source imagery by David Mark, Tracy Angus-Hammond and Bishnu Sarangi all from Pixabay Image


All enquiries to sgnorris@hotmail.co.uk

Revealing the past may be the only way to
see the future

**For Di, 1965 – 2017**

# CHAPTER 1

∞ § ∞

Standing outside my father's house, I question why I feel like the bad penny returning home. A fraud who returns only when circumstances are such that I can no longer avoid returning. Today, though, isn't about me, so it is of no consequence what I think or feel.

It's five years since I stood in this spot. Equally afraid, equally sad that it has never been home to me. I arrive with the wind, blown off course from my flimsy excuse for a life.

Death has issued its summons and for once I cannot pretend it's too hard or too far. I've always been good at excuses when it comes to family, especially since I've modelled myself on the nomadic approach to existence. Wherever I pitch my tent is home. There's always been sufficient distance to make an argument for staying away. But now I am back in England, sort of where I come from. But I've only lived here for a few student years and was actually born in a field hospital in pre-modern Singapore. So the question of where is home is better answered with where I am on that particular day of the week.

My late father's bungalow sits at the end of a quiet street. Much smaller than any of the family houses we occupied on our travels but the electric buzzer and heavy automatic gate suggest that Dad was still conscious of security in his older days. Another legacy of our past.

Funerals. I can't bear them and I'm late, which is a source of further stress. I lean against the wall across the road, not ready to take the plunge into recollections and retribution swimming like waves of nausea. We were never that functional as a family. It's not regret or the sense that I missed something but I always feel a sour taste when anyone asks what led me to where I am now. Rarely do I spend time reflecting as I can't explain much of it to myself, never mind anyone else.

I find one reminder useful to force me to live in the now. I think of it as my moment of truth. Like everyone, life is littered with hundreds, maybe thousands of moments where a decision is needed, a signpost for a new direction. Some people bookmark these, like the time they got engaged or even divorced. Mine was completely different, probably the time I took my first flight after university to Ghana to work on an aid project as a volunteer. That was my present and my future, there and then, marked like the large bend in the lifeline in the palm of my hand. A moment of truth.

But then my nomadic life was only a progression from our family life on the road as kids. Dad dragged his family from one expatriate assignment to the next. The life of a tobacco executive with a past that held far more dubious questions than answers. Inevitable perhaps that when the future was offered as a selection of choices, I might not make the easy one.

Coming out of university, back in London for the most substantial time I ever spent in the UK. I missed the excitement and drama of being something different, especially the last few years at school in Nairobi. London, well England, felt like the Nanny's apprentice, all strict and proper, where as I was on the road with a rock band, discovering new and interesting ways to expand my world, play to new crowds and to grow pretension like a second head. I am still knocking out those same old tunes. Metaphorically, I am banging out 'We are the World' to my legions of fans and everyone else looks at me as the girl who went somewhere and is from somewhere and no-one really cares. As soon as I open my mouth and name a place or a person or a country, the message drops like a stone on the old fashioned weighing scales. It doesn't take long for people to see the scales tip towards arse. Heads turn and the only person I'm left to impress is myself.

Africa is my penance and my salvation. If both can be true at the same time. It's easy to see now, I have always been keen to remove the cloak of privilege and walk the same streets as those on the other side of the house gates. I don't bear it like a cross, though Dad always told me that's what it was, in his puritanical way. I felt and still feel, life has to be lived in a different way if you want to make a difference. You can't fix problems with the white gloves of compassion. It limits discovery and creates charity. Charity is the presumption of failure, that the unfortunates didn't follow the same rules and therefore whilst we offer our tears, it's never our fault. Whilst I can claim to have slipped off those gloves, my privilege still gives me a plane ticket home, just like now.

Talking of charity, there's someone at the funeral who doesn't need much of it. There is a large bright blue Range Rover parked in the street. Really ostentatious one with large wheels, blacked out windows, gleaming bright. Didn't think Dad had such showy friends.

I still haven't ventured from the wall opposite. The funeral was earlier but my flight wasn't back in time. I told them to hold the service without me as it would have meant delays for other people. I didn't protest, even as the eldest daughter, I don't feel like the most important guest. There was nothing I could do to get back earlier with the mess of flights, I just hope not to have upset anyone. Dad wouldn't have minded. He would have seen the funny side.

Not that I am expecting any great excitement.  Though I am intrigued about the man coming out of the house.  Probably similar age to my dad in a decent cut black suit. Tall and slim, well kept. He walks to the Range Rover surveying the street around him. He doesn't seem to notice me. An equally smart man appears from the driver's side and opens the rear door. A chauffeur. Really. Completely missed that. First action when I go inside will be to ask after him.

The car drives off and I get up to cross the road. Time to face the music. At the same time I see a familiar face coming down the steps to the gate.

'Pearl, you're here.'

I smile weakly and stand to hug my sister. I feel her arms tight around me in a welcome that feels genuine and warm. I am relieved when she lets go but feel a little guilty that I'm not as pleased to see her. I don't know. The vacuum has started up and now it's going to suck me in.

'How are you?' I ask.

'Oh I'm ok, better now you are here. There's so much to do. I just need to pop to the shops and get some milk. The cups of tea are totting up. Go inside, everyone's there.'

'Who was the guy in the Range Rover,' I ask?

'Someone Dad used to work with apparently. Says he remembers us from being kids.'

'Oh really,' didn't seem familiar to me but then probably he wouldn't.

'He was asking after you. Said he had hoped to catch you. Bit cryptic, said something about matters needing attention and that he would be in touch. Right posh accent, you know like some butler out of Downton Abbey, that type.'

I shrug my shoulders and Ruby heads off down the street to the shop. I am curious about Range Rover guy but assume if he wants something he will track me down.

With the gate open, I walk up to the door and knock lightly, hoping I can sneak in without anyone noticing.

Sadly my plan fails, as the door creaks loudly and heads turn. I enter a large open plan kitchen and lounge with a room full of people all watching me.

'Pearl.' I hear my name shouted in unison.

The first to come to me is my brother-in-law Jake. 'So good to see you,' he says, grabbing my arm and my bag. 'Ruby, has just popped out. You just missed her.' He's taller than I remember, seeming to be frequently dipping his head to converse with anyone around him. His hair has thinned. Ruby has a thing for tall men, yet it is comical with her five foot nothing. But Jake is a good guy, clumsy but harmless, constantly apologising for being in the way.

My three Aunts are sat round the kitchen table, like a panel of judges passing judgement on the events. My cousin, Rebecca, stands up and lets me take her seat by my Aunt Doreen.

'Hi Pearl, look at you. Love the bright red hair. That African sun does you no harm by the look of your rosy cheeks.'

Unfortunately a consequence of Irish blood is that I don't tan, mostly burn. Bit of a challenge in a hot country. The red hair is the easiest way to hide the creeping grey.

'And a dress. Don't you look smart?'

I ignore the jibe, feeling self-conscious enough. Haven't worn a dress since...since some fancy corporate event I went to years ago. My usual uniform is cargo pants and a strapless top. Practical and comfy, my middle name. I had to buy this black dress whilst I was transferring in Dubai. Not something I had in my wardrobe.

We hug briefly and politely before I take her seat. This hug is brisk with no warmth and welcome. I'm glad to see her ex, Andy hasn't made a return. That would have been awkward given that I am mostly the reason he is an ex. One previous trip home had seen me enjoy an unfortunate moment with him. Sadly Andy fessed up stupidly in an argument and that was that. She didn't blame me apparently. Another example of me laying family cohesion to waste.

I can hear mother still cursing from the grave. The way she would turn her head so fast in judgement was a sight to see, her Irish maternal origins obvious. A split second glance intended to put the recipient in the confessional for the rest of their days and in mother's case, it was mostly me.

I see the family photo above the fireplace. Last time we were probably a family. Not long after we came back to the UK in the nineties. Mum and Dad, looking content, myself and Ruby looking like we are bored of the process, allowing our long youthful hair to cover much of our faces. And then there is Walter, looking boyish, smiling widely. He died five years ago in a tragic accident and his absence haunted us ever since. Especially mother, she never really recovered from Walter's passing.

At least with her illness, she was less harsh on Dad. Not that he ever bothered. It was water off a duck's back to him. There was many a time, when he was younger, when an exchange between them involved raised voices but eventually he learnt to just ignore her. He gave up and sought a peaceful life in his own circle. Mother was food and conscience, life was something he found elsewhere. She passed away a year after Walter. Misery lining up victims.

I wish I knew more about what had been in Dad's head back then, why he switched off from the family. He rarely said a word about work and his travels, despite considerable provocation and pressure from everyone. He was enigmatic. There was a brightness in his eyes, an energy that sparkled under the heavy skin of sagging eyelids. It was contentment, confidence perhaps. It told me he didn't need us.  In those beautiful diffident eyes was a story involving someone else, sadly it was never us.

I don't begrudge his happiness. I don't begrudge anyone's as long as it's not at the expense of others. I hate it when people begrudge me mine. I don't believe I let anyone down, though others round the table probably think otherwise.

I hadn't seen him for four years. Too long for most people to neglect a parent. But he had Bea, short for Beatrice, his companion and partner in recent times. Not that I ever met her, but Ruby kept me informed. Dad would never have held my absence against me. That's why I was able to do it. He was like me, a look forward sort of person, like the past was an unnecessary hindrance. Though it manifested itself as a lack of need for me, I respected his outlook. Even after Mother died, he kept on, exactly the same. It wasn't going to change his way. He didn't need me and I didn't need him, it was as simple as that.

But now he's gone and I'm here to close the book like everyone else. I wonder, looking at my aunts chomping on Ruby's catering attempts with their false teeth, whether Dad would be cringing in embarrassment at their crowing judgement or loving the attention. Perhaps, like for everything, he just wouldn't care.

He'd shrug his shoulders, turn his back and go on with the dalliance in his head, the party to which we were never invited.

I reach for a bottle of beer on the table, uncap it and take a drink. I toast Dad, raising the bottle slightly and give a silent nod. It's the best I can offer him.

I look for who Bea is but there is no-one fitting the obvious description of a large black woman round the table. I decide to ask Ruby when she's back, but I suspect she may have felt rather less than welcome as the family pick over the post funeral cucumber sandwiches.

The front door swings open with a crash. We all turn. A large man with a stick forces his way in. I get up to go to the door to help him. He wears a baseball cap on his bearded head which look at odds with his white shirt and black trousers. Though the fact that his shirt is untucked probably is more fitting.

As I close the door behind me, he reaches out his left arm to shake my hand.

'I'm Terry,' he says, 'next door. Come round a lot. I know the security combination.'

I accept his hand with my left realising that his right arm doesn't move. He stumbles across the floor to the nearest seat. Studying him a little more I realise his right leg is also false explaining his clumsy posture. Immediately I think military. All the stereotypes of the modern injured soldier jump to mind, including the brusque manor in which he seems to occupy space, uninvited.

He pauses to look at me and then acknowledges the people in the room who smile and wave back. Clearly he's more in favour than I am. His attention doesn't linger long but returns to me.

'You'll be Pearl then,' he says with a smile and nod as if he's just got a question right in the pub quiz at the Derby Arms.

'When I heard you were coming from Africa, expected you would be a good shade darker. Like that Bea woman, glad she's out the way in case anyone cares.' He laughs at his own joke, checking for a response, fortunately pauses before it becomes too embarrassing.

I don't like to think I'm superior or snooty, but I probably am. I'm awkward, I'll admit it, but I don't feel the need to laugh and humour any ignorant arse who thinks it ok to joke about race. Dad seems to have some varied friends that's for sure. Between Range Rover man and Terry, there is a defining spectrum of difference.

'I'm not like that,' he adds, his voice softer, probably realising that the subject might be inappropriate. 'Just saying some of the dudes I bunk with... Don't matter anyway.' It's obvious he isn't getting anywhere with his line of anecdotes. 'How are you doing? Your dad loved you, you know. Every day he said something about you.'

At the mention of my dad, I soften and smile. 'Thank you,' I respond politely and feel a blush coming on. I know dad would never say a bad word about me, or even Ruby. But it's nice to know that he didn't stop there, even with this blunderbuss of a soldier, I was his topic of conversation.

'I hope you don't mind,' he says, standing up to grab a beer from the table. He keeps his attention, on me, showing no intention of moving onto anyone else.  For balance, he leans on the back of a chair closer to me and leaves the stick to one side so he can hold beer in his good hand. It feels a bit too close for my comfort as his size is overbearing. His trousers are big even on him. A black plastic belt works hard to hold back the stomach hanging over it. As he talks, he leans towards me. It's forgivable with his bulk and disability, but it's intimidating or even creepy, though I know he's trying to be nice.

'I know you've been away. You work for one of them charities, I heard,' he says, 'anyway, I was good mates with your dad…helped me a lot with…' He looks down to his arm and I get the point. 'Ever since I was discharged and I've been disabled, been difficult to get work, so I'd pop in here some days for a cup of tea and a chat and … it was good, you know. I…' His voice wavers.

I place my hand on his good arm as a note of sympathy. Whether he was a bother to Dad or not, it was clear Terry really appreciated the time with him. The least I could do was respect that. Besides in the last few years, this man knew Dad far better than I did so who am I to judge?

'Were you in the army?' I ask.

'Yeah, served twenty years, pensioned off now though. Honourable discharge. Not much use for a cripple on the front line.'

He laughs at himself but I don't feel like joining in. In fact, the description makes me feel distinctly uncomfortable.

Time to make my excuses with a bathroom trip. Easy one to drop in and buy me a few minutes of breathing space. Terry, goes back to his seat as I leave the room.

I run the water in the bathroom for a few minutes extra, pulling out my phone for no better reason than wasting time before facing them all again. It's not that I don't like them, it's not that I don't want to be here. I can't even explain it to myself. I don't hate people, for the most part I love them, but sometimes when people have a moan I have a desperate urge to say something. But there I am being a superior bitch again, like I know the answer to life, the world and the universe.

Then there's Terry, he has plenty of reasons to be unhappy. And if I've seen a lot of life in a raw form he has as well, and maybe been in far darker holes than me. Whilst I hated bravado particularly in men, who've seen the worst of life? What's worse, a refugee camp full of half-starved people or the aftermath of a bomb blast when you're picking up the discarded limbs of your mates? Who wants to win that race to the bottom?

Stepping out of the bathroom my dad's bedroom door is open and I decide to go inside. It feels like a dreadful intrusion but this will be the first of many intrusions into his life as we sort out his papers. The indignity of death itself is awful but then the thought of those you leave behind picking over the leftovers of your life and the inevitable judgements makes me shiver. The thought of people knowing all my truths after a life time of self-selection on what I share. Dad was the same, I know and he would hate this.

The wall has a full size art work of elephants at a watering hole. A classic image of the savanna. Makes me feel a little nostalgic. All around the room there are lots of souvenirs. Masks which freak me a little, coloured embroidered cloths, pots.

A small blue Tagine sits on the dressing table. Mum and Dad had that for years. I remember my mother putting all sorts of rubbish inside. It was too small to cook with but was great for storing coins or bits of cheap jewellery. Sweet memories. Feels like another life time. When we were a family, before we came back. Before everything changed.

I sit on the large bed, a patterned red blanket covers it. There is little light with the closed curtains and it seems peaceful. Instinctively I reach for the bedside drawer wondering if Dad still keeps his bible close by. He was always quite preachy when we were young. Had the local pastors round wherever we were based, not a part of my life I enjoyed, but I don't hold it against him.

In the drawer there are some papers, some handwritten notes and some loose photographs.

There are some of me and Ruby as kids, and then Walter. He was not unlike me, a thirst for adventure, though he was far more rebellious. He had a bad chemical habit and fate caught up with him. He died in a car crash in Kenya. Even worse was that I didn't even know he was there. That was Walter, reckless and selfish. Never thought that his mother might want to know what country he was in.

There are a few more picture of Mum. They must be from the seventies and eighties given the big bundle of bushy red hair. She was so pretty then. When I was younger I always thought her so boring, dressing like she was going to church. I flick through more of the same until I come across a larger photo, modern paper print with a recent shot of my father.  I wonder why it is mixed up with the others. There are three people stood by him. Two smart men, one similar age to Dad in a suit, the other younger and more casual looking in a white shirt and chinos. It takes me a second or two to realise that the older man is Range Rover man but then I study the familiar features of the younger man.  I curse then quickly check the other photos for more evidence. There is another obviously taken at the same time with a large black lady stood beside Dad. I assume this must be Bea. I focus again on the younger man concluding it can't be anyone else. The high forehead, mottled skin over his eyes that always made him look older. The eyes are bright, eyebrows lifted as if enjoying the moment the photo was taken. If Bea is in this photograph then it must have been taken in the last two years.

That means my brother, who I cried so many tears of guilt for, is not dead.

My heart is beating fast as questions race in my head.

He was here. With my father, with Bea. And a very rich friend who Dad worked with. They were here and I wasn't. I need to find Ruby. She must know, but then why would she have not told me.

Terry is standing in the doorway as I come back to the kitchen. 'All ok Pearl,' he asks. He looks at the bundle in my hand and trying to hide them from him, I drop them.

'So sorry,' he says, as I scramble on the floor. As he leans towards me he spots one of the pictures. 'How the hell did that you get that? Thought I had burnt all the photos of that black bitch.'

He is about to grab it and I stop him. 'Wait', I say and take it off him. I'll ignore his racist outburst whilst I get the answers I want. 'Do you know who these people are?'

'The men, no,' he says, 'but her…' He glares at me, his forehead creased in frustration. He stumbles to speak as if his anger is over taking his capacity to express his opinion.

I brace myself for what's coming.

'She killed him. That bitch killed him. I'm telling you Pearl, one day I'm going to find her and I will beat the life out of her, one punch at a time. What she did. I can't even say it.' His accent and stress is emphasised by his chopping h off him and her.

'But this guy?' I ask. 'Do you know him? He's flash, with a chauffeur and a blacked out Range Rover. Have you seen him here?'

'Him, no. Just her, bleeding him dry. She's been living here two years now. Like a parasite. He wouldn't have it, but I told him straight. She's robbing every penny you got. But he shrugged his shoulders like it didn't matter.' His face went from fury to sadness. I could see the disappointment that he tried and failed.

I look back to the photo and then to Ruby coming back into the house, wondering if she had seen it as well. The matter of Bea was one thing. But we said prayers for our brother five years ago and now he's standing beside dad smiling like it was his birthday.

I can't decide if I'm furious or heartbroken. My resolve weakens and I am welling up well before Ruby gets to me.

***

# CHAPTER 2

## ∞ § ∞

Ruby stares at the photo and I sense the same reaction as me, so pull her into the back room away from whatever rubbish Terry might spout.

'I didn't know,' she says, 'I swear.'

'I assumed you didn't,' I say, 'I know we don't see a lot of each other but I am pretty sure you would have shared that our brother was alive and kicking and knocking on Daddy's door. Oh and posing with the lovely Bea.'

'And I've never seen the posh guy before today? Do you remember him from when we were young?' she asks.

'I don't think so. He's kind of family but there were so many people coming and going in those days. I didn't take much notice.'

We sit beside each other on the bed. Ruby is crying so I put my arm around her. My tears have dried, anger is building in me. Though I am not sure if I am angry at Walter, Dad, Bea or even with myself for missing this whole charade. An enormous crevice has been open and visible in my family for years and it completely passed me by. And Ruby as well.

There's another picture on the wall opposite. A smaller one. I notice only because I'm staring ahead whilst I hold Ruby. It's a painting of a peasant girl typical of African art. Pale background and taut, slim black figure holding a basket of fruit. The shades of dark brown contrast easily with the scenic, dawn landscape. A burning sun rises in the background. Under an African Sky is boldly written in black lettering across the base of the frame.

Kind of corny view but then at least they didn't try to pack a giraffe or an elephant into it. At least, for all the things that could be depicted under that stunning sky the artist chose a peasant girl. I am comfortable with that.

Next to that is artwork with a whisky barrel and a winged angel supping at a small glass. The Angels' Share is written over the barrel. Oh Dad, and his love of whisky myths. The Angels' Share or was it the Devil's Cut where the whisky evaporated in the barrel. Silly but it has a certain charm.

My eye is drawn to a large spider's web that has developed beside it, quite sizeable for the small barely centimetre sized spider who sits at the corner waiting for a fly.

Ruby lifts her head, disturbing my distracted thoughts.

'Tell me about Bea,' I say.

'Dad said she made him happy. I had to respect that. You did too, Pearl.'

Her sniffles dry up. She wipes her eyes with a tissue. I brush her hair back away from her face.

'You told me on the phone ages ago that you didn't trust her, Come on Ruby, you can tell me. Dad was as deluded as he was a good guy. We both know this.'

'She told me not to come round if I wasn't going to do things her way,' Ruby says, quickly. 'It was like, this was her patch and if I was going to upset Dad with my telling him off or what he should eat then I wouldn't be welcome in the house. To be fair, she took a lot of weight off my shoulders when he got ill, cleaning, feeding him, shopping, but that didn't give her the right...'

Her tone is low and feeble as she talks quickly. I think Bea made her feel ashamed. That's awful and Dad wouldn't even have noticed.

'I know, damn it, and of course Dad would wave you off as if it was just women talk. Nothing for him to get involved with.' Dad was so passive sometimes. There were so many times when I wanted rage from him. When Mum was rude to him, when she complained about the slightest thing, I wanted him to react. But he sucked it up and went back to his chair, like it was all too hard.'

'Bea must have loved it,' Ruby says, 'he would let her set the agenda and spend the money so I went round less and less I guess, feeling more and more that Dad didn't need me. But as soon as he passed, she left a note and I haven't seen her since. Not a call or a message. No address. I don't even know her full name.'

'What was she after do you think?'

'Money,' she says, 'but he didn't have that much and that was only good to her if they got married. He could have left her stuff in the will but it's seriously not enough to house sit an old man for years.'

It does seem a big leap to suggest money was a motive. Free bed and board is one thing but living with an old man is not a free ride.

'Takes all sorts,' I say, shrugging my shoulders. 'Where did they meet, again?'

'She was in some sort of community care team. After his heart scare. So he told me anyway. She was doing the rounds and it seems one day she brought some milk round and never left. Dad said she scared him but he was joking… I think… she was quite dominating but he said he loved her company. She was funny and a great cook and he seemed happy. What can I say?'

I nod along. I've heard it all before but I feel it a little deeper. Two years ago when she was first on the scene I was busy with a field camp in Ethiopia, refugee shelters and setting up a camp. It's what I do but I rarely have a phone signal until I get back to base. Can be days and sometimes weeks. I remember Ruby moaning about her, but I didn't take much notice. I called Dad and like she says, he was happy. Kept telling me to take care of myself and not to trust anyone. Definitely the truth, I thought.

'Best go back to the relatives.' She stands up and heads to the door.

'Ok before you go. What do you reckon about Walter? How can he still be alive? What was he doing here?'

'I don't know, honestly. Ten minutes ago my little brother was dead and buried and now he's not.'

'That's it,' I say, 'he was never buried. Remember they told us after the accident that the body was already buried as a John Doe. They didn't know who he was. It was only after we declared him missing that the DNA match showed up. He must have faked his death.

'How do you do that?' Ruby asks, 'that's really not easy to do.'

That's my sister, naïve. That's harsh and not quite true, maybe just doesn't see what's going in front of her eyes. It's like when we watched a movie as kids and we got to the end, I'd spend the next ten minutes explaining what happened. Ruby missed nearly every clue. She stands in the door way, her petite stature enhanced by the long black dress. It doesn't suit her at all. But then this isn't the day for high fashion and who am I to talk. Got to love her, she's everything I'm not.

'Trust me, in Kenya, with money, there isn't much you can't do.' I say, 'In an accident with badly burned bodies, there's no great investigation.  The right amount of money would persuade the coroner to sign the death certificate, I'm sure.'

'But where would Walter get that kind of money. He was a kid, barely in his twenties. He was bumming in hostels and sleeping rough half the time. Remember the stories his mate Olly used to say. They survived off nothing, begging and working for bed and board most of the time.'

'And then why? He must have been very scared of something to do that? Mustn't he?'

Ruby nods and then turns to go back to the party.

I stay on the bed for a moment trying to work out how and why Walter would fake his death. The lack of clear answer or even the vaguest clue makes me realise how little I knew about him and my father. I could pretend I never saw this and go back home. But then there is a past that I don't know about and ultimately affects me. I can't ignore it. And Range Rover guy knows more about it than I do especially as he came visiting with Walter.

Looking at the photographs once more, it suggests that whatever happened, the first place to start is Bea. She might not know the family stuff but she can answer my first question about Walter.

I look back to the spider and the whisky barrel painting, not sure why; it's not going to give me answers any more than staring at a photograph.

# CHAPTER 3

∞ § ∞

I've been awake for two hours and it's still only seven. Trying every angle to sleep in some comfort hasn't worked but I refuse to give up. There's nothing wrong with the bed, bar replacing a saggy mattress and a few less frills in Ruby's spare room. But it's not the bed, I've slept deeper and longer on a concrete floor. The problem with sleep is stuck in my head not my body.

I'm not worried… at least I don't think I am. Worry is something I try to avoid with a positive attitude. Negativity like regret spreads like cancer and then it stops me doing anything. I feel pompous even thinking this stuff, like I'm the only person who ever wanted to avoid negativity. I definitely avoid saying it out loud especially when someone talks about first world problems… Wi-Fi has gone down. I am oh so tempted to bring out my list of third world worries but then I really would have no friends.

I try to play it back in a more constructive way. I have concerns, questions. I might reason that the best answer is to get on a plane back to Tanzania, where I have been living for the last six months. I am trying to coordinate a flood relief project, moving masses of earth to try to protect whole villages from floods and at the same time improve irrigation in the fields. Apart from the horrors of monsoon rains and what that does to life in these hotspots, anywhere sustainable food can be developed is a vital improvement. Whilst I enjoy nothing more than being out there digging alongside the locals I need to be here. There are too many questions and not least if Walter is still alive. I need to see him. Family business if nothing else.

I remember the day I found out about Walter. I was away, as always, but this time at a conference in the US on planning logistics. Nothing new or remarkable in itself. Except I remember, as the phone rang, that I was imagining it being Mum or Dad who I would get that call out of the blue for. It was early morning. The call came from Interpol in Netherlands. I was on an all-night bender with a French girl, Alycia. We had been enjoying the conference a little too much. I was trying to speak to the official whilst holding a bottle of Jack Daniels in one hand, the phone in the other. Alycia was dancing naked to some music videos on the TV and I had to tell her twice to shut the thing off.

I sobered up quickly trying to take in what was being said. Poor Walter and there I was, acting like a dickhead teenager. I shiver at the memory. One of the most important moments of my life and I was stone drunk partying. That's where pompous smart-arse Pearl takes her falls. Deep and hard at the bottom of a bottle of Jack Daniels screwing some random stranger, boy or girl, although these days it's more the girls as too many of the men I meet disappoint me or want something I am not about to give. I tell me myself it's the price I pay for my lifestyle and I earn the right to let go now and then.

Oh my, once I am drunk I am just about the worst human to be around. Giggling like an idiot then fighting like a rabid dog. The morning after, the day after that and for months after my body feels like a cesspit. I let in all the crap that I fight so hard to keep out. The demons that pound like African Djembe drums in time with daggers as my mind switches from one misery to another. I try to be the pragmatist and the optimist, the get up and go girl, but sometimes I shut the door to the light and wallow. It's not worry but more a self-obsessiveness about how I let myself get out of control. I push people away and tell myself that's how I like it. Being alone, being just about responsible for myself is pretty much all I can cope with. I'd be useless in a relationship. I am useless in a relationship and this is well evidenced. I haven't quite murdered anyone in their sleep but have thought about it and I am quite sure those that spent more than a few days on a bender with me, did too.

Still that's who I am. I get by as long as I don't have to justify these outburst to anyone else.

Walter was declared missing weeks before an Interpol investigation turned up results. In January 2014 he called us from a bus depot in Botswana saying he was heading north. He was going to Zambia to see a friend about a job after a few months on the beach in Cape Town. Like me, he had that urge to travel, to experience, though his urge was to work only enough to keep him until the next bar opened. He'd drop a line once a month. Sometimes a message, sometimes a call. His friends came back from Durban in South Africa a few weeks after he had gone. Apparently he'd left with a local girl who was going to get him some work in a ranch. After that he would see where he got to. His last message told us nothing except all was ok and that he was in Gaborone, just over the border into Botswana. None of us paid any attention until it was spring and we still hadn't heard back. We took it in turns calling and getting no response.

By June all we could do was report him missing. I reported him to Interpol and got Mum to send a DNA sample. Interpol said it was unlikely anything would turn up but they would search databases and let us know. It took a few weeks probably because they were looking in the wrong place. In the wrong country in fact. He was in Nairobi, had been there for some time.

It is still odd to think that despite our similar passions for travel and shared history of Africa excursions we had a completely different attitude to it. Me trying to be the martyr whilst he saw himself as the adventurer. Perhaps he didn't want my conscience for company, which I couldn't blame him for. I am not sure it always served me that well either. So he wouldn't seek me out and I didn't push it. I had enough to deal with.

The official explanation was that there was a car crash. He was in a taxi which collided with another vehicle at a junction. Car was a complete write off. There was a blaze. Injuries beyond recognition. Horrible, shocking story. They had cremated the bodies after the coroner's verdict. And we had to live with the consequences.

The shock was the start of the end for Mum. It was sad to see her descent from matriarch to a nervous over anxious shell. Cancer took her body, but Walter's loss took her mind.

Walter was good looking and a charmer. He wasn't the secretive type, though he mostly never said much in his calls and texts. But on the odd occasion, he was engaged or the signal was good, he was happy to share everything. Who he'd met, hotels, odd people, taxi drivers. Sometimes girlfriends.

I sat up in bed, once again looking at the photograph. Bea must know something and she couldn't be as bad as Ruby portrayed, surely Dad wouldn't have allowed it. He obviously did at some level.

After talking to Terry, Ruby has taken the same point of view. Bea is a bad one and she is more than happy not to have her around anymore. I might think the same if I had met her but I need to see beyond that. Bea left for a reason. Could be something sinister or she is just a coward. Whatever, she is avoiding us which means there is something to hide.

Terry says he will help me, though he doesn't feel like the wisest person to be relying on for information. He is too hung up on his past and his disability. His attitude and racism is not something endearing to me at all In fact, I think he says it for effect as he knows it winds people up. Attention seeking comes in many forms. Though I respect his passion for my father. The way he talks about the help Dad gave him and how much he appreciated someone not judging him. I can't ignore that.

The fact that Dad allowed someone else to run the house and his life is no surprise. He was quite simple up front, uncomplicated, though for those that knew him better, there was much more to him than meets the eye. He saw joy in a tin of baked beans... if anyone offered him the indulgence of a ten year old whisky he'd think his life done. He wasn't a romanticist, I think his upbringing saw to that. His father traumatised from the war, was too handy with his fists, his mother more likely to cower for fear for herself than protect him.

Dad never complained or talked much about it. What he did instead was offer advice. The front room was his courtroom. His chair coloured in some old pink fabric, Mum had chosen. He disliked it but couldn't care less as long as he got to sit in it and no-one blocked the TV. It was as much as he needed control over in life and no-one begrudged him that. Me, Ruby and Walter soon learned to curry favour by bringing tea and late night toast before bed. He wasn't a Dad we needed to fight for affection, he was free and easy with many a good word. But it's not the main thing I remember.

It was the philosophy, this was the bit hidden from the everyday view. His musings were not academic or even referencing some quote but like a wise owl. He'd never tell us what to do, but something like ...to do today is to regret tomorrow. Then next day, it would be something completely different and conflicting. Especially if I had homework... don't put off until tomorrow what you can do today. It was stuff you could easily ignore and mostly we did. I mean if Dad wasn't telling us then we didn't have to listen... but it did have an effect. He made my decisions my own. It was advice, a passing of responsibility. 'Pearl', he would say, 'your life belongs to you. Only you can make yourself happy, only you can make yourself miserable. You get to choose what works for you.'

And I do, frequently. Though right now I am struggling with what the right choices are.

***

I'm back at Dad's.

I give Ruby a day off to deal with her family. I think she finds the house too empty or too many memories of Dad. Whichever way, it's upsetting for her. Whereas, I am more on a mission of discovery. Looking through wardrobes and drawers. Reading letters. Everything and anything to give me a clue.

Not that I find anything. There is a desk and a drawer full of household bills, credit card, phone bills. None outstanding.  I've spread them all out on the kitchen table as I go through them. No reference to Bea. The dull and inconsequential council tax listed a single resident. She apparently lived here but you wouldn't know it from searching the paperwork. For all the suspicions, of her motives she didn't leave a footprint.

Apart from the bedrooms, the bungalow is open plan with the kitchen and living space shared. The French doors onto the back garden give some light, whereas the door at the front is dark and uninviting. I wonder what I need to do once I can get round to selling it. The red wallpaper is less than appealing and dad's African art will all have to go before it is put up for sale, despite his love for it. It is a house of contradictions, just like Dad I suppose.

The doorbell rings and check the gate video. It's Terry so I release the gate, wondering why he didn't just come in. Yesterday he said he had the combination.

'Hi,' he says, once he reaches the door. 'Thought I better knock. Your dad didn't bother like, but you're here now.'

'It's ok,' I say, looking back at the bills on the desk. 'Dad trusted you, so I will.'

'Cup of tea?' he asks.

'OK.' I let him make it, if it makes him happy.

I know he's disabled but he moves around like a walrus throwing his weight from one limb to the other. And I know I should have sympathy for his struggles but I can't help thinking he should have learnt to be more efficient, lighter on foot. I don't know. I can barely bring myself to look up at him as he blunders around, yet it's also addictive, waiting for something to go wrong. I really am a callous bitch... but...

I follow his movement whilst making the tea. With one hand occupied he can't use his stick so he frequently leans on the unit for balance, but when he does let go he seems to be more balanced overall; I wonder if his stick is not really helping him and if he lost some weight it might be easier. Either way he is still clumsy and his ability to bump into every edge and obstacle in his way is testing my tolerance for irritation.

'Here you go.'

He places my cup on the desk and returns to get his own drink. He carefully places it down, his hand shaking a little. Even with the care he takes, he knocks the cup and spills some on the table. I pretend not to notice even though the very remote tidy part of me wants to get a cloth to wipe it up. Fortunately it isn't sufficient for the tea to spread to the documents I have spread out otherwise I really would have had to react. Once the cup is safely in position he pulls out a chair and slumps down. The table wobbles but the tea remains safely in cup. Phew!

'Thanks for the tea.' I say and force a wide smile onto my face to hide my callousness.

'What you doing?' he asks.

The smile goes instantly and I resist the urge to bite his head off for stating the distinctly obvious. What else would I be doing with a pile of phone bills in my hand?

'I'm checking back, phone records. I don't know. Just looking for stuff.'

I take a sip of tea and feel a chip on the rim. It's a small mug with a Robin on. He has a large purple, man-size one and I can see that has a chip as well. Mental note to buy some new mugs when I go to the shop.

What a wonderful day, drinking tea in chipped cups with a man I am struggling to look at. Joyous

Though perhaps I can make Terry's presence more of a productive interaction. Same question I asked Ruby.

'Tell me about Bea. Why didn't you like her?' I really hope there is more to learn.

'Hated her, hate her sort. You know.' He spits the words out and then pulls the chair back.  The table wobbles as he moves. He reaches for his stick. His face screws up as he lifts he weight off the chair. I wonder if he wants to stand because he's uncomfortable or because he can't talk about Bea sitting down.

'You didn't like the colour of her skin?' I ask. More like poking a dog with a stick and it is definitely not going to help calm down.

'I didn't mean it like that and you know it.' He says loudly. If it wasn't awkward for him to lift the stick he might have been pointing it at me. 'Don't put words in my mouth. You're smarter than me, I know that but I'm not like that, but you don't know me so I will let it pass.'

His South London accent is strong and I fear I shouldn't get the wrong side of that rage. I haven't taken time to study the numerous tattoos on his forearm but I suspect that they are organisations or connections that might not have the most altruistic of intentions.

'Terry, you don't have to tiptoe round me, I've heard it all before. But if you are going to sit here and tell me you don't like her just because she was a bit blacker than your tender racist mind can tolerate, then this conversation is going to be a short one.'

'I meant her attitude. She was so damn cocky. She was like you. Looked down her nose at me, treated me like I was a tramp, an 'anger on, here with a begging bowl. I got my pride you know. I served. I don't deserve to be spoken to like that. If I spilt my tea or beer and she would be all over me like I'd pissed on the floor. She'd screw up her face and shout at me. When your dad covered for me, she would shout at him too.'

I nod, not sure what to say. I get the image.

'Do you think I like being like this?' He says, stomping around. His stick clattering alongside. 'I got my pride. Your dad understood. He listened; talked to me properly. The pain. The pills. They do stuff to your mind. I can't help it. But he understood.'

'She sounds fussy, rude, but you said she was robbing him. That's a stretch isn't it?' Probably better to get him onto more neutral ground.

'I didn't trust her at all. Why was she here? You tell me. What did she want? She didn't love Spencer... your dad. He even joked about it to me... saying she'll kill me off one day. And ok I didn't like her blackness. I don't mean in a racist kind of way, told you, I'm not like that. But what was she doing here, a black woman like her, with an old white guy. Why wasn't she hanging round with her own sort?'

He sits back down and I don't react. There's no point trying to preach but it sounds like he doesn't have actual reason for his suspicion other than crass jokes by my dad and his casual dislike of obnoxious black women. That's alright then.

'There must be more to it than that,' I say.

'She was always going through his papers, going to the shops. Spending. It was all his money, like. Never heard her putting her hand in her pocket.'

This isn't going anywhere.

He sits back down and I see his lip quivering. I am surprised not just by his anger but the emotion on his face. Tears are not far away. Whatever Bea was, she really hurt his feelings.

'How did you get your injury?' I ask. I need to change the subject and perhaps I need to be a little more patient. His ignorance is wearing but I should feel little sorry for him.

'An IED,' he says, 'same as lot of the lads. You know it was fucking horrible. I can't even say it. Normal patrol. Walking down a street in Kabul. Did a shift in Ireland, same then. Daily patrols, watching and listening, but most of the time nothing happened. But then out of nowhere. Walked past a car and it just goes up. Fucking Taliban, evil bastards they were. My arm went there and then, my leg later in hospital. Got infected. Had to go. At least I survived. Tell you Pearl, there is no words I can say to tell you what it's like to see your mate in bits.' He shakes his head and starts to speak again. 'I can't say more and you don't want to hear it. None of it's good,'

'It's ok,' I say, 'Sorry I asked.' I am sorry as well. No-one deserves to experience that horror.

'Don't be sorry, don't ever be sorry for asking. Don't want no-one to pretend this didn't happen. Ever. I get that no-one wants to talk about war. Me too, but don't pretend it didn't happen. '

'Sorry,' I say again before realising it was the wrong word.

'Need a beer,' he says, 'is there any more in the fridge.'

'Help yourself,' and then decide it's more trouble than it's worth. 'Stay seated,' I say, 'I'll get it.'

While I'm there I get one for me as well. I hand him the bottle and then take the papers from the table. As he drinks, I collect them together in neat order and put them back in the drawer. After a few minutes, I sit back down and take a sip of beer myself.

'I know you don't like my views,' he says. 'But I got my reasons, I seen what some of these types will do.'

I don't need to be an expert interrogator to work out where he is going with this.

'But that's what I don't get,' he adds. Some of them locals were perfect. Would bring us food, gifts. They had nothing but would invite us in to their houses. Share the only bit of food they had for a week. Not many would do that here would they? It's why I am not a racist like you think. Some of them are really good proper people but those here abuse the good luck they had being in this country and blame us Brits for everything.'

Despite slipping back into racist equivalence by the end of every sentence stating why he wasn't a racist, I at least understood what he was saying about Afghanistan. The poorest in the world were often the most generous.

'All them terrorist sorts, evil bastards, there and here. They are not doing this for the poor folk. These people are nothing like martyrs, they're just fucking evil, sick fucks. The worst scum. I would kill them, stab them, strangle everyone with my own hands, because I've seen it Pearl. It's alright sitting here in your nice arm chair with your judgement. But I've seen it.'

And I have too.

I drink the beer as he continues his rant. There isn't much to his thinking and he's not wholly wrong. Sadly he's added in a mix of English general xenophobic nonsense and here we are, in twenty first century Britain, looking for enemies in the wrong places.

Time for a change of conversation. This is getting nowhere. I will ask him about his family.

'What happened to your parents?'

'Mum, was a class act. Bowel Cancer got her in the end. She was strong as an ox. My dad was Navy and left us after the Falklands. He went a bit crazy I think and ran away. She just accepted it and carried on. I hated my Dad for that but since I came back from the tours I know now. I'm not saying he was right to do it. But I know how hard is to cope. Other people they never can handle it. I hope he's alright but wouldn't be surprised that he's one of those that ended up in front of a train or jumping in the Thames. It's what it does to you. Mum got through it. She was a master at keeping the flag flying. Like the Queen. We say our prayers, remember our friends and we get up and do what we have to do.'

'Shame I never knew her,' I say. I'm not sure we would have got on, but with Dad moving to this house only after we'd all left home, none of the neighbours are familiar to me. She sounds like a good character, probably classic matriarch, holding the family together whilst all the men fuck it up.

'You would have liked her Pearl. She was strong like you.' Not sure where he got the idea I was strong but I let it pass. 'She kept me sane you know, first time I came back after all the treatment. I remember,' he laughs, 'any sign of bother from me or moaning, she'd sit me down at the table. Hands where she could see them, she'd say, even though I only one hand like. Out with it there and then. All of it had to be said then. Once it was over, she'd clip me round the ear but mostly she'd get up again, make tea and just carry on as normal. It wasn't love or sentimental like. It was just the way it was. Can't tell you Pearl, how easy she made life. She sucked it all up. Every last bit of it. She was a saint.'

And how easily we forget the importance of women in our lives. Behind every good man and all that.

'She sounds amazing actually. Thanks for telling me about her.' I must going soft. For all her good as a mother, she'd have been chastising and complaining about every brown face or gay in the village. But as people always tell me. Different generation.

Terry finishes his beer.

'Bit cheeky, I know, but need a favour. Have you got a car?' he asks.

'Hire one,' I reply. 'Why?'

'Star,' he says. 'Bleeding marvellous. Couldn't give me a lift somewhere could you? Save me a cab fare.'

I say yes, before I can think of a reason to say no. Except that enduring more of this kind of conversation is like having a bra reengineered with nipple clamps. I don't have any plans but not having plans didn't mean I was ready to fill the gap with more of Terry's misery. 'Where am I taking you?'

'Cheers love,' he says, 'Conservative club in town.'

'No fucking way.' I say. Apparently my nipple clamping bra comes with an auto tightening function for every time I want to scream.

'Ah you'll be fine. It's cheap beer and I need to sort a few things out with some types there. They'll never spot you're a leftie if you keep quiet. Plus some of them there knew your dad.'

Do I have to do this? Apparently yes.

# CHAPTER 4

## ∞ § ∞

Terry reckons I will go down well here. He's taking the piss.

I am speechless as I get him in the car, slamming the door hard shut behind him, still asking why I am doing this.

'You might enjoy it,' he says.

'Someone said the same about smoking some pot in a club in Columbia once. I was sick for a week. Since then I choose my vices more carefully. Vices are supposed to be fun. I'm not sure the Chevening Tory club comes into that category.'

He laughs. 'You're such a fucking show off.'

'Tell me again why you like these people?' I ask as we drive, 'they wouldn't give you the time of day, most of them.'

'Seat of power though isn't it,' Terry replies, 'and I tell you what. No-one will question me. Most of them like to claim their military patronages but they never saw the wrong end of a gun. They see me as a useful idiot, fund raising and sympathy vote. That's fine, means I can get favours. You know. Guy at the council when it comes to allowances. Universal credit hearings… it's handy to know someone. Get one of them to speak up for me. All the people you want to know. Right there in the room.'

'I would have thought the Labour Party would have more an ear for your needs.'

'Not round here love, it's like the set of Antiques Roadshow? Labour just makes up the numbers, no-one takes them seriously. Tory council, tory seat. Want anything doing round here, stands to reason you need a Tory not a Trotsky do-gooder.

Like those preachers in the street with the bible. Take no notice.'

For all my judgement on Terry's views, I get his thinking on this. He's adapted and whilst he is obviously still navigating his way through disability, his pain and fight to cling on to his pride cannot be understated.

I find my way through the dark streets of the town and to the club car park. I can smell a curry place next door and I am wondering if I should go there whilst he goes to his club.

'Blair was the only one who had balls.' Terry is still rattling on, but I am barely listening. 'He knew he had to call a war. Didn't shy away from it. Everyone said he was wrong but they didn't have to take responsibility. He did. It was a fuck up but that was the yanks. At least he stood up and was counted. But the rest of them weren't worth hating, honestly ineffective bunch of nobodies. No-one listening. Brexit, Europe. No-one listening. We won, get over it. Liberals were worst of the lot, they didn't have any MPs or virtually none and yet we get told we have to listen to them.  That ivory tower they put them in is high and mighty. So high no-one on the ground can hear their whinging.'

He laughs as we park up. I shake my head. Pointless even arguing with that.

I watch him negotiate walking with his stick as he heads towards the entrance, still thinking he makes it harder than it needs to be. His movements look plain awkward as he shifts his weight from his good leg to his false one. Perhaps the false arm creates an imbalance and this is how he compensates for it. I won't ask him. Who am I to advise on what's right and wrong with how he moves?

I walk to the bar first and order half a bitter, still got to drive back. Terry takes a pint. I carry it in so he doesn't have to struggle and spill it like he did with the tea earlier. That would be more than I could take. Though I have to say this hand-pumped, flat bitter with no head is a challenge for me not to spill. As I put it down on the table I can smell it on my hands. I think the bleach in the toilet has better aromatics. Our seat in the meeting room is thankfully near the back. About thirty people of all shapes and sizes turn up, though no-one looks less than forty. I try not to sit in judgement. I fail within seconds as I see the first white twin set and pearls. I should love pearls with my name but I think of the times I pretend my name is sort of cool are ruined at this exact moment. Whether the pearls are originals or not is a moot point as it's a question of whether her teeth are her own and whether the blue blazer chap with her requires some extra strong blue pills to keep her in surgical engineered smiles. Or perhaps he reserves his blue pill investment for the car park behind Tesco's. She's not the only one. Most of the women sport fake tans, blonde hair and rings that look like they came from a Bring and Buy sale on the market. There is definitely an end of the pier show missing its audience.

As well as blue pill Blazer Boy, the men look like they were drummed out of the golf club for incorrect tees or playing with the wrong balls. They spread out like men do to take up space, confident that the continence pants will keep them dry whilst they tell their wives how they could show the young 'uns a thing or too. Do I really think that badly of people? Yes. Talk about out of place.

I think about my mates out in the field. I already texted a few to say I was going to a Tory party meeting. A few messages came back 'Spying on the enemy?' or 'sold out now you're home'. Or the funniest one yet from Vanessa in New Zealand. 'Remember when we had that lecture on how pickpockets could shake your hand and at the same time be nicking your purse.' She suggested that I could be home and counting the cash before any of them realised it was their round. Vanessa is not wrong but I am not that desperate to get close to any of the specimens. It's enough having Terry for company. So much for not judging.

I have no intention of saying anything at the meeting nor asking anything. Though if I was in the mood for a wind up of the snowflake sentiments of these people, now would be the perfect moment. My gut is bubbling like a geyser wanting me to let loose on the privilege but it's definitely not the time. Good job I am driving. A few more beers and my restraint might have to take an early taxi back. A few verbal hand grenades in the room would be so much fun

'Call to order,' another blue blazer man at the front shouts. His white hair slicked back with an 80's style Brylcreem flick is hard set back on his head.

Conversations stop. He holds his head firm, eyes searching the room, checking for the last murmur to be stared down. His beard is white, his nose boyish, contrasting with his slick hair

He runs quickly through the agenda for the meeting, which I don't hear too well. I do hear the word subs and I whisper to Terry. 'Do I have to pay?'

'Guests free first time.'

'Ok,' I reply, relieved to that I don't have to pay to be bored.

'Any guests this evening?'

Terry puts my hand up.'

'Welcome,' he says, 'would you be so kind as to sign the book at the break please. Always good to have new members.'

I smile back politely but quite clear I am not signing any book. This is a strict one-off, whatever Terry says.

They've got a speaker in. Apparently experienced in International Trade. Telling all of them about the WTO, World Trade Organisation. It's been 3 years since that damn Brexit vote, not one of them gave a crap about international trade before then and now they are all on wet dreams about free trade on WTO, thinking it somehow is better than the nasty bullies in the EU who got their own way. Apparently only Mauritania trades fully on WTO terms. I've been there just the once. And if there is one place I don't want to be compared to its there. It's like claiming you want to exchange the toilet in your en-suite with those in the public park, complete with graffiti, leftovers from local druggies and other indescribable discharges. Someone is yanking these people's chains and they are falling for it, like lemmings queuing for a cliff jump.

Terry's all in as well. Listening intently.

I resort to my phone as a distraction. There is a message.

Number unknown but it is a UK mobile phone.

*This is Beatrice. I need to speak to you before you go back. It's about your father. Can you come to London tomorrow? There are some things I need to tell you.*

I reply, yes. And then think about whether to ask some more. The phone vibrates with another message almost instantly. I look around conscious of the noise of the phone and then discreetly check the message. It's an address in Greenwich. Deptford Towers. 11 O'clock.

I put the phone back in my bag. Nothing more to know now. But tomorrow there should be a whole lot more. I nip out discreetly to the toilet so I don't have to listen to this crap. Maybe I will text Terry from the Indian after all. Whatever purpose might have come from the Conservative Club, I don't think I need it.

# CHAPTER 5

∞ § ∞

I take the stairs down from the DLR and cross the road. Looking up at the flats, they appear ultra-modern and slick, relatively new built even in an area which looks like if you sneeze a new block will appear. Bea must be doing alright if this is her place. She definitely doesn't need Dad's money. That's one Terry myth blown out the water. Is this where wealthy Range Rover man comes in?

I didn't tell Terry about the message from Bea. He would have wanted to come with me and that would have been a disaster, both for him and me. His clumsiness would have meant me leaving him on the train and telling him I'll pick him up on the way back. I dropped him back last night. He was so grumpy with me for dumping the meeting for the curry place. The rant was almost worth it. Almost. He kept telling me how clever the WTO system is and how we all should be embracing the new way of working. Mental note to never go there again and especially not with a nationalist idiot who believes anything wrapped in anti-something vitriol must be true.

I ring the outside door of flat 70. Top floor a voice says. The door clicks open and I walk to the lift.

Top floor is level 24. Nice, I think as the lift carries me up.

The door opens onto a blue hall. Clean but oppressively warm. The heat clearly rises. I see a door at the end open and a large black lady holds it open.

'I'm Bea,' she says, 'I'm sorry about your father. He was a lovely man.'

'Thank you,' I say, 'sorry for you as well. I understand you were close.'

She reaches forward and hugs me. I didn't expect that. Her large arms feel quite oppressive but I take it for the goodwill intended.

Once she lets go, I follow her into the open plan room. The view hits me immediately. Wall to wall vista of Canary Wharf, Greenwich Park, East London. I can see for miles. Olympic stadium as well, my eyes are drawn further into the distance, trying to pick out new landmarks. Tearing myself away, I take in the flat's interior.

It's sparsely furnished. More like a show home. Not very lived in. The furniture is showy but doesn't look very comfortable. There is a bright blue sofa with more of chaise longue look, can't imagine slobbing out on that. A large TV adorns the far wall and table and chairs form the connection between the kitchen area and lounge. Done for style, probably some West End boutique place. Definitely not lived in and not sure it suited someone like Bea. But what do I know. Though it's clearly expensive and more spacious, it's hardly a million pound mansion. It's an ultra-posh version of the bedsit I rented as a student not too far away from here. Having said that, it probably doesn't have the black mould decoration on the walls and a toilet seat soiled with all known diseases.

'There is a bedroom and en-suite bathroom upstairs, it's a maisonette as well as penthouse in case you were wondering where the facilities are.'

I think she's reading my mind and noting my cynicism. Not sure why she feels the need to inform me of the extended living space though. It's for me to be curious but hardly for her to have to explain.

'I can see why you bought this place,' I say, still a little in awe of the view. 'Must have cost a fortune.'

'Oh it did, but it's not my place,' she says. Bea pauses and I turn waiting for the clarification. 'It's yours.'

'What? How come? Seriously?'

My heart is racing. I reach for the back of the white dining chair to steady myself. I take another view of what she says is now mine seeing it all in a slightly new light, thinking if this is mine, I will need to make it far more gothic, dump the white and get some hard-core black and silver fittings. But seriously, even if I had the money, I would never consider buying a place like this.

Bea watches me, arms folded, diffident, leaning back against the kitchen units. She doesn't have the look of an estate agent who shares my excitement at this discovery. Instead she has more the look of a shop girl watching me try on skinny jeans, waiting for the moment when I can't get them over my hips.

 'You mean it was my dad's and now it's mine?' It's the only logic I can reach for.

'No, I mean it's yours. Come sit down,' she says, pointing to the table.

'I will explain what I can.'

I am pleased to sit down. She sits opposite and smiles. I am drawn to her size. The black trousers she's wearing, stretch as she tucks her legs in. The buttoned black blouse seems a mistake as it stretches across her chest gaping wide revealing her black underwear. Her hair is dyed a striking amber and tied up. Her nod to colour is matched by an amber flower patterned scarf tied round her neck. It's all a bit odd but who am I to talk, I dye my hair red and have a farm labourers approach to clothes. Hope she's not still reading my mind.

'Your father was a senior finance executive in International Tobacco. You probably know that better than me. But he set a few things up after he retired. One of them was a company in your name. I wasn't around then, so I don't fully know his motives.'

I am listening, but her accent is distracting me. Her flat vowels, a slight lisp but she speaks clearly.

'The company is PMC.'

She hands me a piece of paper from her bag underneath the table. The paper is blank but there is a letter head. PMC, registered address, IOD….Pall Mall. Pall Mall. I look up to Bea again. I begin to shake not taking this in.

'PMC, Pearl Management Company. IOD is Institute of Directors, it's a post box address for the UK operations.'

'And what does this company do?' I ask, very tentatively. What was Dad involved in? What am I now involved in?

'Nothing. It's a shell company, the only asset is this place. Actually I'm the only employee. You are the only shareholder. I work for you. You pay me £100k a year to manage your affairs.'

She folds her arms and smiles. Like it's that simple. One hundred thousand a year. I pay her. I am missing something. And beginning to feel stupid. I get up and walk around. I have a hundred questions but feel like I need to get them all in the right order. I came here to find out what happened with my dad and Walter. But this was not what I expected at all.

I want to be confident and assertive in handling Dad's affairs but I feel my pants have just been pulled down and all assurance has gone. I'm wobbling like jelly.

'Ok, you've got to tell me properly now. Assume I know nothing about this, because I don't.' I hear myself speak but I think my voice has been replaced by a child. I'm still hearing one hundred thousand pounds as a salary and wondering what she does to deserve it.

'To be honest, I don't know all about it and I don't think I want to. Spencer, your dad, had some money, he wanted to keep it below the radar so he put it in your name, that's why he set the company up this way. Why he bought this place. Your company needed a UK base.'

'What was he involved in? Is this dirty money?'

'No, not like that. It's not simple I know. He wouldn't tell me but he said it was legit. But he didn't want to draw attention to the money. There were people. People from his past. They came to see him. Not nice people. He told them the only money he had was the company pension and the house. Nothing more.'

'But you knew he was lying and that he had this place. So it must be dirty money. Who were these people?' Then it clicks and I reach for my bag, pulling out the photograph. I show it to her.

She nods.

I stand by the window looking directly down. It makes me a little queasy as the window seems to bend the more I lean forward. I can see the DLR approaching, the platform where I stepped off only a few minutes ago. I think I've aged a year since then. I think about the man with the fancy Range Rover and imagine being invited into the back. Part of the rich club.

'You know about Walter?' I ask, as I turn back towards her.

She is the one who gets up now, unable to look at me. I can see she is tearing up.

'It was horrible,' she says, 'Walter came out of the blue. Spencer was distraught. Furious. Walter begged Spencer to give him the money. And this other guy turned up. Nigel something.'

'But in the photograph, you're all smiling.'

'That was me,' she says, wiping her eyes. People underestimate me. It's why I got on well with your dad. They think I'm a housekeeper, a cook… everything. But I know stuff, hence why I'm managing your affairs. But I'm also a good actress, Pearl. I played the dumb housewife. I made them all behave. Eat, drink tea. It was a charade. They knew it and I did. But I made them all play nice, because if they didn't, they had to admit they were up to no good.'

I can't help but admire her. She is a good actress and I can see how she had them all ordered and managed. She is an imposing figure.

I take the photographs, put them on the table and we look at them together.

'They smiled nicely for my photograph before I let them eat.'

I smile. She talks about it so easily rather than me who sees it as a momentous and unadulterated family unmasking. She says it was horrible but now she seems to be nostalgic. Maybe the picture of dad is catching her feelings.

'Why didn't you stay for the funeral?' I ask.

'Because. You're a clever woman Pearl. I don't think I need to tell you what they thought of me. I said my goodbyes my way. Seeing you is the last thing I need to finish.'

She sits back down at the table and I follow. The dizziness from the moment before hasn't left me so I'm happy to go for safety.

She's right about the family. I have listened to both Ruby and Terry piling on the hate for her and there is no doubt the rest of the family would be the same. I move the subject on.

'So what was the money about? What did they want?'

'Your dad didn't say a word. Not a thing. With Walter it was bitterness. His anger with Walter was something I had never seen from him before. With the other guy it was just pure stubbornness. He wasn't prepared to give into his threats to go to the police. Spencer just kept saying, do what you want. Nothing for them to find. Then he said something about us all having things we would rather others wouldn't know.'

That last point registers with me but first I need to get an idea of what Walter was doing there.

'And what was Walter's role in this?'

'I think he was supposed to be a stooge. Some kind of emotional blackmail.'

'But he was supposed to be dead. Did they talk about it?' I am pressing my hands on the edge of the table, feeling the edge rub in my knuckles. I move my hands back on my knees embarrassed at how nervous I am.

'It was so tense,' Bea says, 'There was a suggestion Walter had to do it. Fake it I mean, I guess this comes back to the money but after they'd gone, Spencer wouldn't explain further. It was more than money, almost that the money was a consequence and he kept saying to trust him. There was a good reason for it but it wasn't the right time. It went back to his old job and the company. Best I didn't know, but just to make sure everything was in my name. That way they couldn't touch him or you.'

'But how could he set up a company in my name without me knowing.'

'Your dad was clever. You saw him as a parent but he was a businessman and he knew how to get stuff done. This company has been around for twenty years, since before you left for Africa. You might have thought you were signing papers for university, who knows. But he planned this for a long time.'

That he did.

'I've probably given you enough information for now, but I will leave you with this. It's your company statement of accounts for 2019.' Once more she reaches into her bag and hands a larger document over.

She gets up to leave. 'You have my number. The keys for the apartment are on the kitchen unit.' She points according to each instruction. 'Paperwork in that filing cabinet on the coffee table. Read it at your leisure. When you want to know more or want to talk, call me.'

'Thank you,' I say getting up to be polite. I expect the same hug as she greeted me with but she keeps her distance whilst she grabs her coat.

'Oh and not sure what this means,' she says. 'He didn't explain it but told me that Pearl would know what to do. She would do the right thing. That seemed to be his way of dealing with it. Passing it on to you I'm afraid.

With that, she departs without looking back. The door slams behind her.

I sit back down at the table and open the document, still thinking about Bea. But then I glance at the summary, trying to find the important highlights. Company is dormant etc. Just words about nothing. Some photos of beaches and pearls. Presumably for effect. I find my way eventually to the numbers page. The profit and loss and the balance sheet. Only one number stands out and I have to read it three times.

PMC has assets of $56,985,000. The amount isn't the only thing of interest. The registered headquarters for PMC is Panama City. This is not possible. It's ridiculous. Dad didn't have this kind of money so how can I. Panama… drugs… offshore money… tax haven. I can't bring myself to look away from the number.

I am a multimillionaire owner of a shell company registered in a well-known tax haven. What has Dad got me in to? And what is this about me knowing what to do? I haven't got the first clue.

# CHAPTER 6

∞ § ∞

As the night progressed, I dispensed with the mixer. A Vietnamese takeaway from the high street and two bottles of JD hasn't numbed the pain.

I check the view of every corner of the apartment numerous times obsessed with spotting landmarks. The bedroom view upstairs is almost more daunting as the bed is by the window looking directly out on the full glass wall. No curtains required. Good job it is the tallest building around in the vicinity and even a perv with a decent drone camera will have to work hard to keep it steady at this height. Not that I believe there is a long queue to see me in the buff.

I am still trying to process the money. The apartment. This is mine. All mine. The answer's always the same and I don't know what to do. Thanks Dad for dumping this on me.

Another glass filled. It's probably my last but I said that the last time I topped it up. The 75 inch TV is on loud and playing a random movie. Something for company. The lights from the night decorate the windows like a moving mural. It's so addictive. I can hear sirens routinely as the night life of London continues. From twenty odd storeys up I can see and hear everything that happens but somehow I'm immune and insulated in my aerial cocoon.

Across the road there is a lower tower block. Only 9 floors. So inferior, obviously cheaper places. This is me, all of a sudden, filling my membership card out for the elite, looking down on those below me. The residents are probably younger commuter couples. Bikes on the balconies, lights in the window making the interior visible. The interiors are probably shoeboxes and they will be paying a mortgage they might get to pay off the day they get their pensions. If they are lucky.

56 million. I am rich. Ridiculously and incalculably rich. When I think about a million pounds it seems an already insurmountable value to count, even when you take a thousand pounds and add it up. Then add another million the same, and another. Say it quick and stop counting. It becomes unreal, academic. Overwhelming.

I never wanted money. Nothing more than I need to cover my expenses. Living in Africa I can't spend my salary on much so it all goes into a savings pot. I'm used to that. Charities sometimes pay well, sometimes it's literally the bed and board and that isn't much more than a veg stew. But I don't do it for the money. No-one does. Even paying chief exec level salaries would put many off going into the camps. I do it because I want to.

But faced with this kind of money. Is that what Dad meant? He knew I would do the right thing? Invest it in charities etc. I can. But even charities won't touch dirty money. And whilst I am still bathing in dollar bills, the logistics of spending this money might become problematic unless I can establish the legality of the money. And how will I do that. I googled it but how to launder million dollars on Wikipedia might not be the best advice to follow. It's a minefield.

I often get calls from financial advisors and feel embarrassed that I don't have that much to impress them with. They seemed quite bored with the whole limitation of small pensions and savings in the tens and hundreds. For once, I might get their full undivided attention.

I check the phone. No reply from the text I sent Bea.

Bea said earlier she would be around.

I take another gulp of drink and decide to try the bed.

Tomorrow I will have to go back to Chevening and think about what to do next. I put the half empty glass down, leaving what's left in it. I'm too drunk to think and suspect as soon as I put my head on the pillow, I will pass out.

***

My head hurts.

But this time it's just the drink and not regret. For once I didn't do anything wrong. Made a mess in my own princess apartment but it's mine and apparently I can do what I like in it. It feels like an indulgence. I've done it before, upgraded myself in the fanciest hotel in town. One night in the Four Seasons Hotel instead of the Ibis. Just because. But then I have to give it back in the morning.

Will I have to give this back?

I'm really not sure.

I crawl out of bed and freshen up. Even with spreading out, my discarded clothes don't stop it feeling empty. Devoid of love. I will have to do something to smarten it up or perhaps bring it down a level.

Walking past the door I see a note pushed under.

A plain envelope.

I open it and find a neatly typed letter.

*Dear Pearl,* it's starts and before reading the content I jump the name at the bottom. Bea of course.

And begin to guess the contents before I read it.

A resignation. Immediate effect. Apparently she feels it's the right moment to move on with her life.

Yesterday, she said she would help me. She lied.

I pick my phone up and ring the number. Auto response, number not recognised.  Shaking with fury I fling the phone across the room. She's ditched on me.

Was what she said even true? Have I been spun a line?

I still have the keys. The company.

Shit! The bank accounts. She better not have stolen the money. I panic now. Picking up my phone. I find the number of the bank in the accounts.

I march up and down the apartment waiting to speak to get past the automated answer lines. The view is worth nothing now. I need to know she has not just run. But why tell me about it and then steal it. She could have done all that herself. Not if she wanted to punish me. That would be no fun. Best to let the precious bitch see what it's like to have all the money and then steal it from under her nose.

'Hello.'

Finally a human responds.

I give my name. And my title. Director at PMC incorporated. That does not sound like me.

Immediately I am redirected. Another voice, another introduction.

Some questions to identify me.

He reads the balance.

I breathe again. Apparently I am million dollars richer than the statement I read yesterday. Interest or some investment. I wasn't listening.

Next question. Recent transactions. Apparently Bea can't withdraw any funds, only action financial transactions within the listed accounts and approved vendors such as the tax office. I whisper a big thank you to no-one in particular and then to my clever, bastard father, who wasn't stupid enough to hand all the control over to a woman whose motives might be questionable.

I then take great pleasure in removing all authorisation for transactions from Beatrice Lovane of Deptford London. Though my guess is that she is currently at or on a way to an airport.

Once the transaction is complete, I sit down. I check out the half bottle of JD left and wonder if another bender is in order. But no. Not today.

I need to talk to Terry. He kept talking about her robbing Dad. He was vague before but maybe I should ask him again.

This woman. Damn. This woman. She might not have the financial sway over me, that I panicked about but she knows more than she's telling. I'm convinced now. She even said it yesterday, straight to my face. I'm a good actress.

***

Terry is waiting at Dad's.

He doesn't want me to come into his house. He doesn't say why and I guess I don't have to think too hard that he doesn't keep it clean and he doesn't want my pity.

Yeah, I feel for him, but I need his help. My mood today was more of business to be done rather than tentative.

Once we are in the house he goes to straight to the fridge again looking for beer. The clock has just struck noon so I guess I don't have to judge too harshly.

'Tell me again?' he says. 'Your dad left you a gaff in Greenwich? Penthouse. He was some sort, your dad. Why did he keep that so quiet?'

I didn't mention the money. I am not sure what that would do to him. Besides that is a secret I am going to keep to myself until I can work if it really is my money or I'm due to be measured for handcuffs in the very near future. Besides the penthouse is more than enough of a bone for him to chew on for now.

'Apparently, Bea managed a lot of his affairs. She didn't seem to care what you or Ruby thought of her.' I don't say it to wind him up, more that I want him to be interested in this. I want him to dig deeper, remember stuff, get past her skin colour to what she actually said and did.

'Told you. She was robbing him. Check the paperwork on that place. And this house. And the will. Wouldn't surprise me if she forged the lot.'

'Is there anything you can actually remember or are we stuck on the merry go round of vague accusations? I need something specific.'

'Did you google her?' he asks. I haven't. So wound up it hasn't crossed my mind.

I grab my laptop from the bag and type in her name.

I click through a doctor of the same name. Some American psychologist. A Baptist preacher in South London who wrote a book on the holy spirit as electricity. But not the Beatrice I met. Maybe even her name is fake.

Nothing on LinkedIn, nothing on Facebook. That's not compulsory for anyone but whatever or whoever she is, she has dodged social media. For a reason perhaps.

Deflated. My fingers pause on the keyboard. Trying to remember the conversation from yesterday.

'Did you talk to Dad about the job at all? International Tobacco?'

'A bit. He mostly talked about the places he'd been to, some stories about the Africans. Rituals. He knew I liked stuff like that. Weird religious shit. Couldn't get enough if it.'

'What about people he worked for? Did he mention someone called Nigel? Has a blacked out Range Rover. The one I mentioned the other day.'

He scratches his head and drinks a few more swigs of beer, the bottle now empty. Without hesitation he gets up for another. I pass on his offer to join him. The post-JD hammer man is busy in my head.

'I remember a Nigel. But that wasn't about work. He moaned about a Nigel Davies, who became an MP a couple of years ago. Orpington way, it was on regional news during the election. Owns a country estate thing.'

'Seriously? An MP?'

'Yeah, proper toff. Spencer didn't like him though. Told me he used to work for him. Real bastard, but then I asked him why and he didn't say anymore. He changed the subject, said it wasn't worth it.'

I google the name and there is no doubt, Nigel Davies, a former senior executive of International Tobacco, owner of Studenham Hall, now a Conservative MP. More importantly is Range Rover man. With that kind of estate I can see where the chauffeur comes in.

I show Terry.

'Fucking hell,' he says. 'What the hell is going on here then?'

'I don't know Terry. I seriously don't know. But I need your help to find out.'

'Thanks' he says, his eyes lift with joy as if no-one ever asked him for help before or at least not for a good while. 'Not sure what I can do, though?'

I laugh.

'Terry, you said to me that being at that club with all those Tory bastards was useful if you wanted anything doing. Well guess what.'

'Fucking hell,' he says, laughing.

Maybe I need a drink too.

# CHAPTER 7

∞ § ∞

Halfway through the afternoon and Terry is snoring. Bit of a relief and gives me chance to think things through a bit more.

Researching Nigel Davies in respect of political stories is quite easy. His voting record is that of the rightest of right wing fellowships. Brexiteer of course….hard-core Libertarian, whatever one of those is. Votes against numerous social initiatives, votes against removing anonymity for men accused of rape. He even wrote a libertarian piece in Spectator on a moratorium on historic sex crime prosecution given the laws and morals were different than they are today. A new legal definition needed. That sounded like some very rich and influential sexual deviants getting a very big free pass.

Oh found a Tweet on Trump, the worst president the world has ever known, being described as misunderstood. The rise of American freedom policies opposing state regulations is a model for us all to follow. Drain the swamp, another of his favourites.

In the big society world of Cameron these so called 'swivelled-eyed types' were supposed to be a thing of the past. Cameron was focussed on one-nation Tories, meritocracy, social justice and underestimated the power and money behind the likes of Nigel Davies. And now look where we are.

But his past in International Tobacco isn't well documented. Just a write up from the time of his election a few years ago, popular in the local community. He got Studenham Hall by marriage it seems, third wife. She was lady of the manor and no doubt wanted a bit of support. He clearly chose well.

So he retires or gets paid off from ITA, probably a fat pension cheque. Gets well in with the local party cultists, finds a rich woman and gets a country mansion thrown in. Plus a seat in parliament and probably the Lords to follow. This chap knows his business.

But what is his interest in Dad. And for that matter Walter.

If he thinks the money is his, or belongs to someone he knows, then it feels like theft. The social CV of Nigel Davies does not lend me to believe he makes a particularly compelling victim, nor my Dad a compelling villain. But Dad had someone else's money and now it's mine. Am I now the villain?

This is so confusing.

And how did Walter come into it?

Where to start with that?

If Walter was here in the UK last year alongside Davies then does that link Davies with what happened in 2014? It must do, otherwise how would he and Walter cross paths. According to Davies Wikipedia record he was still in International Tobacco back then, in the role of a non-executive Director. Did Davies help Walter to arrange the change of identity or did he find out about it after? Without Dad and Walter, I have no-one to ask. Not even Bea is around now.

I will have to start with Davies I suppose. I look at Terry and he's still snoring.

The house feels like a shell after the last few days. I walk around trying to sense Dad in here. His thoughts and musings. His disinterest in much at all except the weird artworks. This situation is his making, his doing. I can't believe that all he left me is a cryptic clue left by an untrustworthy... I'm not sure what to call her. She describes herself as a housekeeper and carer and then in the next breath she is managing international finance transactions and bookkeeping. And then her final role. An actress which makes me think that all or some of the above are bogus.

I sit at the desk and run through the papers I already found. Household bills which didn't tell me anything. The bedroom has the photographs. There was Dad's passport, certificates. There was old bottles of aftershave, socks, underwear, shoes. Stuff that Ruby has been through already. None of them give any indication of his past.

I pick up his passports and flick through. There is a plastic band around older ones. Visa stickers for numerous countries. Older passports before we had our own with each of us listed. Like a history of twentieth century travel from Singapore to Senegal. Papua New Guinea to Panama. Smoking is as international as it gets.

I remember one of the things Dad said about the company was that tobacco companies are brilliant at three things, particularly ITA. Firstly selling and making cigarettes. That is a given but having the right farms, products, tasters is as essential as the network of selling agents. The next expertise is handling cash. For an organisation like this that is cash rich, movement and handling of large amounts of money are essential. Financial investments, asset management and tax avoidance are key elements to doing business. The final and most crucial element of a tobacco company, especially in the last 50 years, is its legal framework. It pays the best lawyers in the business able to defend ITA against US Class actions, worth millions of dollars. Even on a smaller scale, Dad told me they had to dodge legal and regulatory frameworks in virtually every country they operated. Dad was very clear, they always complied with the law of the land, but part of being able to make that statement hid two vital points.

One is that money and influence over local regulation especially in weaker or corrupt countries is easier. It's easy to comply with the tobacco law if the interior minister making the laws was at a party at your house the day before being served the best steak, wine and whatever else came with vast wealth. The other more cynical tactic of every international operator in third world countries is dissociation. Using a proxy to do all the handling, corruption and networking needed to run the business. Local militias are very happy to run a security operation for tobacco plantations using cheap workforce, poor conditions and all deniable for ITA because it isn't them doing it. Pleading ignorance with a powerful lawyer in a court where the judge was at the same party as the legislator is also not uncommon. This isn't all stuff I got from Dad, this was stuff I found in my work.

I'm not saying things don't function or that everyone in Africa is corrupt. It's just that many of the institutions have corruption built in, structured, institutionalised where even good people trying to do the right thing have to use the mechanisms of corruption to get influence or control an outcome. Almost like saying to do a good thing, you have to do a bad thing, but that's ok because the good thing is really important in the overall aim of removing the bad thing. And meanwhile, whilst the good people fight on, the bad ones enjoy their success. And as one avenue for profit closes another one opens easily. If they can't make cigarettes they can invest in mining or diamonds or oil or drugs or any the other demands on the wealth of natural resources that Africa offers. And then, not forgetting the other abundant natural resource Africa offers. It's people, exploited in their millions, for the same financial gain. These people are atrocious and operate in plain sight.

I remember going to parties as a child. We were kept away from the darker more adult elements of them, barbecues, pool parties, and private beaches. As kids we were ushered away to our rooms after dark but we could always hear the noise late into the night. Other times there were parties at sports clubs where we would be taken home by the housekeeper, security guards or the nanny. As an adult, looking back, it doesn't take a genius to work out what would be going on. Mother was so proper, she would rush us all away. But Dad was still there and he went to numerous events that we were never present at. It all happened.

So if Dad was even involved a tiny bit in these parties which were simply breeding grounds for corruption, then it goes to show that Nigel Davies was also there.

As Davies is the only known association I have, I need a way to get to talk to him. But what will I say, I can hardly go big on the corruption as an opening gambit and he is sure as hell not going to talk freely about it with all the posh folk around.

But he came to see Dad last year. So I, as his daughter, especially the daughter with all the money, would be very welcome. It has to be an invitation waiting to happen. Given the uprooting of Walter it's a wonder he's not been round already looking for a way in. Or does he think whatever Dad has on him, died with him.

The house is beginning to depress me but I will stay here tonight. I don't want to go to Ruby's again and I can't be bothered with a hotel when there is a spare room. Looking out over the garden at the back and the open fields, I wonder if I could come back and live here. The house is here and it belongs to me and Ruby, assuming the will is straightforward. I also have the flat but still haven't quite worked out how much of a contrast that is with my lifestyle. The greenery at the back, the flower meadows, farms and passive lifestyle that decorates English country living is there waiting for me. Forgetting about the millions in the bank account, this is a future. No more digging in fields, nursing dreadfully poor women, cleaning up the crap of the world left behind.

I sigh. It's not really me. I would be eating my brains after a few days, drunk with boredom and turning into some old spinster with a rifle pointed at anyone who dared to come on my land. Yeah, that isn't happening. Plus for all my pale skin and Irish resistance to a sun tan, I do like it a bit warmer than this place has to offer.

I can see my fingers leave an imprint on the window ledge. I will have to get someone in to clean it, but also to strip it. Whatever we do with the place it will have to be overhauled. Worries for another day, I think. Back to business.

I walk back to the living room. 'Need you to get me a meeting with Nigel Davies,' I say, shaking Terry awake

'Hey, hey,' he says, 'I've murdered people for waking me up like that. Coiled like a spring. Where's my gun?'

'Funny, if was a bandit I'd have cut your throat before you even open your eyes.'

'Bit out of practice,' he says rubbing his eyes. 'How can I get a meeting with Nigel Davies? He won't meet the likes of me.'

'Thought you said he liked the military types.' I know already what I want him to do, but I'm having fun winding him up.

'I'm good on VE day and Poppy day for a photo op. Likes of them nobs won't let me wipe the shit from their shoes. I'm cannon fodder. Expendable.'

'Yeah, you're not wrong.' I say, 'I think you are being a little generous. But anyway, you just need to get a message to him.

Pearl McCann would like to see him. I have absolutely no doubt the mention of a McCann will not be an issue.'

'Yeah, you're a smart one,' he says, pointing. 'Still don't know how I will get a message to him though.'

'You're a soldier, I'm sure they gave you training on that kind of thing. Or were you not senior enough for thinking?'

'Funny,' he says.

***

I am woken by the security alert for the front door. The rattling of the gate has triggered the sensor and the alarm is sounding like a 4 minute nuclear warning.

I check the clock. It's 6:00 am. I pull on some jeans and a jumper on quickly.

Glad Ruby left me the code, I try to type the number whilst rubbing my eyes. I don't do early starts.

The camera shows two large heads.

'Hello. Can I help?' I ask

'North Kent Court Appointed Bailiffs, am I speaking to Pearl McCann.'

I say yes but don't open the gate. I decide to go out to them. It's just coming light and a bit chilly but instinctively I don't want to let them in until I know what they want.

As I approach the gate, I can see that my instincts were right. I feel most times I can handle myself but there is a reason they choose these bailiffs the way they do. Mostly, so that people like me feel that we best do as they say just in case they beat us up. But truth is, for all their court appointed authority they can't enter the premises without permission and they absolutely can't touch anyone. Still they hire them with dome-head haircuts and a body shape modelled on barn doors. The communication capabilities are capped at growling which neatly avoids more nuanced conversation.

The older bailiff hands me the court document.

I do a quick scan and then decide I have something to argue with him.

'Why have you come here?' I ask.

'Miss, we are at this address as the property of Pearl McCann to take payment or goods to the total of £100,000 as a down payment on a court pending payment as per the below judgement. Are you going to pay up or let us in to start valuing items?'

I look at them both for a moment. Sometimes a pause makes people nervous and I have found a use for it when dealing with ignorant arses. They are so used to a fightback or a feeble response and the pause disarms them.

I stand back from the gate and wait with my arms folded trying to mentally count to thirty seconds. They look at each other, slightly puzzled by my silence.

'Are you going to let us in or shall I call the police?'

Good, they are irritated. I decide to keep it up. 'I am going to respond slowly and clearly and I'm going to record it on my phone here for the record, that I have been perfectly reasonable and open with you. Let's take the points one at a time.'

I take the phone from my pocket to show them my intentions.

'Miss, we haven't got time to mess about. I'm calling the police.' He takes his phone to his ear.

Wonder how we did this before we had phones. I decide to not spend too much time on that thought. The likelihood is in those days they would have used a battering ram to break down the gate and I would be trampled underfoot whilst they robbed what they wanted.

'I am pointing out for the purpose of the recording that I am not being difficult or awkward but explaining my position reasonably and openly. You cannot bully your way into this house and I don't have to let you in.'

My voice is loud and staggered and I feel a bit silly. Good job only Terry's house is nearby otherwise the curtain twitchers would be on full alert. I carry on with my forced speech.

'Firstly, this property is my father's house and not mine. So nothing in this house can be taken as a payment against this debt. Whilst my father is dead, the matters of his estate are not resolved and I have no claim against a single penny.'

'Secondly, if you wish to make a claim against me for this money, then go ahead. Reach me at my address and we can discuss the appropriate debt management. For your information my current residence is in Dar-Es-Salaam, Tanzania if you want to check it out. East Africa if you need more geographical hints. Let's see if your jurisdiction stretches that far.'

'Thirdly, the court order provision is made without me being given a hearing and therefore I should be entitled to appeal it.'

It's hard work this speaking in capitals and have to take a deep breath.

A door slams. I turn to see Terry stumbling along from next door. He is dressed in track suit bottoms and a vest. He hasn't bothered to attach his false arm so looks all the more imposing as the stub of his arm swings loose in the chilly morning air.

'Problem Pearl?' He asks.

'Morning Terry,' I will tell him later but he has no idea how pleased I am to see him. I'm shivering with the cold and trying to outface these two idiots is hard work. 'I am waiting for a response from these two gentleman as to how they want to proceed.' I point to my phone again in case Terry goes off on one. 'I'm recording, for the record, you know?'

He nods back, good that he picked up on that. Last thing I need is a verbal rant and Terry trying to be a hero as they will call the Police in seconds. Though Terry lashing out with one fist might be something of comedy value in years to come.

'Call the police,' he says to his younger colleague. Turning to me, 'I've a letter here that states that this is the address of Pearl McCann and I am legally permitted to enter these premises to retrieve goods to the value of £100,000 pounds. Unless you can prove otherwise, I have right of entry.'

'Sure, what kind of proof would you like? Electoral register, phone bill, gas bill. Council tax statement. In fact let me do that. If you can find my name on any record for this address, I will gladly let you in. Can you wait with these gentleman please?' I hand him my phone through the gate.

I come back a two minutes later with my coat on and a selection of bills. The bailiff takes them into his hand and reviews them. He picks up the phone and seems to be calling his office. He wonders out of earshot.'

'You ok,' Terry asks whilst he is out of the way.'

'Thanks for coming out. I think I've done enough to keep them away, but I'm going to need to see Dad's solicitor today otherwise they will be back or maybe worse round at Ruby's.'

The bailiff returns and hands me the papers.

'I'll be back,' he says and follows his mate back to the van.

I am so glad to get back inside the house. Terry follows me in and I put the kettle on.

I am shaking as I try to fill up the pot.

'That was tough call.' Terry says. 'You did brilliant.'

I still have my copy of the letter from the court. He reads it.

'International Tobacco have sold the debt onto a debt management company. Now your old man is out the way they are seeking urgent payment of the debt amounting to £15 million pounds plus interest calculated at 27% per annum. They require the debtor to set out payment terms and an immediate payment of £100,000. Fuck me. Where you going to get that? What was your old man doing with that kind of money?'

I don't know what to tell him. I really don't want to involve anyone else. We sit down with the hot tea at the kitchen table. I have the letter and the papers spread out on the table and move them around like playing cards. I notice a boarding pass stub among the papers. I pick it up as I continue talking.

'Honestly I don't know. It seems to be something Dad was involved in. Like the order says, he took some money from the company but I don't know why and how much? Well I suppose the how much is written there.'

'Your dad wasn't like that, honest as a day is long. No way had he stolen money.' Terry says getting agitated.

'Look, we don't know the truth. Let's hold off emotions. I agree with you but this isn't going to go away easily. I need to speak to the solicitor and find out about any wills. Something's bothering me though.'

I study the boarding pass. Dean James is the name. British
Airways. Cape Town to London. I wonder where this has come
from. It's from June 2018. Maybe one of Dad's old friends
visited him and this was left behind. I will check who it is later
on.

Terry is still talking and I look up to listen.

'Whole thing is bothering me,' he replies, 'fucking parasites
these companies. Living off other people's miseries.'

 'What bothers me is that it would have been obvious to the
debt management company if they knew who Dad was and who
I was, the house and estate would never have been transferred
to me so quickly. And it might all go to Ruby anyway. So why
would they take a chance and why would a judge even agree to
it?'

'Because they're bent that's why. All pigs in the same trough.'

I stare out the window and think about what he just said.

'I think you are right. They were chancing it. Which means it was
a warning shot. They are telling me they know who I am and
that I have my dad's money. Nigel Davies said he had business
to attend to with me and I guess this is him pushing his
position.'

'Wait a minute, who's they? And you just said you don't know
about the money.'

'Speaking metaphorically, sorry Terry,' I say, back tracking.
Caught out in a verbal joust by Terry. Need to watch myself. 'I
know there is some money, but nothing specific. I need to find
out as well. But to your point about who 'they' is. They must be
Nigel Davies as who else do we know who's looking for the
money. He must be still connected to ITA. He must be behind it.'

'Told you, I am not stupid, it's always the same with these rich types. They are stitching the likes of the working man up. No question. And you know more about that money than you're telling me. If you don't trust me, that's fine but don't lie to me. I can fuck off home and please myself if you are going to be like that.'

'Sorry Terry,' I decide to be more open. He is not my perfect idea of a buddy but he's the best I have at the moment. 'I'm not lying to you. I know there is money but I don't want to scare you or me yet as you've seen the numbers. It's scary. We could be in serious trouble. I mean prison. I don't want you to think you have to get involved.'

'Jesus, Pearl, I'm in for a penny, in for a pound. I knew your Dad and will defend him to my last breath. You don't need to protect me.'

'Sure,' I reply. But I am worried. That bailiff told me how serious this is. I am some kind of target, I have to realise that, whoever is behind it; I have no idea what to do. I have come to a firm conclusion though, especially since they put together the dodgy bailiff order, that they are quite happy to use dirty tactics to get money from me. It doesn't put dad in the clear or make the money he has any less suspicious. It does mean however, that they are as bad or worse. So I am not going to hand it over without a fuss. I know for a fact I didn't do anything wrong so let them bring it on. Bring the police, the courts, I don't have anything to hide. The moment I feel that I am in danger I might have to run to the hills but whilst my knowledge of the circumstances is less than zero, I still feel I have a slight upper hand in being entirely innocent. Maybe that's a little naïve.

# CHAPTER 8

∞ § ∞

The solicitor will see me today.

Terry comes along. He thinks he needs to be my bodyguard. Kind of charming but no. It's comical trying to picture how many ways that would not work. I dismiss the image of Terry waving his stick at an assailant and the assailant toppling him with his little finger. Poor Terry. Still I let him come as I feel I owe him to be at least included in the conversation about my dad's secret, given he is probably the most recent witness to it.

I tell him to stay in the reception whilst I go into the office. No need for him to hear the more intimate details as yet.

The solicitor is a bearded grey haired man. Grey suit to match his personality perhaps, not that it matters. He offers me little of consequence as he advises me that he needs to apply for probate before anything can be done. That has to be done via the executor of the will.

'Who is the executor? I know it's not me or Ruby but I don't know who he trusted outside the immediate family.

'Rebecca Andrews, I believe a cousin of yours.'

'Ah.' Not someone who's going to do me any favours.

'Did my father leave any special instructions?' I ask, 'he seems to have made some arrangements for me that I am not sure I understand.'

'How so?' he asks.

'I'm not sure I can elaborate on them at the moment. It wouldn't be fair. Or at least I don't think it's fair.'

'Not sure I follow.' He says

I sigh. I'm not sure if he's playing dumb or I need to be clearer with him.

'It's possible he did something illegal when he left his job all those years ago. It involved some money. A lot of money and it's now in my name.'

He pauses. 'I don't think there is anything I have that fits into that category.'

'There is maybe something you can help me with though.'

I explain the situation with the bailiffs and what legal basis I have to defend myself. He confirmed that until probate was complete they would be unable to claim on the estate or any beneficiary.

'Of course, they, whoever they are, may have known that.' He says, 'so it's possible they were agitating for a response. But why would they do that?'

'To scare me?'

He scratches his beard. I suspect this is not his normal conversation when handling probate and wills.

'If you want me to write to the court and complain I can do?'

'No, I don't think there is any point in doing it. I suspect I will hear from them soon enough. If they want the money they will find me once more. The question is more the why and whether there is anything I can do to keep them from it.'

The solicitor has nothing to offer me so I head home. It doesn't tell me much accept that dad was definitely wanting this business kept outside of any other domain. He didn't trust anyone but me with the money, I have to ask more questions about why.

'Got something for you,' Terry says. 'Rang one of the contacts I have. Nigel Davies has a local surgery on Saturday mornings. He holds them in the offices at the gate house to his estate. How fucking la-di-da is that?'

'Did you mention my name?' I ask.

'Didn't need to. Apparently he's a sucker for a good war story so swapped a name with my mate. We're booked in.'

'Perfect. Tomorrow then.' I knew Terry would come in useful for something. It's actually a relief not to be using my name. As the day's gone on, I get the feeling that he wouldn't welcome me so openly.

***

It doesn't take long to drive there, probably half an hour from Chevening cutting across country. The gate is open and there is space to park next to the familiar blacked out Range Rover. Looking over to the driveway, I can see the house. It's not actually that big, five large windows either side of a central grand entrance. The manicured gardens and views over the local countryside are expected for a property such as this. Nice work if you can get it.

I let Terry register with the secretary. He gives his mate's name and address in the constituency in case they check the electoral role. For all the problems the army gave him, it also gave him a social network second to none.

The room in the gatehouse is like a church with no pews. Cold stone walls and a tiled floor. The vaulted ceiling is smart but the room with the chairs round the edge is boring. I wonder if his office is more appealing as this is like queuing to be told the year I'm scheduled to die.

Terry's whistling some random tune to himself which is grating a bit.

'Tell me what I'm supposed to say again,' he asks.

'Tell him that you are not getting the right money on universal credit,' I say, 'tell him what the problem is and when he asks for your statement say you left it at home. Tell him your disability allowance and Army pension are not properly reflected.'

'But he'll just send me away then.'

It's the tenth time I've explained this.

'This is about him seeing me and me seeing him. I want to see if he knows who I am.'

'Don't know why the fuck you don't just go in there and slap the posh fucker round the head. Bloody deserves it coming for your money like that. Look at that palace. Not like he needs money.'

In some ways, he's right. About me slapping Davies too. But that won't get me anywhere. Truth is at some point I will have to have this out with him but I don't want to be handicapped with lack of knowledge before I have to. Damn you Dad, you could have at least sent me a damn letter, I don't know. Even a sodding treasure map with X marks the spot. All I have is a cryptic crossword clue suggesting I do the right thing.

It's our turn and I follow Terry in.

Davies is sat behind his desk and politely stands for us. He is wearing a smart blue suit and matching tie. He is more imposing close up, tall and slim, moderate tan. For someone in their late sixties he looks fit and able. I have met him before but only when I was young.

'Hello,' he says, 'please come in and sit down. Jack Burns, isn't it.'

That's the name Terry gave him.

'Yeah sir. I think my benefit is wrong.' He says, stuttering a little. 'My army pension is too little and I can't afford my rent. It's wrong is this, man like me who's served and all that.'

Good start Terry, keep it up.

'Yes, yes. And indeed thank you for your service.'

He's not looked at me, which is disappointing. He's focussed on getting his story straight for Terry. Fair enough, one thing an M.P. has to be quite good at is putting up with people having a good old moan, not looking bored and then having to suggest or take some action that might meaningfully move forward a situation.

'Look old chap,' he continues, 'I could check your statement but I'm not really sure I'm the best option. I would suggest the DWP office in town. They can look into it.'

'It's wrong,' I say, jumping in, 'after all he's given to this country. Look at him, disabled, in constant pain and he can't get enough money to pay his rent.'

He looks at me, staring for a second. He recognises me but doesn't place me.

'Quite,' he agrees. 'If you give my secretary your details I will write to the local office and get some more information if that's ok.'

'OK,' Terry says. I think he's happy to get out of here, but I need more from this meeting. A scene is appropriate.

'Not good enough,' I say, 'you can't fob this man off just like that. Not important, waved away. You should be outraged by what he's telling you. I am. Damn hero he is. Bet you never got your boots dirty. Public school. Nearest you got to service was playing plastic bayonets with the school chums.'

'I don't have to listen to his,' he says, standing up to let me know this is over. 'I've offered to help and I will, now please...'

He stops to study me again.

'I know you.' His forehead is creased, red faced as he looks to the window. The view over the meadow must be his source of inspiration as he then turns back to me. 'Pearl McCann.'

I am standing as well. Ready to leave, not sure what happens next. 'I am.'

'You owe me. Your Father as well,' he says, pointing. 'You weren't at the funeral but I've been waiting to speak to you.'

'I don't owe you a penny, I don't even know who you are, what you did. But my dad's gone now and there's not a thing you can do.'

'Get out of my office,' he says, his fist clenching. He's reaching for the buzzer for the next visitor.

'Hey what about me?' Terry asks. 'I still got my problems.'

He looks between us, trying to work out if he has just been had or Terry's genuine and I've just disrupted the session.  But then Terry bursts out laughing and our cover is blown.

We head for the door but I can't resist one last stone to throw at Davies.

'You stay away from me and my family,' I say, with the door open ajar. Not sure if people can hear in the hall but what the hell. 'I've got the evidence. My father gave it to me. You stay away from me or I will send it to the press.'

He walks over and slams the door shut before I can get out.

Now furious with anger, spitting his words directly in my face.

'You've got nothing. You're making it up. If you had anything, you wouldn't be here play acting. Now get out. And you,' he says to Terry, 'you're a disgrace, using your service to bluff your way in here. Absolute disgrace.'

He opens the door again and ushers us through it.

'Fuck off,' Terry says, as he staggers past him with his stick. He gets very close to his Davies face and moves to nut him but stops short. Davies winces and moves out of the way spooked.

As we exit the hall, everyone is watching and we rush to the car. Just as likely Davies has called the cops. We get to the car and drive off quickly.

We both laugh.

We are at back on the road back to Chevening before either of us speaks.

'He don't like it up him,' Terry says. 'That's one stuck up bastard.'

'Thank you,' I say. 'I'm not sure what I expected from it, but it confirmed one thing. This is not about money. There's a secret and Davies doesn't want anyone to know it. That's worth far more than cash in the bank.'

'But how you going to find out? You never even mentioned your brother.'

'I know,' I say, 'I know. But I hate the fact that he probably knows what happened to Walter and I don't. I didn't want to give him that leverage over me. If I can take one positive from that meeting. I am 100% sure that whatever Dad did, he did for the right reasons.

But I'm also running out of sources of information. Bea has run off, Ruby and Terry know nothing. Solicitor knows nothing and the only person who knows something is Nigel Davies. I'd rather rip my guts out with a rusty knife than go back in that office and ask though.

The next time I see that obnoxious prick I want it to be him resigning or in a court room weeping as a judge discusses whether the key to his cell can go in the recycling bin or not.

***

I arrive back to Dad's house, feeling exhausted. All the way back from Studenham hall, I felt that I could rest my head on the steering wheel and have a nap. Pity that urge for sleep escapes me at 4:00 a.m.

I am back in the house and Terry goes home. Thankfully. I could do with the time to think. I put the kettle on to make some tea. The boarding pass stub I found yesterday is still on the top of the papers I left out and reminds me I was supposed to check on the name.

I get my laptop out and put the name into google.

Dean James, Fleet Sales Director for African Logistics Company. I click on the LinkedIn profile and see a photo of my brother staring back at me. He has a suit and is looking smarter than I've ever seen in my life. So this is him and his new life. I'm annoyed I missed this the other day.

I hear the gate and look out the window. Ruby's car's on the drive.

I top the kettle up for an extra cup of tea.

'Where've you been?' she asks. Her voice is raised and she looks as if she has been crying. She's in jeans and a t-shirt. No make-up which is unusual for her. She obviously come over in a rush.

'Just out,' I say. I will postpone the business with Nigel Davies. I show her the laptop instead.

'It's Walter.'

'Yes.'

'Unbelievable. Look at him. Carrying on as if none of us exist. What an utter contemptable...Pearl, why would he do this to us?

'I can't imagine why except that he got into serious trouble. But if you look at that profile he's living his best life.'

I carry on making tea but begin to feel lightheaded. I collapse into the chair. I rub my eyes and push the tiredness away

'You ok?' Ruby asks.

'I don't know,' I say. 'I think all this is catching up with me.'

'I know what you mean. I've hardly spoken a decent word with Jake this week I've been so out of it. Let me finish the tea.'

She continues as I push the tears from my eyes. This morning's adrenalin is fading and I'm getting emotional again. My stomach feels like a washing machine. Ever since Dad passed, there has been a barrage of new revelations to handle. Every day is a day on the wheel of fortune. What particular trauma will I have to face next?  Maybe I need to go visit the doctors and have a full screening. I'm sure on the record of this week, I'm due some kind of cancer diagnosis or more likely for me, liver failure.

'What's going on Pearl?'

'I wish I knew,' I reply.

I get up and put the papers back in the drawer. A useful distraction from her enquiry.

'But you know something? Not just about Walter,' she says. 'Pearl, I can read you like a book. You are keeping something from me. You always do it. Walk away. Never just sit and talk. Something to be done, something to be avoided. Never mind messing with those documents, come back and talk to me.'

Fuck, she knows me too well. I need to give her something. I can't tell her about the money can I? I seriously can't process it myself so how can I bring her in. Or is it selfish me who wants it all myself. Is that me?

She looks at me. Her forehead creases as she instinctively brushes her hair back behind her ear. I sense she's looking through me, trying to read my thoughts.

'I met Bea,' I say, without thinking too much. It seems the easiest to blurt out. 'In London. She was sorting Dad's affairs.'

I carry on tidying the papers, not ready to look her in the eye. I'm actually still thinking about Dean James and Walter's new life. Without us.

'So why didn't you tell me that? What did you think of her?'

'I didn't think much at all. She said, she stayed away from the funeral as she knew she wouldn't be welcome. She talked about Dad in a nice way, explaining that she was going away for a while.'

Gosh, I am now lying to my sister. I fill the cups, unable to explain why I feel the need to lie. Is it her I am protecting or me?

'Did she mention the photograph or Walter?'

'Yes, she told me how scary the meeting was. Dad was really upset by it. But she didn't know what it was about. He didn't share it with her.' At least that isn't a lie.

Fortunately, my sister is also easily readable. She wants to know more but I suspect she is not sure what to ask or whether she really dare ask for fear of what interrogating me might bring.

Pragmatic me has already come to a conclusion. I can't stand still and I can't wallow. I need to do something positive.

'I'll go to Cape Town,' I say. 'We need to get to the bottom of the affair with Walter and the best way to do is to go track him down.' Even as I say it I'm wondering if it's the right thing. But why not? What else would I do?

'Really? Should I come too?' She says it quickly and I can her eyes shift to the left likely thinking of a hundred reasons why she can't do it.

'You stay here,' I say, to help her out. 'Someone needs to look after this place.'

'Yeah, it doesn't need both of us does it. And I can't leave the kids with Jake too long. He will go spare. I'm just off to South Africa for a few days, kids will be fine. Yeah, I can do without that stress.'

You could just call him couldn't you?' she adds at the end.

I think of a response. 'I could,' I say, 'but I think he would probably put the phone down on us and do a runner. Plus I need to have it out with him. It's better face to face.'

'Yeah, it feels like a long way but it's definitely better to do it in person. But you must tell me everything when you come back. Pearl, I mean it. No more secrets.'

'Yes,' I say. I'm becoming as slippery as Walter now. 'And we can go away together, spa break or something like that when this is all sorted. Dad's money will resolved at some point and we can spend it on a treat for ourselves.'

'Sounds good.'

It does but I wonder if we'll ever do it.

'I'll check the flights, see if I can get one tomorrow.' I say before she can pick me up on that.

'What will you do when you find him?'

'I'm not really sure,' I say. 'Once I've murdered him, I will bring him back to life so I can do it again.'

'Think he already did that,' she says.

We laugh. Good we still can.

'But seriously,' she says, 'don't waste any time on Walter. He doesn't deserve it. Find out the truth and then come home.'

'You're right. Let me get there first and find out what's happening. I'll decide then.'

She's right about Walter. Though she doesn't know the next call I will make as soon as she's gone is to put a decent wedge into my bank account to cover this and the other costs I'm going to pay out in getting to the bottom of what's going on. Legal costs to deal with whatever Davies comes up with me, travel and who knows what else.

A gaping hole is growing inside me where the truth of my family is supposed to be. That centre of gravity we all crave as a baseline for our lives. It was always flawed whilst there more questions than answers about some parts of the past but I was satisfied that there was little that would change me or change

the world around me. How wrong I was? Now all I can think
about is to get the answers before that hole grows so big I can
no longer stop descending into it.

# CHAPTER 9

## ∞ § ∞

## South Africa

Sunday morning. I am half way through my first bourbon courtesy of South African Airways. I never fly business class but today I am. I spent my first money from PMC, my business, booking the next available flight and caring little for the price. It felt so empowering. The first time in my life where I never asked the price. Actually, I did look again when it came back at five grand, but then I am not going to dwell on it. It's a pin prick on an elephant's arse. My ethics, hard wired into me are going through a temporary outage whilst I rediscover magnetic north on my moral compass. With all this chaos, it may take some time.

It felt weird at the check-in desk. Though I've had a few air-miles in the past which allowed me to bypass the queues now and then. This time the nice check in lady with the slightly better make-up reserved for those with platinum travel cards did actually smile. I didn't get the look that wonders how come someone travelling with little more than a rucksack gets access to the premium lounge.

Terry wanted to come. How sweet. I've kind of got used to him but don't feel quite ready to have him as a travelling buddy just yet. And fork out a ton of cash, even though I could. But no, what purpose would he serve?

Plus sadly Terry is hard work on the physical side and my patience gene is not that well developed. How did I ever become a charity worker with this little empathy? I'm fine with

my customers I guess, it's just friends or hangers on I lose it
with. Maybe, the sense I have that Terry doesn't help himself
with his weight and his beer and his way of just being clumsy.
Sigh!

So I scared him with stories of black beggars pestering him in
the street and he went off on one about spongers and liberals
letting them get away with it. My work was done at that point
and I didn't even have to get into explaining the nuance of
apartheid where the law supersedes the politics of liberals and
spongers. A lecture for another day perhaps, once I get past
explaining the simple point that loving your own country doesn't
mean you have to hate all the others.

He is content to keep an eye on the house in case any more
bailiffs come knocking. Plus he can ask around his Tory mates
for gossip on Davies. I figure that someone knows his past.
Someone always knows and there is always gossip. If Davies is
scared of something coming out then it must be criminal, not in
the white collar, fraud type of way. That would be inconvenient
but not shaming. It's something darker than that. Diamonds,
drugs, corruption, people trafficking or sex. Or all at once. That
kind of mud sticks especially if the evidence is damning.

The steward brings me some food and asks if I would like
another drink. He is already filling my glass before I get to say
yes. I click through the movie options and settle on something
action packed. Fast and Furious perhaps where brain doesn't
need to engage and I can reinforce my judgement on their low
morals and lack of understanding of world affairs. My
superiority complex could do with the same boost as my whisky
glass.

So I'm going back to Africa. I didn't anticipate that quite so
quickly but it's almost a relief to be away from the chaos of the
last few days. Though I can't help thinking there is far more to

come and taking a 10,000 mile plane journey is not going to solve it. At the same time, it feels like the right thing to be doing. Something like that anyway.

Going to Cape Town and tracking down Walter doesn't faze me. I hope it's simply a case of turning up at his work and finding him waiting with a cup of tea. Of course it isn't going to be that easy. And who knows what he will say or do. I could say the same for myself.

The movie begins and the moment comes to disengage the outside world.

***

I check into Tsoga Sun hotel at the Waterfront in time for midnight. It's convenient for eating at night and also for city centre. I've booked in for five nights though not sure if I will need to stay for that long. I suspect this is not going to be fast thing.

I slept awhile on the plane. A few drinks saw to that and one crap movie does encourage me to do the sleep thing rather than pretend I'm enjoying it. Plus the fact that I hardly slept Saturday night, meant I was well in need of decent rest. Now I'm here I feel pretty much the same. Tired, out of place, on a journey and not just in a plane.

Rattled is a good word for it.

I'm rattled.

I spend my life in control of all that I do, even in circumstances where I shouldn't be in control, like a raging flood or a sandstorm. I know what to do, keep calm, keep everyone around me calm and keep the world turning.

This is different, totally disarming and I have no idea what to do next other than go with what comes to me in the moment. A strategy is missing and will have to be found. Perhaps if I knew what this was all about then I could do something like that.

I open the bottle I picked up in duty free and sit by the window, checking the lights over the bay. Fancy apartments, stunning views all around. A few miles down the road and it's the townships, the social systems that exist as an underworld to this vast wealth. I understand that world. The deviance, the innovation, the will to survive. The priorities of food and water, of basic pride. They live their lives without riches but often with joy. I sometimes wonder where the joy comes from, often from some illegal still in the back of a shack somewhere but that's their joy. I look round at the riches from my window and joy isn't my first thought.

I'm in the wrong world. I am not meant to be rich. I could pay for and run a hospital in Djibouti or Somalia, do something truly mesmerising with this kind of money. But it doesn't feel like my money and for me to decide. Certainly not ready to nail my sign up on a new hospital wing. The Pearl McCann Wing. In some ways I can't wait to give it away, it'll be anonymously or through some intermediaries. I don't want the focus on me or anyone asking where it came from.

Drinking again. Alone again. Story of my life.

Though I can go look up some friends, I won't. I'm not ready for that yet. Walter first, then take on the rest of the world.

***

Africa Logistics is in the city centre. The company rents a floor of an unremarkable office block. I walk in and am guided to the second floor.

I expect it to be a glossy reception like any other city centre company. When the lift door opens I'm surprised to find something similar to a kitchen cupboard with a coffee machine, a sink with dirty cups and a buzzer on a plain wooden door.

I'm about to knock when the door opens. A bearded Asian man comes through.

'Is this reception,' I ask.

'Just go in,' he says.

Inside, there are a few desks. There are a few staff but many desks empty and the equipment looks dated. No-one pays much attention so I go to the first desk where a large black woman wearing jeans and a T-shirt is sitting. This seems the most casual unprofessional office ever. Whatever African Logistics is, I wonder how it makes money. This doesn't look like a place clients visit.

'I'm looking for Dean James,' I ask the lady.

'Don't know him,' she says. She taps on the computer and shrugs her shoulders.

'You sure,' I ask.

'I'm sure. He's not here or in any office in South Africa.' Her local accent sounds dismissive and her general demeanour is rude. I look around for some extra help but no-one seems interested. There isn't much more I can do so I turn around to leave. I pass the Asian man at the door again.

I take the lift down and walk out the door completely disappointed. Back in reception I wonder what to do next. That woman just completely blanked me. What an odd place.

The lift opens and the Asian man comes out. He walks over to me.

'You're looking for Dean James?' he asks. 'Don't worry about Sherrie, she's a bit…. Well she's not used to visitors.'

'You know Dean?' I ask.

'Yeah but he's not on the system. He works direct for the boss. You won't find him here. He's kind of on the road.  I can give him a call if you want?'

I think for a second. Do I want to give him a warning?

'I'm not sure,' I say. 'I've come a long way to see him but I want it to be surprise. If you let me know where you are going to meet him, I could turn up and surprise him.'

He mutters a response.

'I'm his sister and I haven't seen him for a while.' I say, trying to tempt him, 'I would like to surprise him.'

'Hmmm ok. Look we have a car sales and rental lot just off the freeway. Out towards the east of the city. He will be there at some point this afternoon. You'll find him there if you want to surprise him.'

'Thanks,' I say, 'can I ask what Dean does?'

He smiles. 'You really don't know do you?' he replies. 'Lots of things I suppose. We rent cars, vans…supply equipment, people. Anything that companies in the region need we get it. Dean is kind of freelance. He deals with clients' specific needs, let's say.'

That sounds really vague and suspicious.

He gives me the address of the rental shack and I leave. I wonder if he will call ahead to Dean or not, but too late now. I will have to take my chances.

***

An hour later I am on the freeway towards the airport, glad I took a hire car when I arrived yesterday. I wasn't sure I would be needing it but felt like a useful insurance policy.

As I get close the townships out of the city, there is a road junction. The navigation guides me off to main road and a few hundred metres along I am by the car lot. I park the car off the street and check it out. No sigh of life though the gate is open.

It's not unlike any typical used car sales lot except these cars were even more dated. This feels more pound shop car sales than an international logistics company. I'm already concluding that car sales or rentals is the least of what is for sale.

I wander through the gates tentatively wondering how I'm going to handle this. Is he going to be sat in the office chair with a pot of tea waiting for his next punter? Is he out delivering and I'm going to take him by surprise when he comes back? Will he panic or run? What will I do? I haven't thought about this.

I approach the door of the Porta cabin. Nervous, looking all around. Still no sigh of anyone.

Placing my hand on the handle, I pause. Deep breath.

The door opens and I have to step back. A small black man appears and barges passed me without a word. I don't even have a chance to say anything before he is in a pickup truck and drives away. The door has swung shut in the meantime so I need to open it again. My heart is beating fast and I grab a tissue from my bag to wipe my head. Too hot.

I push the handle more confidently this time

Inside there is an office with a number of files on the wall, a locker cupboard and a desk. Behind the desk is a black woman. She is large breasted, rotund and leant over fixing her tight red dress. Her red lipstick is smudged and I think one of her fake eyelashes has fallen off. It doesn't take an expert to work out that she has been providing services.

The office smells musty, stale with a hint of body odour from whoever frequents the office on a regular basis. It's unclear whether the odour is from the woman or her visitors.

'Can I help you?' she asks, whilst picking up a mirror to continue her facial restoration. She doesn't seem embarrassed by what I might think of her so I carry on with my request. I look the other way and study the contents for the office. It is like a car lot office but a really shitty one. The baseball bat in the corner provides further evidence of the customer facing challenges that this business deals with. An international logistics business doing deals with a threat of violence. Quality.

'I'm looking for Dean James?' I say.

'Not here today,' she says.

'When will be here? Is there somewhere I can find him?'

'His business not mine? I don't keep a diary.' She says. 'If you are paying for something, get on with it, otherwise I got things to do.'

Her voice is abrasive and dismissive. What happened to lovely friendly Cape Town? Between this place and the office in town I'm beginning to think the musical joy of the local accent has been replaced by nastiness.

'It's ok,' I say.

I don't fancy another minute in her company, so I step outside. I walk back to the car considering my options. This feels slow and unproductive. But he can't be that far away either. I take one last look round before I leave the lot. What a desolate and desperate place. Why would he be here among all this garbage?

So much for faking his death to end up here. A distance from his smart LinkedIn profile.

A police car pulls of the road and into the gate. I step back out of the way as it pulls up. Two white officers get out. One goes towards the office. The other remains by the car. He sees me and decides I am worthy of attention.

'Who are you?' he asks.

Shit, I hadn't anticipated questions.

'My name's Pearl McCann,' I say. 'I'm looking for my brother, 'Dean James. He told me I worked out here but think I got the wrong place.'

As it splurge the words out quickly I realise the mistake I've made. He is not my brother in his new world.

The cop looks at me like I just spit on his shoes.

'Do you know where he is?' The cop asks.

'No, I came looking for him.' I reply, as assuredly as I can but his hard stare is making me more nervous. I think I'm digging a hole very quickly.

'When was the last time you saw him?' He asks.

I'm sure he's reading my reticence. Now what do I say.

'Quite a while,' I say, hoping something vague will help. 'I have been working out the country for a while.'

He thinks about another question. I'm feel my armpits dampening with the tension and the heat. Why am I lying for this shit of a brother of mine?

'Ok you can go.' He passes me a card. 'We need to speak to him so when you find him, call that number. You'll be doing him a big favour.'

'What's he done?' I ask, feeling braver.

'Just tell him to call us.'

I decide to follow his instruction and rush back the car. I'm relieved to get inside and take a deep breath. But instead of driving off, I decide to stay and watch events unfold from a safe distance.

The officer joins his colleague in the lot. A moment later, the same officer returns with the woman. She is being held firmly by the arm and is protesting. He places her in the back of the car and returns to the lot at the same time as making a call. The other locks the office with a key and joins the other one in the car. They drive off together and the lot is quiet again.

I shake my head in wonder. What is this all about?

I put the car in gear and look back down the street to check for traffic. I catch sight of a movement at the car lot. I stop again and get out of the car for a better view. Someone, looks like a white man, is walking between the cars and going towards the office. He staggers, stepping awkwardly from side to side using the cars to steady him.

Quickly I go back towards the entrance as the robust looking man reaches the office door. It's Walter. He must have been hiding among the cars. Or looking at his state, probably sleeping.

I rush over to him as he struggles to open the door with the key.

'Walter,' I say.

He turns quickly.

'Pearl, shit. What you doing here?' he says. The door opens. 'Get inside quick.'

The same smell permeates my senses and whilst I was already feeling dirty, being back here I feel the aroma is coming from my clothes.

He collapses into the chair the woman was seated in moments before.

'So here you are,' I say, 'my dead brother.'

As I speak, the anger grows inside, I can't hold it in. I walk over and slap him on the cheek.

Other than him placing his hand on his cheek, it barely registers on his face, yet my hand is stinging. He looks towards me, his eyes half open. Dark holes centred on the pale skin of his face, stretched with an inner pain.

'Pearl,' he says, 'I'm sorry. But did you have to hit me. I thought you would be pleased to see me, you know.'

His words are slow and laboured. It's not drink, it's drugs. There is no alcohol smell and the dead eyes give me all the clues plus the pale pasty skin. He is stoned.

'You're dealing from here?' I ask.

'Fuck you,' he replies, spitting the words out. 'What you doing here anyway. Don't need you telling me what to do. What did you tell the cops just now? How the fuck did you find me anyway?'

'I didn't tell the cops anything,' I reply. I want to leave. I can't face him like this. It's making me sick. I can't decide if I actually want to be sick or really just pick up the baseball in the corner and bash his head in. I am so damn angry with him.

'Your father's dead.' I say, 'he had a heart attack. His third in as many years. This one was the end for him. I came to find you because you went to see him.'

'Fuck,' he says, 'Sorry he's dead, but he didn't do me any favours. Caused me some shit when he wouldn't hand over that money.'

'Seriously, that's all you've got to say.'

I grab him and push him to the floor. I step back worried that my anger is getting the better of me. I've never reacted like this to anyone, ever.

Not that he seems to care. He slowly turns over and clambers back into the chair mumbling his annoyance. My anger is wasted on the drugged up bastard.

Turning my back, thinking, I grab a piece of paper and a pen from the desk. I write down my number.

'Call me when you come down.' I say.

I walk out the door and back to the car. I don't know what to do next but I can't be in the same room as him in that state. I can't really believe it. Did I come to find him, expecting some kind of sibling redemption? Probably not. I didn't also expect to wish he was still dead.

***

It's inevitable that the phone rings.

Six thirty a.m. I don't recognise the number but even from the foggy depths of my early wakened brain it doesn't take a rocket science to work out this is Walter, given it's a local number'

'Sis, they caught me. Can you come to the Police station?'

I don't even ask why and what for. I don't really need to know much more at this stage.

Rubbing sleep from my eyes, I get in the shower. I came here to find Walter and get him to tell me what he knows about Dad. Which means I need to get him out from the hole he is in and get him to talk. Then I can return him to his cesspit and move on. Or at least that's the theory

Two hours later I am at the police station.

Asking for him at the desk I am guided to an interview room. I can speak to him before he is taken before the judge for charging and bail.

He's in a white single piece overall and looks even rougher than last night. How did it come to this? The aesthetics of the room are predictably plain. No colour, no frills, all the rooms featured are focussed on restraining someone. A table and a chair fixed to the floor. A screen divides us so I can't touch or hug him. Not that I feel inclined.

I hadn't expected this moment to upset me quite as much. Yesterday I was angry. Today it feels like a loss. Walter has taken the well of grief I had gone through and now dug it deeper. There is no joy in seeing him like this. Just absolute sadness for what he has become.

'So tell me?' I say.

'You got money sis?' he asks, eyes flickering, looking up and beyond me. He can't look me in the eye. His hands are shaking. Not hard to see he's coming down from the stupor of yesterday.

'Anything to say to me?' I ask.

'I'm sorry. I haven't got time to explain sis, I am desperate. I need to get out of here. I need...'

'Yeah I get what you need. I didn't come here to feed your habit, Walter.'

'Dean, it is. Dean James. Don't call me Walter here. I will be screwed.'

I stare at him, observing the horror in the pit of his eyes. The desperation. He looks at me, his sister but that's not who sees. He's lost to himself as well as me. I listen to his words and the fear, but the fact that he is tugging on every heart string I could possibly have means that he has no love for me. Just for his habit. Just as Ruby said, he's not worth it.

'Please sis,' he says, the words more feeble than before.

If I had any doubt before, it's all gone. This process has become transactional. He needs money from me to get him away from jail, but I need information and I am determined that will be my price.

'You dropped me in it with the cop. They wanted to know why you were a Brit with a different name. It's your fault as well. Had to make something up about you moving to UK when you were a kid. So come on, if you hadn't been here, I might not have got caught.'

'You are seriously unbelievable.' I shake my head as I get up to leave, feeling nauseous again.

Turning away, I avoid the further pleading of a fucked up druggie. I will give him what he needs but I don't want to give him the reward of seeing me say yes there and then. I don't want to reward the manipulation he's attempting.

If it wasn't for the information he has, I would be more than happy for them to throw away the key.

'Sis,' he shouts as I get to the door. I am already back in the corridor with the door slamming behind me before I breathe again. I'll get past this one way or another but it will be struggle not to want to murder him in the process.

***

A few hours later we are in a bar. It's the first place I could find outside the court house. He is drinking water and I decide, given the circumstance, not to order alcohol.

Walter is still agitated and he probably needs a fix. He won't admit it yet but he does. But I want his attention and then I will let him return to his cesspit.

I handed over 1 million rand for him to be released. I surprise myself that in the business of running my card through the machine that I didn't think more about the amount I was spending. But either way, having put myself in the room, I have to see it through. Dean James, Walter as he now is, surrendered his passport and must report to the station each day. Trial date will be set in due course. The story of a South African passport will be another conversation I need to have.

'So tell me. What happened?'

'They're not my drugs, honest sis. It wasn't me. I've been stitched up.'

'I don't give a shit about your drug habit. Damn Walt, I want to know why you faked your death. You have no idea what that did to me. To Ruby. Mum, she died of a broken heart, you know. Honestly, you are so fucking selfish.'

He looks around, nervous.

'Don't call me Walt, please. No-one calls me that these days. It's Dean. I need a fix. I can't focus, can't think. Give me a couple of grand, promise I'll be back and tell you everything.'

I grab the jug and throw the water in his face. I don't care that people are staring.

'You think I'm going to let you walk out without telling me. If I have to take you into the gents and ram your head down the toilets you are going to tell me.'

'I don't have to tell you anything,' he screams, 'you came looking for me.'

'If you want money from me or not to be back in that jail tomorrow, you will tell me. Jesus, Dean, whatever your name is, you owe me and Ruby to tell us what happened. It's the least you fucking owe us.'

He won't look me in the eye. I hate drugs. Excess alcohol does something similar but the drugs, especially hard stuff provides a physical embodiment of the mental destruction. With the deadened eyes, the drawn pale skin as weight loss and general reducing health manifests itself. It's a self-inflicted poison and whilst I can confess my own weakness to excess booze I can also manage my relationship with it and walk away for long periods of time. Walter or Dean is now the visible representation of what happens if you don't walk away.

'I had to,' he says. He gets up to dry himself and knocks his glass over. I wipe it with a mat. He sits down again. It's like dealing with a hyper child. 'I was in trouble. I was gambling. Big wins. I mean serious wins. I was doing well sis, getting myself straight. Had a girlfriend. Getting settled and everything.'

Let's add gambling to the list of vices. Perhaps there's something of the addictive personality in the McCann's genes.

'Why didn't you tell us you were in Kenya?' I ask, trying to keep on the important stuff.

'I just didn't. Was busy. Lot happening. And Nadia was amazing. And then I lost everything. She left. I lost some more. I was in danger. Seriously. They were going to kill me there and then. They had a machete. I was so scared. Then one of the owners spoke up. So he had a better idea. He did me a deal to get me out of the Kenya and into a safe place. In return I needed to run some drugs for him. Told me he would take care of things for me. New name, new identity. He would pay for everything. I said yes. I was desperate Sis. They were going to kill me. I was so scared you have to know I had no choice.'

'Who was in that car Walt...Dean?'

'There was no accident, sis. Whole thing was faked. You have to know these people. They control everything. Got contacts everywhere. It was easy to fake a news report and pay off the local police. Couple of stolen cars, burnt out. Supplied DNA for the death report and a fake crematorium report. I figured after a while I could own up. Come home and make it alright. But it didn't work like that.'

Yeah, selfish prick didn't give a fuck about anyone else. To be honest, I can see there is little evidence of the necessary backbone to do something about the trap he was in, but I will keep digging for more.

'So how come you came to see Dad?' How did you get involved with Nigel Davies?'

He gets up again and sits down. Guilt eating him inside. Or the cocaine. Who knows? Or cares?

'I found out about Davies later on. It wasn't just the casino owner who arranged everything. Not that I knew who or cared about the details at the time. But it was all a setup to convince me to go into being a drugs mule ultimately working for Davies. I got a call last year. He knew everything. I mean everything. He told me to meet him the next time I was in the UK for one of my drug trips.'

Oh joy, he was he even coming into the UK regularly. Ruby could have bumped into him in the street. Unbelievable.

'And you naturally said yes, like you seem to say yes to anyone who has your balls in a vice. You've got the backbone of a garden slug. How the fuck you are my brother I don't know.'

'Sis, he told me that he would recreate the car crash for real if I didn't comply. He had that posh accent but he was evil, I'm telling you. He knew exactly what screws to turn. In another life he'd be a Nazi torturer, smiling and laughing as he pulled my nails out.'

'And what about Dad? What happened when you went to see him?'

'It was horrible. I was sick after that. He forced me. Dad was furious with me. I've never seen him like that. Not that I blame him. If it wasn't for that black bird, I don't know if his heart would have gone there and then. She calmed everything down. Made it easier. She was looking after him, trying to keep him calm. Thank fuck for her. She and Davies did the business. Dad wouldn't even speak.'

'What did he want from Dad?'

'I don't know I swear. I just know that Dad denied everything. Refused to even discuss. It was unbelievable. Davies was furious, but he couldn't' do a thing. Not with her there. She got him out the door. I ran off once we were out the house. Got the first plane back out again. Davies never contacted me after that. I was no use to him it was obvious. Dad didn't care what happened to me, he wasn't going to deal with him.'

'You sure you didn't know what he wanted. Money or something else?'

'Oh, money for sure. But Davies has money already. It wasn't all about money. He kept saying that if he didn't hand it over then he would made sure he'd regret it. But with that black woman he wouldn't say what it was. It was weird but in the end he left it alone.'

I am trying to imagine the scene. I didn't' trust Bea but her presence, her acting skills as I remember them meant that Dad was protected. Davies would have had to admit what he'd done to get Dad to succumb and then they all would have known, no matter what he did to dad. And he couldn't touch us because as soon as anything happened, it would have been public knowledge that he'd threatened us.

'And that's all you know?'

'It's all I know.' He says, 'Sis I need that fix now.'

I hand over some notes. He shoves it in his pocket and heads out the door. I won't see him again today.

I order a whisky and ice. I feel drained. My brother's a wreck and I'm not sure what I can or should do. There is no point me trying to drag him out of his cesspit but having now handed over a significant amount of money, I feel the need to hang around and decide what to do.

It's a Tuesday afternoon in Cape Town. Thirty odd degrees outside, I should be finding something to enjoy outside. But I'm inside and not inclined to go anywhere or do anything.

As the glass empties, I order another.

# CHAPTER 10

∞ § ∞

Eventually I am bored with myself and my misery and decide to take a walk.

My tendency is to head to towards the waterfront like most tourists but first I want to walk the old streets further up the hill towards Table Mountain.

With Walt, now probably out for the count in some bedsit somewhere, time is a plenty and it would be good to see how things have changed.

I've lived here off and on. The first time I was eleven years old. We stayed here a year. Apartheid was falling apart, though still functioning. I was well used to our lifestyle being privileged before then, in the three countries I had already lived in before coming to South Africa. The private schools full of international students. The private taxis, maids, security. It was part of life.

But in South Africa there were even more rules for special status. Whites and non-whites. There were no black kids at the school. Even living elsewhere there were rich black kids in the special schools. But it wasn't allowed here. Against the rules.

Of course, as a kid, I asked why. As I got older much of this began to make sense. I was too young to be part of that revolution but I like to think I still carry the flag of equality. I imagine the likes of Davies exploiting their circumstances just as he is in the UK now. It makes me wonder how that might manifest itself.

As I approach the university, walking round the lower slopes of the mountain, I get distracted from Davies. Without much more information, I am guessing and I'm bored of that. Walt just confirmed his influence is far and wide and he is happy to exploit anyone and everyone to get what he wants. It doesn't though tell me what he was hiding. And things were not going to be resolved until I get past that.

The streets are more familiar now.

I can see the path into the forest walks where we would hang out as kids. It's good to see the communities much more mixed. Back in the 80's a black face would have been moved away quickly, unless they were a maid or cleaner. Cape Town is a much more international place these days. A beautiful spectacular city but whilst black and Asian people were well and truly established in the middle classes of these estates, as you go back to the city centre, to the projects and townships out of the city, there are no white faces. Poverty is rarely the outcome for a white person and that doesn't seem to be changing soon.

But I never let that be a reason not to enjoy the city. Guilt of others actions doesn't have to be my cross to bear. I have good memories and for all its troubles I don't think I've ever lived in such a spectacular place.

The mountain often shrouded in cloud, reveals itself on the best days, like a theatre curtain opening for the show. There is no denying the aura it has. From every angle, the steep cliffs are visible. Sitting below, I contemplate its vastness, a piece of art that presents something new each time you gaze at it. I feel shrunk as I look up and understand why mythology is generated by inordinate objects. Not to believe the mountain has power of its own when it presents itself in such a stark way is almost a contradiction.

I return to the walk and find our old street.  Standing at the corner, I feel sick. I recall Walt as a child, playing round the pool. The innocence. Dad and Mum hosting barbecues or braais as they are known locally. But now, the memory brings it all crashing down around me and decide to walk back to the centre.

At least, walking round the modern transformation of the Victoria Waterfront, I don't feel the past as a millstone.

***

Outside the courtroom the next morning, I call Walter. The rain is pouring down today. Supposed to be summer but even here I attract the bloody rain.

He's not here. No surprise there. If it's one thing he's reliable for it's his unreliability.

There is no response but a WhatsApp appears instead. Five mins, it says.

It's closer to ten but I don't quibble. At least whilst I am here I am making sure he reports for his bail terms. Otherwise they will come looking for me. I am his guarantor.

Once he's back out, we go to the café over the road.

At least he's looking better today. I suppose he's suitably coked up and can function normally for a few hours. He's still agitated and his arm pits are damp with sweat but that's probably his normal look. I will ignore it.

'What's your plan now?' I ask once we are at a table with coffee. I lose count of the sugar he adds to his latte.

'Don't know.' He shrugs his shoulders.

'But you will do prison time once there's a trial. I heard there was a serious amount of coke you had stashed there.'

'Got a few months until the trial, something will happen.'

Two minutes with him and I already want to punch him. His arrogance has taken a boost today.

'What? Someone will get you out the country or get you off? What exactly are you expecting to happen?'

'You have no idea have you? Someone will get me out. They always do.' He laughs.

'Then if they so easily get you off, why call me.'

'Hey, Hey sis, you chose to come look for me. Figured you might want to do me a favour.'

He leans back in the chair like his work is done. I'm fuming again. I'm looking at my hot coffee and thinking it might go the same way as the water I threw yesterday.

'Why didn't your friends bounce you this time then?'

'Sensitive like. It's not so easy to do it here. Usually a few bribes takes care of it. Takes some time in South Africa. So needed to stump the cash up front. Know what I mean?'

I get up to leave. I can't bear to be in the room with the arrogant selfish bastard. Each time he does it to me. I want to know more but the anger rises so quickly I can't hold it back.

'Sis,' he shouts.

'Fuck off,' I reply as I get out to the street.

I walk to the car. I had planned to go out for the day anyway. I will just leave earlier than expected. In ten minutes, I'm on the freeway north.  I drive past the townships and out into the greener landscapes of the city outskirts and eventually I reach the spectacularly scenery of Stellenbosch. It's only as I pull into my favourite winery that I begin to relax.

Stellenbosch has the feel of a theme park. The rain has stopped so it looks better already but in the perfect sun it's a landscape designed for a post card. Mountains surround a lush green valley. White housing, colonial style street designs give the sense of a historical movie set. And the surrounding landscapes of the wineries which have been tailored to maximum effect. The neatness of the lines of vines adds the extra pattern details to the artificial picture.

For all that, I love it especially the contrast with the city nearby.

I walk to stall style café on a deck by a picture perfect small lake. The wooden veranda has a view from where you can see all the way down to Table Mountain and the bay. It's a truly special spot, surrounding by the rocky mountain landscape. Being a Tuesday there are not many people around.

The young man at the café beams, obviously pleased to see a customer.

We pass the time of day whilst I order a burger and a glass of red. I don't stay chatting, grateful for the opportunity to take in the tranquillity of the lake and forget about the nonsense that's currently battling with me.

I pick at the fries, one by one. Definitely in no rush to scoff it all down. Happy to take the pace of the day as a slow one. I need to make my wine last as well as I have to drive back and can't have another. Once I am done here I will walk over to the winery and pick up some wine to take back.

I wish I knew what to do next.

I take the phone out to check for messages but it rings in my hand before I've unlocked it. It's Ruby on WhatsApp.

'Hi Pearl,' she says, 'where are you?'

'Still in Cape Town,' I reply. Her voice is uneven.

'Stay there for the moment,' Ruby says.'

'What's going on?'

There is a pause on the line and I get the sense she's gone to another room to talk.

'Sorry,' she says, eventually. 'I needed to find a room. Pearl, the police were here. They want to speak to you.'

'Shit, that bastard Davies, has complained about me and Terry.' I say, 'but that's no big deal. We didn't do anything. We can sort it out.'

'No, no. It's to do with Dad and money. They were asking me if I knew money had been fraudulently obtained by Dad and that this was now in your possession. Pearl, they asked about money laundering and whether I had any knowledge of how you might be doing it. If you come back, they'll want to speak to you.'

'Sure, sure,' I say, calmly, trying not to react to what Ruby is saying. 'It's ok, I'm safe here. I can stay for a few more days and try to sort things out. I've got to sort Walter as well.'

She asks me about Walter and I tell her what happened. I try to minimise the drug stuff but I don't-hold back on how obnoxious he's been and impossible to deal with. I'm glad when the conversation is over.

'Has all this got to do with what you didn't tell me the other day?' Ruby asks eventually.

'Ruby, I'm not keeping things from you.' I respond. This is tricky. What to tell and what not to. 'I don't understand it myself. It's why I didn't tell you. I don't want to upset you.'

'I'm not a child, Pearl, please don't patronise me.' But she is to me. Not a child but my younger sister who I'm supposed to protect.

'There is some money tied up with Dad but I am trying to find out more about it before saying more. I don't think it's illegal or stolen but I can't say.'

'But you should have told me. Where did it come from? How much is it?'

'It's a lot but that's not the most important. I will tell you more as I find it. I promise.'

She lets it lie at that thankfully and we close the call on good terms.

I sit quietly looking over the beauty of the lake thinking that once I drive back down to city I will be leaving tranquillity for some time. The pressure is mounting up, bailiffs, debtors, police and Walter and his dodgy history. Dad's been dead for two weeks and the world is falling apart. I wish I could stay in this serenity and make it all go away.

But there is no point dwelling on it. I finish my drink and walk up to winery. Time to face reality and make a new plan.

# CHAPTER 11

∞ § ∞

Back in the hotel, I sit at the bar.

I'm drinking cocktails tonight. Whisky sour. I'm trying to be good and make my drinks last a little longer given the amount of shorts I plied through in the last few days. Yeah, I know, who am I kidding? But I can start slowly at least.

'Want another?' The attractive black girl behind the bar asks.

'Sure,' I reply. That was too easily done. There's another universe where the words 'no' and 'early night' are in common usage but it seems I don't occupy that one. What was that I was thinking early in the day about preaching to Walter about his addiction and me in control of mine?

'You here alone?' she asks, as she places a fresh glass on the bar.

'I am,' I say and then look back to my phone, reading news and updates, pushing thoughts of my casual alcohol addiction to one side. I look back up and she's still stood close, watching me. The bar is quiet tonight and I realise she wants to chat. I wonder if I do.

'Just hanging out,' I add, saying something without saying anything.

'You working or here for pleasure?' Someone else comes to the bar so I don't get chance to answer.

What do I tell her? It's not exactly work and I can't say it's a pleasure either.

My phone pings. It's a message from Walt asking if I would go to the bail office with him tomorrow. He wants to say sorry to me. I will go, but not because I have high expectations. Sorry is a start but I don't see how we come back from this.

The bar girl twice gives me a sideways glance whilst she's serving. I smile back, naturally thinking whether that was me being polite or am I inviting more conversation. This is something I have not planned for. But then surprises are always more fun. I take an extra draw on the straw and notice the cocktail is a little stronger than the last one. Again, she's watching for my reaction. I laugh to myself.

I could do with something fun that's for sure.

She's busy with more customers so I go back to my phone and reply to Walt. As is common at the moment, I can't stop my brain turning my conscience round like a dryer, stopping every so often to change direction whilst I ponder that particular mystery of my past. As usual when I get into a pensive mood I remind myself that I always wanted life on my terms so I have to take the pain and the good bits as mine and mine only. There is never going to be anyone else to blame for the lowlights. It's why I fight to keep the past stuffed in a bin liner in the back of my brain rather than up front and personal as it is now.

Another smile and something whispered. Assume she means she'll be with me soon. I can wait I guess. Nowhere else to go.

Living alone is not always fun but at least I don't have to compromise for the whims of weak partners with their own obsessions. I have loved before. Men and women. I've never really seen the separation of people I like and fancy and their sex. I much more enjoy the connection and the moment. It's probably why I'm less good at relationships, the moment fades too quickly and I get bored of sharing and compromises. I have tried proper relationships, but not for long. I met a guy in a Haiti camp when I was working on a contract out there. He was classic good looks, heroic hippy type called Luke. Muscular, blonde, fluffy light beard, unkempt but also perfectly cool for the organic style he presented. He was a bit like me, posh kid looking for a cause. We didn't take each other too seriously and it worked. I followed him around for a few years. Luke worked for Oxfam and managed to persuade them to take me on a contract for a few trips. But then I got tired of competing for his attention. Goes with the territory of a pretty boy like him. Women around the camps loved him, his natural charm and hard work. He was made for the work, hero status frequently bestowed on him. We got on well but neither of us were nest builders and I wasn't the competition type either. It is or isn't a thing. I got a call asking for me for a job back in a Southern Africa task force and I decided to take it. We both agreed if we missed each other enough after a few months apart then I would come back. But I didn't.

I got on with things as I always do. Live in the moment or something like that.

Ruby is the opposite of me, always wanted to be back in the UK. She was happy to meet a local guy and settle down. Whereas I am cold and selfish never wanting to share anything. Why are we so different? We grew up in the same house, same parents, same relationships, two years apart and we are completely different people. She couldn't manage in my life and I couldn't manage in hers. Though I love her as a sister. She's a beautiful woman, a perfect mother and Jake is a good guy.

Walt though. He has the same streak of selfishness as me. It was never obvious before now. Oh was I learning that.  I like to think my selfish streak was for good reason and his for self-destruction, but I am not the judge. I know mother was never happy with either of us for leaving. She used to say, your father needs you, as if it wasn't her asking. But the opposite was true.

Dad didn't need me, he made that plain. He was more than comfortable with me pursuing my own path. I didn't think too much about it either way.

Maybe she felt the pain as someone who had to follow her husband round. From country to country, dutifully never complaining. We always had a maid, a gardener and sometimes a cook. She was largely bored, I would imagine. She read books and did puzzles. There were often social outings with the other wives but she complained about them as much as enjoyed them. I remember her dismissal of many of the wives as deluded and rather nasty. There was a social hierarchy linked to their husbands' and we were never top of that tree. I didn't pay much attention at the time but I see it now.

The bar lady returns.

'Sorry about that,' she says.

I notice her badge. Elly.

'Want a drink Elly?' I ask.

'Can't,' she says leaning close to me. 'Though to be honest I'm gasping. Boring as shit tonight and places I'd rather be.'

'Is this your only job?'

'Yeah, I do this. Husband looks after the kids in the evening. I come here. Need the money. Need a new fucking life,' she says.

She is thirty something at a guess. Silky chocolate skin that glows. She has heavy eye makeup, glaring green glow which kind of works with her dark green branded T-shirt she wears for work. She's nice.

'What do you like to do after work?' I ask.

'Ha, what I'd liked to do and what I do, are two completely different things.' She laughs and goes to serve another customer.

My glass is getting empty and I could do a runner. But perhaps Elly has hooked me in.

'Another,' she asks when she returns and I nod accordingly. She giggles as I say yes. 'I'd be pissed if I had what you drank and there you are, looking all perfect and straight.'

'I'm not far off with the extra shot of whisky you dropped in there. Anyone would think you're trying to get me drunk. You chose your victim well. I must have pisshead as a label on my t-shirt.' I laugh as she brings my drink back.

She lifts a glass of water in my direction and says cheers.

'You must be tempted to drop a shot of vodka in there.'

'Fuck yeah,' Elly says, 'but they measure everything here. Boss is like a bloodhound. Would sniff it a mile off, if he comes round here. Like my husband, if I go home and have had a drink, would get the same lecture. Where you been? Who you been drinking with woman? You're getting fat'

'Fat?' I say, 'no way are you fat.'

'Oh he throws that in for good measure. Just the way it is right. Keep the little woman down.'

She goes away again. I sip my whisky, feeling a little loose now, forgetting about the past few days.

Elly is back again.

'Look, I know it's not strictly speaking the done thing in hotels and all that, but I've got a bottle of bourbon sitting lonely in my room and no-one to share it with. I've got some good mouth wash to get rid of the taste of alcohol before you have to go home.'

She laughs and then leans forward as close as she can get. 'I thought you'd never ask. I'll send a text to my husband telling him they asked me to do a party tonight so will be back late.'

I lift my glass to offer another cheers.

***

I wake up naked, the bed covers ruffled but empty beside me.

I hear a noise in the bathroom and slowly remember what happened. I smile at the memory. As soon as she arrived with an ice bucket and fresh glasses she'd dropped her bag and gone to the bathroom. Whilst I was pouring the drinks she came out stark naked.

'Let's get the party started,' she said, 'got any music to dance to?'

It was good fun.

I reach for my phone by the bed but it's not there. I get up in the haze looking around for it. Not on the floor. I pick up my discarded clothes and throw them on the chair. It's not on the dressing table. Is it in the bathroom I wonder?

It comes like a wave. I stand still. Shock. Fear. What the hell am I doing?

I bang on the bathroom door.

'Elly,' I shout, 'what you doing? I need to see you.'

'Hey girl, I'll just be a minute.'

I bang again.

A few seconds later the door opens. She's fully dressed and looking just like she was in the bar earlier.

'What's wrong with you?'

I see my phone by the sink and push by her to get it.

'Did you touch this?' I ask.

'No, lady, you left it there. Got nothing to do with me.' She looks at me and must be able to read the anger on my face. She looks shocked and cowers from me. 'I better be going,'

'Yes, you had.' I turn away from her and go back to the bed. My voice is flat and I know I'm being cold. And maybe she didn't touch the phone but I swear I didn't remember taking it to the bathroom. She's gone in a second and I breathe again.

What have I turned into? Suddenly I'm paranoid. But then maybe I'm paranoid for a good reason. Because my life is being turned upside down. That great big hole inside me grows with everything I learn. Especially after seeing Walter the last few days and the darkness he's created. Is that going to happen to me now that I seem to be the next target of these greedy money men?

And then I'm annoyed with myself. I switch on the TV to find a movie. Half a bottle of bourbon is gone from earlier. I feel bad for Elly. She probably wasn't doing anything and I just turfed her out like a discarded whore. What did that make me?

# CHAPTER 12

## ∞ § ∞

I'm back at the courthouse at ten though my head is still climbing out of the bottle from last night. No amount of water drank at the breakfast table is going to flush it out.

A surprise is waiting for me as I step out of the taxi. Walter is not alone. He's joined by a tall older man. White hair and white beard. He must be six foot six, slim build but appears fit and strong.

He's dressed in a light grey suit, casually but most importantly, very smart. I imagine him in his younger days as very much a looker.

'Hey sis,' Walt says, 'this is Henrik Dahl, by the way. He's a local businessman I know.'

Henrik reaches out his hand and I take it. The handshake is firm. I flinch with the grip and I'm happy to let go. He smiles but the eyes don't say the same. Why the pretence?

We enter the court house together but I follow a little behind. Dahl puts me off. I get the impression I'm inconsequential. A feeling or sense, those emotionless eyes; the lack of warmth in the greeting. I can't exactly put my finger on it. Though if he thinks I'm of no consequence, I wonder what his opinion of Walter is.

Walter takes his place in the queue for registration. Henrik doesn't speak to me whilst we wait and I don't speak to him. He takes a call thankfully which relieves the enforced silence, though I notice he is talking in Afrikaans. Of course we are in South Africa so it shouldn't be surprising hearing him speak.

Though listening to the harsh rhythm of the language keeps me on edge. It's not the softest or most musical of tongues. Sounds like everyone is permanently angry.

Thirty minutes later we are back to the same coffee place as yesterday. Henrik joins us at the table like our new best friend, though he tags along silently, checking his phone and looking around regularly. He's obviously not one for social pleasantries as he doesn't offer any small talk. I am nervous, unable to ignore him completely yet not wanting to converse with him either. I try to analyse how I feel. Humidity is the word that comes to mind, oppressive perhaps, making it hard to breathe when he's around. Can a person have that effect?

Walter speaks to break my reticence.

'Look sis, I am sorry about the other day. The shit was affecting me. I'm good now.'

I nod, without speaking. He thinks he's good but it's like putting butter on burnt toast. It might be more palatable but the toast is still burnt.

My sense of discomfort continues and catching his eye he grins a little as he holds my gaze. I look away not really interested in a competition. It does show his nature though. Glancing back I see he is watching me avidly. Though, in the absence of my counter stare, I catch his eyes drifting south in common with most men. Given my T-shirt is round necked and my chest size doesn't exceed the boundaries of average I suspect the investment return on the glance is disappointing. How sad for him.

'We're cool then sis?' Walter asks, breaking my musing. 'Tell Ruby I'm fine. Please don't give her a bad impression of me. I don't want her to worry. You know what I mean right?'

'It's ok. I've spared her feelings. Though, honestly Dean,' remembering to use his new name, 'I'm not sure Ruby can lower her opinion of you much more, you know what I mean?'

I lean forward with a forced smile, the sarcasm displayed loud and clear. It's a callous response but he earned it just as he did the slap yesterday.

He laughs but stops quickly and avoids eye contact with me. That landed firmly. He looks to Henrik for support but I see that Henrik's expression is not changed.

Walter is too much of a coward to have a comeback so he moves on to other matters.

'Anyway sis, you don't need to worry about the money. Henrik will take care of everything? You can go home. I will be fine.'

I look at Henrik, who nods and then smiles. He is weird.

'Is he always so quiet?' I ask. 'Is he going to write me a cheque for one million rand then? Just in case you disappear again?'

'I can speak,' he says. The Afrikaans accent is so strong, I feel like he just spat at me. The undertone of aggression though doesn't just belong to the language. 'Dean and I have common interests. I will cover his costs.'

'And why would you do that? What possible common interests would that be?'

Walt tries to speak but Henrik is there before him

'Not your concern,' Henrik says, though this time he forces a smile through the white beard. The skin on my back crawls a little. 'Dean and I will work it out.' I wonder if I should care.

'So, I'm surplus to requirements?'

'Sis, you've been amazing. I couldn't have survived without you.' He's talking to me but he's looking to Henrik for approval. I really am surplus to requirements.

'And the one million rand I paid the court for bail? You going to give me that back?'

Henrik's smile is gone. Instead his face reddens.

'Take it from the money your fucking thief of a father stole.' He stands up, cold and abrupt. Maybe he's had enough of me but I'm not going to let him get away with saying that. I stand up to confront him despite him being so much taller.

'Don't speak about my father like that? And how come you're such an expert in my father's money.'

I'm shaking as he leans down into my face.

'Pay the fucking money and shut the fuck up little girl.' He holds his stare for a moment and then turns away before I can muster a response. Two fucks and a bit of misogyny thrown in. Is there even a response to give?

Walter gets up to follow him.

'Don't mess with Henrik,' he says as he tails him out the door. A puppy following his master.

Is this the last time I see my brother. There is no doubt that he's sold whatever soul he had to Henrik Dahl. Oddly, I feel nothing. It's just an end. And in that sense, tomorrow will be the same as today.

But Henrik Dahl is the devil in this story. Local businessman and professional oversized arse is one thing but he revealed more in that exchange than I've learnt since I first came back for Dad's funeral. Whatever grievance dad had with these people, it's very much live and raw.

This Dahl character is either a foot soldier or an instigator and I sense that it won't be the last time I meet him. I promise myself that if there is a next time, I will be ready for him, whatever that means.

***

I walk back to the hotel. I need to clear my head. The breeze in the air helps blow away the cobwebs and I once again start planning. I need to make a few calls and do a bit of searching on the internet.

Back in my room, I open the laptop and search out Dahl.

LinkedIn gives me a brief CV. The local businessman is in fact the Operations Director for ALC, African Logistics Corp, the same people Dean works for. Is Henrik his boss?  Looking at the company site, I am seeing it as being a bigger operation than the dodgy dealing at Dean's car lot. Transport, travel, operations, buildings, warehouse, staffing. That must give him contacts throughout the continent. A business of logistics is all about moving people and produce around. Drugs under the radar, but does it include Tobacco as a legitimate part of its business? I'm sure it will do.

Time to make a few calls. Terry first.

'Terry, how are you?' I ask.

'Pearl, it's not the same without you round here.' He says. It's oddly reassuring to listen to his south London roughness. Good to listen to something bland and honest and also, I never thought I would consider attaching such an emotion to someone like Terry, but homely and friendly. Especially given where we started a week ago. My world is well and truly turned upside down.

'How you going on down there? Met any nice locals. I hear those black guys have impressive... '

'Terry, stop now.'

I know he's winding me up, though he is so far off base. I'll get him back with that one day.

I think of Elly last night and flush a little. I was awful last night. I left a note for Elly behind the bar to say sorry. Not sure I dare walk in there later but want her at least not to feel my paranoia and outburst was anything to do with her.

'How's your brother?' he asks. 'Did you learn anything?'

I give him a brief rundown of the drug issues and how he faked the whole death thing.

'I've seen the drug addiction before,' Terry says. 'Some of the lads got addicted. Look the PTSD is bad. Pain like you wouldn't believe from the surgery as well as the mental pain. They take anything for it and get addicted. Terrible. Families can't handle that kind of shit. They end up on the streets. I think I was a whisker away when my arm went. I don't mind admitting that I was close to ending it.' He pauses and I sense that the conversation is going far deeper than I was comfortable with so I change the subject.

'Did you get any gossip on Davies from his mates?'

'It was crap, Pearl. No-one's saying anything about him. Not a thing.'

'Really. There must be something?' Not what I was hoping for.

'The only thing I got was that he isn't liked. One of the old captains told me that he's the sort who would be first to life boats whilst his ship goes down. I asked him, how come? And he just said, you can see it in his eyes. It's the way he shakes your hand when you're in line but he's already looking at the next face. He doesn't care. That's all I got, Pearl.'

'Yeah thanks.'

'But Pearl, I talked to Ruby. You're best off staying away. Police have been round. Something dodgy is going on. Old bill is sniffing round but they haven't found anything yet. Let me know if I can do anything?'

I think for a moment. It's a good question. I need to decide what to do next. Going back to UK feels wrong until I have answers for the police. So what to do instead? It comes to me in a second.

Surely not…Where it all began…Maybe it's the best plan. I don't have a better one. But I don't want to go alone, I feel I need someone to tell me I'm not paranoid, that I'm doing the right thing. I have friends all over Africa, I could call on but I don't think they would get what this is about. Ruby would stop me doing it. So is Terry my only option?

'Terry, is your passport up to date?' I ask.

'Yes,' he asks, 'where we going?'

'Kenya,' I reply. Even as I say it, I wonder what I just suggested.

# CHAPTER 13

## ∞ § ∞

### Kenya

I'm standing outside the arrivals terminal waiting for Terry.

I'm sweating even in the shade. His flight's delayed and I've walked up and down a few times trying to avoid the attention of the security guards. It's not like I don't stand out here with my red hair and pale skin. Every second glance from them feels like it's on me.

I'm not the only white person arriving here but I can count them all on one hand as far as I can see over the taxi ranks.

White folk here tend to come in two forms. The linen suits and Fedora hats who fell out of a 1920's movie about the Raj, missing the pipe and slippers. And then there are the twenty something boys with fuzzy faces and a pony tails and a lifetime membership to Fitness First. Their girlfriends would be wearing a yellow bikini under a white gym top and shorts.  Stereotyping I know but I'm proud to be neither of those things

I came here yesterday and rented a private house. A week at a time. I figured it was a bit more secluded than a hotel and if I am going to have to stay for a while, it is better to have somewhere more substantive. Plus it has a garden and a pool and feels more of a hideaway. It's got a secure gate and will be a decent base.

I could have gone back to Tanzania and my apartment there. It would present more of a logistical challenge for any pursuit of money from me but isn't going to help to solve my issues with the past. Dad was in Kenya when he worked his last major stint with Davies and I suspect whatever bad blood was between them developed here. It also annoys me that I was actually living in the same house as much of this could have happened. I completely missed it.

Eventually Terry appears.

I try not to laugh.

A young local comes out with him. Pushing his suitcases and managing the rotating doors. Terry is managing with his stick He looks like he's on a trip to Margate on the hottest day of the year. His face is puffed up, canvas shorts with a button that's clinging on for dear life and a white shirt that is pretty much liquid. Only thing missing is the white handkerchief replaced instead with an Arsenal baseball cap.

Terry uses his false arm to hold his wallet against his body as he rip off notes and hands them over to the boy's demands. Give him his due, disability or not, he works stuff out.

'Fucking hell,' he says, as I reach to hug him. 'I think he just robbed me that boy. No fucking idea. Seriously Pearl, what am I doing here?'

I laugh.

'What's wrong, did you have to sit next to black people on the plane? Has it upset your English sensibilities? Or did they give you a seat all on your own, so you could place your privilege beside you?'

'Don't fucking start, Pearl. I'm disabled. Veteran. Know what I mean.'

Actually for all my teasing, I am happy to see him laugh at himself a bit. A week ago he'd have gone off on one if I'd even mentioned his sensibilities.

'Got the row all to myself,' Terry adds. 'Makes me laugh though. People look at me and think they might catch it. Like having a limb chopped off is infectious. So I need a drink, a long one and then another. Where's the cab?'

'I got a car,' I say, pushing his trolley over to the car park, dodging all the cars picking up other people.

'You're brave driving here,' he says, as we trundle along slowly. I let him step slightly ahead so he can get a full swing on his body as he manoeuvres himself forward.

'I'm used to it. Got us a nice big Toyota Land Cruiser. Comfort, air conditioning and most of all, we won't feel the bumps in the road quite so much. Most of the time it's point the car in the right direction, keep your wits about you, your foot close to the brake pedal and your hand close to the horn. It works.'

An hour later we are sitting in the in the shade of the house's garden.

Terry is well into his second bottle of local ale, Tuskers. The first didn't touch the sides.

The garden isn't large but it's very pretty. It's neat with a sprinkler so the grass is half green and there is plenty of blooms in the flower beds. Easy maintenance geraniums seem to be the main feature. The pool is more of a postage stamp but it serves the purpose of being able to cool off in the face of the baking hot sun. But most importantly I stocked the fridge with enough alcohol to keep an army drunk which I'm sure Terry will see as a challenge all on its own.

'Tell me again, so I get it. What we doing here? Or more to the point. What am I doing here?'

'And I thought you wanted a holiday. Some excitement.'

'Pearl, girl. If I wanted an 'oliday, Tenerife would have done me fine. I've had enough excitement in my life to last a lifetime. I'm happy to watch the Arsenal bore me on a Saturday afternoon and even that gets my heartrate in the red zone.'

I sip my beer, smiling. He's so easy to wind up. It's like mention Brexit or even liberals. Light the blue touch paper, stand well back and wait for the rocket to go off. He's so damn predictable.

'Kenya is where it's at Terry. It all happened here. We left here just before I went to University in the early 90's. I remember it all being a bit rushed. After that, when dad travelled, he went from the UK. Mum said she was fed up of being passed around like a parcel. If he wanted to travel he could do it on his own. Anyway, Walt faked his death in this city and Dad kept his secrets from here. As I look back, I get the sense it all traces back to Nairobi.'

'So what you going to do? How you going to find the truth?'

'Me is it? Thought you were here to help me?'

'Oh yeah,' he says, holding his empty bottle to me, 'you just told me I was on holiday. Get me another of these whilst you're at it. They don't last long, do they?'

'I'm not your servant, don't get used to this,' I say. Still, I go and get him the drink. Today is a day of rest for him and for me. 'We're going to see a few people and ask some questions. Some contacts I have.'

'Seriously, what you do need me for? You can do this on your own.'

'I wish, but I don't think I can. Look Terry, in the nicest possible way, we are poles apart, we think completely differently. But you're honest I'll give you that and you say what you see. I need that. Someone who will look at all this with a more cynical eye than me? Am I making any sense?'

He turns to me.

'You want me to call a spade a fucking spade, is that it?' He says. 'Round here that's going to be the easiest fucking job ever. Cheers to that.'

I shake my head. I'm sharing a house with Jim fucking Davidson. I'm trapped in a 1970's Working Men's club. Sadly he's all I've got. And that's pretty tragic.

'If you could keep your crappy racist jokes to yourself for the duration, I would appreciate it. And if you succeed, I'll take you to see a Giraffe for being a good boy. Deal?'

'Cheers,' he says once more.

Opening a fresh bottle of bourbon from duty free, I'm reminded of Elly and I cringe a little with my last encounter. In the note I gave in at the bar, I left her my phone number if she wanted to message me. I got a message back but it was just a photo of her middle finger raised. The end of a beautiful friendship.

# CHAPTER 14

∞ § ∞

Nairobi is not that different to most cities. It's not even that big really compared with other capitals. It's dense and overpopulated but so is London. It has awful slums alongside vast riches, but anyone who has ever been to Tower Hamlets will be familiar with that contrast. Even my brand spanking new penthouse luxury apartment sits alongside Deptford high street. It might not be as harsh as an African township with houses made of mud and various bits of metal, but there is some raw poverty down that way. Penniless immigrants, street beggars, homelessness. None of us have that far to fall.

Saying that, I can't treat being here like a London high street. I've got to be on guard. When I'm not working, I stick to the tourist and business areas like everyone else. I don't make myself a target. Keep money and bags close. Don't go out wearing my best sunglasses or fancy labels. Like everywhere, robbers are looking for the easiest targets.

That's the downside. But the upside to the city, is the fun, the energy. Even more than Cape Town, barbecues are everywhere. Street sellers, fancy restaurants and music on every corner. It's quite a party atmosphere on the streets. Most people, when I mention Kenya, know little or nothing about it but assume it's slums, poverty, terrorists and safaris. And it does have all of those things, but it's a modern city with a modern night life and tourist scene. And it's hot most of the time. What's not to like?

But today I'm going to the darker side of the city. It's still residential and it's not all slums. My old housekeeper lives here.

I still have the address. Christmas cards and letters exchanged over the years. She was and I am sure still is, a sweet lady.

As I pass the centre the Toyota's large wheels hit the frequent potholes and debris. There are many people hanging around vendor stalls, cafes, car maintenance, and phone card shops. Just like the fancy streets on the main drags only smaller, lower rent and a completely different audience.

I keep an eye on Terry beside me.  He holds the hand rail tight and seems to be wincing with every movement.

'Like Kabul this is or Belfast on a bad day. See a day on the Falls Road when the locals are pelting you with the Molotov cocktails and there's shit everywhere. Did that as a rookie. Fucking scared the shit out of me. First time I realised what it felt like to be hated and that was in my own country. Marvellous. '

Other than that he doesn't add much to the conversation. I think he's nervous.

I find Johanna's place on a side road. After parking I walk round the side and help Terry out. Immediately I'm surrounded by three boys wanting to mind the car. They are school age. I give them a hundred shillings each and they seem content with that.

'Sure they aren't going to nick it?' Terry says.

'Leave it Terry, will you?'

It's a bungalow, sand coloured with a window either side of the door. A couple of metres garden at the front and probably a yard at the back. It's not big but I know she lives alone.

I knock on the door and wait a few moments.

The door opens and she stares at me as her brain slowly registers who I am. Her hair has greyed, no surprise there and the lines on her face look well established.

'It's Pearl, isn't it?' She says. 'That beautiful East African lilt in her voice. Honey and toned and that touch of exasperation as impatience lingers at the end. 'Why didn't you say you were coming to see me? I would have made a meal. All I got is a tea on the go.'

She invites us inside.

'And who's the young man of yours. He looks like he could do with some shade.'

'I'm sure he could,' I add. 'This is Terry, a friend of mine.'

Johanna moves easier than Terry I note. Inside the bungalow there is small sofa and a chair. A TV on the table with some local news on.

She looks tired and a little flustered. Not surprising given we've descended on her. I remember her as such a dignified lady, in the face of the onslaught of teenagers and rich families always demanding. She would give us kids a telling off but I don't recall her ever complaining about anything. I see the determination in movement, always playing the servant as any good host knows how to do.

'I got some water if you prefer,' she says.

We both nod and wait whilst she goes to the small kitchen and brings back two full beakers.

Once everyone is settled down, she leans forward to speak.

'How is your father?' Johanna asks. 'I was so sorry to hear about your mother.'

'Dad passed away two weeks ago, I'm afraid.'

She makes a simple sign of the cross and utters a prayer.

'I'm so sorry to hear that. He was a nice man.'

I tell her it was his heart and it was probably his time.

'How are you doing Johanna?' I ask, wanting to change the subject.

'I'm doing fine, I am. Not worked for a long time but that's ok. My sister lives round the corner and her boys see to it that I don't want for nothing. It's all fine. But you don't want to know about me. I can see that. You came to ask me something.'

'She seen you coming, Pearl,' Terry says. He stutters a little and is sat up straight. He doesn't seem comfortable and is looking round at every part of the room. Wonder what he's expecting to see.

'I smile back to humour him.

'I did come to ask something. Of course, but it is nice to see you. And also to say thank you. Those days back then, we were pretty rotten kids. We must have given you a terrible time.'

She smiles and nods along.

'Kids, I've seen it all. Think I don't know how to handle spoilt white boys and girls. I knew you well before you knew yourselves. But Pearl you were a special one. Old head on those young shoulders. You were the only one who checked on me and the maids. Only one who said sorry. Honestly the other two weren't bad kids, they just didn't see me. I was invisible.'

'Maybe,' I say, 'but I think you are being nice because I'm here. I must have been always complaining.'

'You wanted to go outside,' she says, 'but it wasn't safe and you didn't understand that. Trusted too easily. Posh white girl on those streets was like an electric light. All the flies will come buzzing looking for the heat. But look at you now. You grew up big. Look at those shoulders. Where did you get so strong?'

Don't come and see an old Kenyan lady for flattery. I smile and Terry laughs.

'Tell her you've been weightlifting, Pearl,' Terry says. 'Johanna, your house is very beautiful and I just want to say thank you very much for letting us be your guests.'

'Alright Terry, don't have to be all formal with Johanna.'

'Thank you Terry,' she says and then looks at me and winks. 'It's nice to be treated with some respect, such a nice man. And you look like you have had a very bad time of it.'

'Err, Johanna, I had some things to ask you.' I say before Terry starts with more of his tales of woe.

I should tell her about my work and travels but as I just cut across Terry for doing the same I should get to the point.

'Do you remember Mum and Dad?' I ask. 'How were they as a couple? Was there any issue when we lived here?'

She thinks for a moment. She mutters under her breath before she speaks, like she's rehearsing her lines.

'As a man and his wife they were fine. Your dad was much the happier but your mother was nervous. I got the impression she wanted to do more and having me there got in the way. She wasn't a sit around and do nothing type and that meant sometimes frustration would boil over.'

'What about Dad?'

'He was a private man, he didn't boast or brag like the other men. He worked hard as they all did but he just absorbed the stress and cared for the family.'

'And what about his work. Who did he mix with?'

'Your father mixed with all the business men and politicians just the same. It was the same at many of the houses and parties. Drink and food in abundance, behaving badly as the night went on. I had ears, I caught it all, not that they cared what I saw them or could hear them. I saw everything those boys were up to. Not just your dad, but those white boys and politicians. Every time they were round, they were cooking something up. They looked at me like I was trash to be put out whenever I was around.'

'What did they do? What were they up to?'

'Three things they were always talking about, business was one and then sport. They would go down the clubs and play tennis and squash. Football would be on the TV or rugby or cricket. Always alcohol and shouting. When that was over and the wives had left them alone, they moved onto talk about girls, women. Sometimes even the maids.  Each time when I was leaving for the night, they would be outside by the pool or the barbecue. They wouldn't see me or even if they did, my opinion or dismay was worthless to them. If I told anyone about what they were planning or saying I would be fired, simple as that. So I kept quiet and let them get on with their boasting. I kept hoping your father was just on the side-lines and whilst I never saw him doing anything out of turn, he was there in the thick of those conversations. He never told them to stop and I didn't like that. But it wasn't my business. I did my job.'

'I think he knew I didn't approve as he apologised for their behaviour sometimes, but he wasn't going to stop being involved to spare my blushes. It was like a great pretence for him to fit in without selling his soul to the devil. I was glad when it all stopped.'

'What stopped Johanna? What do you mean?'

'You must remember, a local girl was killed. Found dead in road side gutter. It was a big noise at the time.'

I recall something. Yes, we talked about it the school because she was same age as Ruby. Just a school kid and nobody knew why she was out there on our estate.

'I think I remember. It was terrible murder. But what did that have to do with Dad and his friends?' I am starting to get worried as I joins the dots. Surely not?

'I'm not saying anything for certain, but what they didn't tell you, was that young girl was raped before she was murdered and she was discarded like cheap shoes. All I know was that some of those men who came to the house weren't good Christian men, if you know what I mean.'

'Yeah of course,' I say. Men have always been corrupt and exploitative in big groups. All ages and wealth are much the same once they are in a group. 'I still don't get the connection.'

'They never found who did it. Like everything round that way, money talked and the problem went away. But then for a time after that, there was less parties, less of macho groups, less laughing. Doesn't that tell you something?'

I nod, thinking as she speaks. Maybe a few them had a conscience. I decide to read up about it and see if I can find anything more.

'Do you remember someone called Nigel Davies?'

'Oh yes,' she says and her face darkens a little, 'he was the ring leader if you ask me. I think he was the boss at the office if I remember. But he had this voice that carried, so English. I don't want to be rude, but his voice was like the old days. The courts, the judges. You know you English have the ability to be so polite and make everyone feel like you are there as the best friend but that's just so you can get close enough to slit our throats. That was what he was like.'

'And was he around at the time of the murder?'

'Yes, but then there were a few of them. Sometimes twenty men and various women would come round, hang round the pool. Drinking, laughing. You must remember the parties.'

I do remember, but I mostly stayed inside reading or playing games on the computer. I wasn't allowed to join in the barbecues after dinner time and no-one talked to us kids so we would come inside out of the way.

'Are any of them still here?' I ask, 'probably all retired and gone home.'

'Yes I think so. But from what I hear, it still goes on. Those parties, the drink, the sex. It all still goes on.'

I'm sure she's right.

'Do you know anyone who I can talk to about those days? Who might know about more of the people and what happened to the girl?'

She pauses and thinks. Then looks at Terry. Finally she leans towards me.

'You can't take him with you. They won't let him in. She grabs a pen and paper from a cupboard behind her and writes an address out for me. It's a women's refuge.

'Go there,' she says. 'Those women will tell you all you need to know about those times. I am not the best person to ask about the past. Too long ago. Ask for Jamila. Don't say I sent you. Just ask for her.'

We talk some more of the past but I'm already imagining what I might learn from this girl and how I'm going to feel about it afterwards. The bright light of my memories around my father are fading.

But we carry on.

***

'You were quiet and then oddly formal?' I ask Terry as we drive back.

'I didn't know what to say. I didn't want to put my foot in it.' He replies. 'So I decided to do it like I was visiting families on patrol. Be very polite.'

'She's not the enemy you know, you can be natural.' And then I think about his racist joke back catalogue and decide that maybe polite is the better option.

A bump in the road forces us both forward. The seat belt digs into my bare shoulder and I push it over my arm.

'Thought you were used to this?' Terry says.

'OK, one nil to you. You got me there.'

'I know she isn't the enemy. I listened to her. But she knew more than she was telling. I can't tell you why she didn't tell you more, maybe out of respect for your father or something else.'

'I'm glad I'm not the only one who thinks that.'

'Pearl, I got to be honest with you. I thought your dad was a top bloke and all that but when she started talking about that girl getting murdered. It rang bells for me. Scary ones.'

I look at Terry and then back to the street. This conversation isn't going as I expected.

'I was in the army, you know that. It's a gang, boys together. There was banter. Boredom. Some of the guys were obsessed. You know real hatred for the Muslims. Especially after bombing attacks. Next day on patrol, it could be brutal. I know for a fact some of the lads would go into houses and do some terrible things. Not me. Let me get this straight, it wasn't me. But I can't say it didn't happen.'

'But you didn't say anything?'

'Jesus Pearl, what do you think it was? It wasn't a kindergarten where you go tell miss and everyone puts their hands up and says sorry. If I'd had grassed on those boys I'd have gone home in a coffin draped in a flag. Scratch that, they'd have pissed on me and probably dumped me in the river along with the Taliban scum they'd just blasted. I'm not saying it's right. But it was what we did. All for one and one for all.'

'Even if they were rapists and murderers.'

'We was all murderers Pearl. Don't forget that. We had a badge of honour but I knew what I signed up for. It was to kill people. Queen and country and all that but every one of us signed up to take up that gun and shoot people. We did it because we were happy to do it. I'm comfortable with that. I can say it more now. With reflection. In the heat of the brigade we pretend it is honour and we are doing our duty. The fact is, it gave us a purpose. It's why so many guys struggle outside the service. They lose the purpose and then conscience kicks in. Creates the doubts.'

He pauses. Looking straight ahead, talking to the windscreen but it feels like he's talking to himself as much as me. It's fascinating to see the passion come out. Scary when the truth speaks but then I feel like it's setting him free.

'A girl got killed. One of our team did it. It was a young girl from a farmer's house. She was raped. We reckoned the farmer had tipped off the Taliban the exact time we would pass the farm. Probably there was more, but I remember this one because it cut right through our camp and our unit. We'd gone in, I wasn't there. I was over the other side patrolling the fields but the lads said they took a while in the house before they torched it. They found the girl outside, clothes torn, a bullet in the head. It was like they did it deliberately. A warning to the locals. We denied it. Absolutely defended it to a man. Like I said, it was that way or… just didn't happen. You understand right?'

'Not really.'

He slams the dashboard in anger. It scares me. I turn the wheel erratically and I look across at what I've unleashed.

'Pearl, don't judge me on this.'

'I'm not judging you,' I say. Though I'm lying. 'I get the mantra, the team ethic and all that. But it scares me.'

'Yeah, then you are beginning to understand. It scared me too. Every day I was there I was scared like. You got to be there, Pearl. People looking at you every minute of every day, hating you like you're the devil. Snipers, bombs all waiting for you. If you weren't scared you were already crazy. That was a fact. The only thing you had was your mates. You learn it. It's drilled so hard into you that you never question it. The only people you can count on is your mates, even if they scare you more than the fucking enemy.'

And maybe then I do understand. I can't condone it but I understand it.

'And now when that old lady were talking. It all came back to me. The pack, the hunters. That's how they think. I'm sorry Pearl, you need to start believing that no good is going to come of this. What with your brother and all that, you're going to walk into the devils parlour and your old man might be sat by his side.'

And in that he may be right.

I flick the automatic gate and drive onto the forecourt of the house. Terry gets out as I stop the car. He moves so quickly he almost falls before he gathers his balance. He obviously wants time alone so I let him go.

I sit there for a few minutes. He has his demons and perhaps for the first time in my life I realise I have my own.

# CHAPTER 15

## ∞ § ∞

I decide to walk to the refuge. I try googling the address but it tells me nothing. The note from Johanna was quite specific about the location. Behind the Muthurwa open market. Cross the carriageway, past the police station and the bus station. Walk behind the main building and you will see an apartment block and an old warehouse. They look derelict but there is an entrance at the back.

Go alone. No men. Wear a scarf or face covering. People are watching all the time. Wait at the door, someone will see you.

Johanna said all would become clear once I got there. Driving my car seems a bit like advertising.

I wear a full trousers and a long sleeve top. Luckily I had packed a few for the UK. I wear a handy light scarf covering my hair and neck. I'm boiling but I feel at least a little discreet.

It's good to get away from the tension around Terry. He's hasn't said much since yesterday. Did I press him too much or was it all locked inside anyway and I just lifted the lid? Makes me wonder how useful counselling is for the soldiers and clearly explains how PTSD has terrible impacts. A mentality built so much on a single minded ethic, drilled hard into everything they do. Is it so hard to imagine the post-service impacts that will have? Counselling will work for some but trying to unpick all that horror and tension and soften the personality so it can function in a civilian environment is more the work of brain surgeons.

I do feel for Terry and hope that he is learning to live with himself as well as his disability. Still, being the selfish, needy cow

I am, I have given him some work to do. It will stop him basking in self-indulgence because I would never do anything like that.

His task is go to the central library and do some research. I need to find as much out about ITA as possible in Kenya. Any companies that partnered with them. Plus search the media sites and see if there are any headline events that might be important. Who they worked with in local government, sponsors etc.

Of course he complained but then he nodded. I called him a taxi and let him get on with it.

I move quickly through the bustling and busy market. It's a colourful energetic place like all these city markets but it's also very crowded. People push and get in the way all the time. It's a bit in-your-face for my liking and will be happy to get to the relative safety of the open street again.

There are beggars hanging around the fringes and seeing my white face they make an extra effort to get closer. I ignore them and keep my focus on getting to the other side of the market.

I see the police station and think I can guess the flats she means. Coming closer, everything is boarded up. Graffiti and street sellers loiter round the outside. I navigate my way round the building and walk down a dusty alleyway. There are some boys playing the street and I try to keep my face covered as I walk along the side. There are men hanging around and I try to avoid any eye contact. I keep checking over my shoulder, holding the scarf in place, really wanting to be discreet but feeling very nervous and exposed down this narrow street away from public gaze. Despite my scarf, my white skin stands out like a street light.

Eventually, half way down, I see a blue metallic door and above a camera shielded in a metal frame. No doubt people will steal anything. I wonder if this is the place. There is no more obvious entrance and door way so I wait a few seconds to see if anything happens. Johanna said all will become clear. Not quite sure what that means as it's hardly an automatic glass door with a concierge waving me in.

There is no handle on the door, no video call system. No clue as to what lies beyond.

I look up and down the street and back to the camera. This is feeling weird. The people in the street don't seem to be watching me but then there could be someone hidden from view.

A buzzer sounds and I look back to the door, relieved. The door swings open inwards. I step inside and it shuts firmly behind me.

Once I'm inside, I'm amazed. From the building outside, it looks run down, derelict, boarded up.

Inside it's bright and clean. The walls are painted a light green and well lit, more like an office corridor. I follow it and reach a turning. At the end of that next corridor there is another door and another corridor. Reminds me of corridors at the university campus that were connected via so many intersections that I had no idea once inside the building where I actually was. I assume in this case the disorientation might be intended as I already seem to be quite some distance from the entrance.

Security is paramount, not a surprise but maybe the total hidden from view access and video protection is more extensive than I expected. These ladies do not want anyone coming in that they have not assessed. I'm reassured about that. But what do they see me as. Starting point might be that I am not a man.

The next door opens into a reception area. A large black woman sits behind a desk, leaning back, fanning herself with a plastic document cover, enjoying the draft of the air con. She wears a bright yellow dress and matching head covering.

'Welcome,' she says.

I'm invited to sit down on the chair by the desk.

'Welcome to our residence? Can I ask your business here?'

It feels very formal, but that's ok.

'Firstly, my name is Pearl McCann, I'm English but live in Dar Es Salaam. I'm a charity worker for a local logistics charity. But I'm actually here on personal business.'

I decide it's better to be honest with these people. They have experience with lying and manipulative men and it feels like an environment where truth works.

She makes some notes.

'I was given the name of Jamila from a contact in Nairobi. I am looking into the affairs of my father and some other business men here. I was told that Jamila might have some experience of those men and what they did. I am not going to judge or argue, just to listen. It's important I find out the truth because....' I pause, not sure how to explain this. Then it drops easily. 'I want to be able to do the right thing. It's quite clear there are some things that need to be put right. I may have some small means to do that.'

She looks at me, but shows no emotion or reaction.

'We don't desire any attention here. Our guests would simply like to get on with their lives free from the harassment of men. We are not campaigners or seeking rights. Our only wish is to protect.'

I think about how to respond. I'm beginning to sense what they are about and I decide on another tactic. It's a vulgar one, but something I have prepared for.

'I want to be clear, I represent no-one but myself. I seek only to find the truth so I can decide what to do. Part of the decision is money related. As I explained, I am involved in a number of charities as a worker. I now have the chance to become a financer, not for my glory, but because I can. But I believe some of these men that Jamila or others may have come into contact with will make it impossible for me.' Still she doesn't react and maybe I need to throw another card on the table. 'They are trying to get me arrested for fraud as a way to deflect from the truth. As a show of goodwill I will leave 100,000 shillings today whether you talk to me or not. I know how important these places are and I completely respect your discretion.'

I open my bag and place the cash on the desk.

She immediately removes it and place it in a drawer below the desk, which she locks with a set of keys on her belt.

'Give me a moment.' She opens the door behind the desk and steps away. The angle of the door behind the desk is such that I can't see anything. I'm now alone. It's a soulless office. Very brightly lit but no windows. It must be right in the heart of the warehouse. Another door opens from the corner and a slim black girl emerges. She's not young or old in her looks but dresses very western style with a vest top and short skirt. She wears heavy make-up and her nails are coloured. She looks like she's been getting ready for a night on the town.

'I'm Jamila,' she says. 'Come with me.'

She takes me down another corridor and then to a kind of lounge sitting area in the image of a doctor's waiting room. No-one else is here. There is a large TV screen on the wall showing a video of a fish tank as if that gives it some kind of atmosphere.

As I get deeper into the building I forget my university reference point as the security feels oppressive. It's closer now to a reminder of mental health training I went on during my nursing course. I went to a secure mental health facility where the dangerous sociopaths and predators are kept. Every room was sectioned off from another. In one room, I had no concept of what would be in the next as it as was completely secure. Plus you were never allowed to be alone with a patient but obviously that doesn't apply here.

'Sorry, this place is a bit strange. A bit overwhelming and disorientating.' I say.

'You get used to it,' she says. 'I've been here nearly thirty years so had time to get used to it. It's to protect us. Honestly the residences in the apartments are better, you get natural light there. But you can't go there. Only guests allowed.'

'Thirty years,' I say, surprised but then if her problems trace back to Dad's time then it has to be. That means she is in her fifties. She looks barely out of school.

'Not everyone stays that long. The place has developed a lot. I didn't have anywhere to go so as we grew up, I took a job here. That's how Mary knew who I was immediately. Because there's only one of me. I work in accounts. I do the banking and payments.'

'Right', I nod like it is a normal every day activity. But I guess it is. Like all charities and voluntary organisations. Not only do they have bills to pay like everyone else, they are subject to maximum scrutiny by Trustees and auditors.

'Mary said you had some questions for me. Going back a whole while. Not sure what I can tell you but I'll try. But just so you know. Neither of us can write anything down, you can't record me and I'll never speak at a trial. It's the rules here. You have to agree to that.'

I think about what she saying and it becomes a little clearer. This place is under the radar, no name, no address. I wonder how people know it exists or even how it is funded. But the point I am learning is that the women come here because they know they are protected and will not be forced to give evidence or compete with their families. Remarkable.

'Ok,' I say, 'I have a few names to drop on you and see if you know anything about them or they were involved with you in anyway.'

She nods. I get the impression the questions are not new to her. I guess if some of the things I suspected that happened were common, then quite a few people will have come with questions before.

'Are you familiar with the Tobacco Company, ITA; International Tobacco?'

'I never took any notice of who the men worked for. It was tobacco, oil, drugs. Then there were teachers, lawyers. Just sweaty guys who wanted girls.'

'Do you remember names?'

'Names? 'She asks, 'When someone has you faced down on a bed for him and his mates to take turns, the last thing on my mind is checking their passports.'

'Sorry,' I say. 'Can I show you a photograph?'

I had one of Dad from the 90s.

She looks at it and shrugs. Then I have a photo of Davies from the internet in his younger days. She stares longer at him.

'They are familiar, but I couldn't tell you much. It was a long time ago. She looks again at Davies. I remember him for his eyes. Something about him. But he never touched me, or I don't think so. I might have been too old for him.'

'What do you mean too old for him?

She pauses.

'How much do you know about this?' she asks, 'I thought with these photos you knew stuff. Do I have to tell you everything?'

'Look I'm not naïve. I know men but I'm trying to be specific. It's important I know what I'm dealing with.'

'Ok. I was fifteen when this started. Sixteen later and seventeen when I ran off. I was a big girl for my age,' she says, looking down at her chest. No doubt she was voluptuous, probably amazingly beautiful as a teenager.

'Men liked the way I looked, big chest, and big ass. It was all that was needed. They didn't come for the conversation right. But some… him… they wanted them younger, smaller. Sick men they were.'

I'm stunned. I'm not sure what I expected from this conversation but I'm listening to this girl talk about gang rape of an underage girl as if she's relating a teenage bad date and then switching into systematic paedophilia. I want to be sick. Certainly these four walls feel oppressive. Davies liked young kids. Dad must have known. That's why Davies was scared of him.

But Jamila just told me she isn't going to go on record so I have no evidence and could never repeat it. But then Dad must have had something otherwise how did he keep Davies at bay. Oh my. This is big. I can't sit on this. I need to go, but I need to ask more. I'm not sure I will get the opportunity to come back.

I sit down again.

'How did you get into this?' I ask.

'Are you being deliberately stupid? Mary said you worked in Tanzania and other places, you know the way it works.'

'I do,' I say, but I think I'm missing something. I don't know, Jamila. I think I do and then suddenly what you are telling me is turning all my assumptions on their head. Please tell me.'

'These companies, the bosses. You can't touch them. They're rich. Fancy families. Big houses. Police are on their side, judges, and politicians. Everyone wants their money so they are untouchable. Nothing will ever happen to them. But they also need locals to do their work. You are in charity, most people are poor. You go to the villages, families are desperate for money and income. Gun men, militias all run the farms. You're not stupid. You get it. Everything has a price even daughters.'

And now I get it. What she is telling me was true and I have seen it. But it takes no imagination to work out that desperate fathers will have been forced at the end of a gun to let a daughter go so he could feed his family. He may not even have known where the daughter would end up. Some would refuse but others wouldn't. The girls would have been bargained off to a gang, moved into the city and then rolled out for private parties like sweeties. This is what Jamila is talking about. It is sick and they could do it with impunity as if anyone ever complained, it just got pushed under the carpet.

'My friend, who gave me your name mentioned a girl who was murdered, left for dead. Do you know about that?'

'That was my friend, Bernadette. She was younger, smaller. I don't know what happened. At the end of the night after a party we would get collected in a bus. But she wasn't there. I don't know why.'

'And this guy, was he at that party?'

She nods. 'I don't really remember in detail. I just remember he was at a few and he probably was there that night. Once it came out that she was dead, him and another were the first people I thought of. Just because she was what they liked.'

'What do you think happened?'

'She was scared, we all were. But she cried with fear every night. Maybe she ran. They would have chased her. They didn't like loose ends. It wouldn't have ended well for her. It was horrible. The bossman hit us after that. He beat us up, one by one, telling us that worse would happen to our families if we tried to run.'

'But you ran?'

'One of the women at the houses gave me the name of this place. I didn't know about it until she told me.'

'But weren't you scared for your family.'

She laughs.

'My family had abandoned me. Two years of being raped daily and not a word from my family. I was only worried for me by that time. I didn't want to die like Bernadette. So I escaped and came here.'

This is like a tidal wave of information. I'm processing it as quick as I can but I fear my time is going to run out. They will be getting nervous if I'm asking too many questions.

'One last question,' I ask. 'And I will leave you alone. I promise.'

She shrugs her shoulders like it's normal. Why am I feeling under more pressure than she is?

'This is an amazing facility here, but how do you pay for it if you are not an official charity or you don't go to courts.'

She looks around, maybe someone is listening in and she needs to be careful.

'They are clever here. The women who set it up are long dead but they carried it on well and hopefully new girls coming in will do the same. All women are welcome here. All faiths all ages. We've got battered wives, women running from forced marriages. Then we have girls like me, prostitutes some mentally ill, mostly everyone who comes here is desperate. We don't have children, mothers with children have to go into another facility or leave them in care. Not everyone stays but we don't shut any woman out. But like you say we need money and it doesn't happen by magic. We don't judge and we don't put pressure on anyone. In their own good time they tell their story and then we get the names of the men.'

'But you don't get the police involved?'

'Half the women in here are running from the police. You don't get the police involved.'

I feel like the naïve child at the back of the class. Where have I been for the last fifty years?

'We use intermediaries. It's clever. The men get a visit. Discreet. No publicity no police or threats. They get told that if they don't provide money to support our guest then they might have some troubles along the way. The history for women is not a good one, I'm sure you know that. We can be persuasive. With the connections right throughout the cities and the courts and the council we know many of the men who have had indiscretions in the past. They will do as they are told and make life difficult for men who don't pay.'

'Wow, it's like a reverse masons where you know all their secrets. I don't know how you get away with it.'

'Two things are important. One and this is the most important. We don't exist officially and no man can get close to this building. You have seen how secure it is. Second, most men will happily pay to keep a secret. It's the easiest way to put it under the sand. They can hide it from wives and lovers, from work and bosses. No-one need ever know.'

'And there is the beauty of it. I'm so impressed Jamila. I would love to know more of your stories but I understand that can't happen.'

I pass her my card with my name on.

'Please if you think there is anything I should know, contact me.'

'Sorry,' she says as she tears it up. 'That's against the rules. I've explained what I know and you should leave now. And you can't come back here. They might not let you in again, you understand. It's too high risk for this place to be known about.'

'Ok,' I say.

'Come with me and I will see you out.'

We go through another door and then down a set of steps. We arrive in a damp underground corridor and walk along.  It carries on for a hundred metres. There are more concrete stairs and then at the top is a door. Jamila releases a catch and ushers me out.

To my surprise I appear through a curtain in a fabric shop. No-one takes any notice of me as I leave and I'm back in the market. Unbelievable.

I'm in complete awe of Jamila and what these women have achieved. Totally unbelievable, I say to myself.

# CHAPTER 16

## ∞ § ∞

Back at the house, I'm pleased to see Terry isn't back. I should go looking for him but I decide in the end to collapse on the sofa. I put on the TV to take in the news and try to relax.

Spending time at the refuge has given me a lot to process.

I have seen many a similar place over the years, that's the easy bit. Usually the refuges were for widowed women from wars or from disease. Aids being a common one. There were sometimes orphan daughters who had no-where to go when their parents died.

These places were humble affairs. The local community finding a way to look after those in need. But this was a much more professional and sophisticated approach. Also the fact that they saw themselves as a refuge and a home made it a much more interesting place. It wasn't a temporary hideaway until you found a better option, it offered a way of life, looking after their own. And the fact that they made the men pay for it was a stroke of subtle genius.

But my pride in the achievement didn't take away from the horror of what brought the women to it.

Due to my less than delicate looks, broad shoulders and larger size I've never felt the male gaze in quite the same ways as petite more attractive girls. I've perhaps been more intimidating. Big boned as mother would say, pig ugly according to a few boys threw insults at school. Hurtful but easily dismissed, especially as I was often as strong as them. But my more masculine looks didn't stop with the gropes and I have even been shoved against the wall with a hand round my neck one time when I shot my mouth off too much. I've been lucky enough to escape those attacks but that was luck of the moment. Every woman has had a moment when they feared the presence of a man.

To dismiss many of these bad encounters as trivial or bad luck allows those feeble, atrocious men get away with misogyny like this but that hardly compares with the treatment of these women. As girls they are treated as a disposable commodity, a luxury the family can't afford and sold onto men as sex slaves. Their innocence stolen, futures smashed. The sliver of a silver lining is that these pigs seem not to have completely crushed the life out of the girls and they have found the courage to survive and rebuild their lives. Yes, some of the men paid a price but only in cash terms, they've never paid in pain, humiliation and removal of hope that the girls had to face.

Considering the men, I had to put my father front and centre of the discussion. He was one of these pigs. It didn't fit with the gentle man I knew. I had to prepare myself to accept there was two sides to him.

The door bangs twice and I hear the familiar associated grunt. I get up from the sofa. Terry bundles in with his stick as a local man follows with two carrier bags.

'Been shopping,' he says. 'Top nosh and a few beers. Found a helper.'

'I can see. Find anything useful?'

Terry rolls off a note with his good hand and gives it to the driver.

'You still don't have any idea how much you just gave him.' I laugh watching him pretend he knows what he's doing.

'Not the foggiest,' he replies 'Anyway found loads of stuff. But let's eat and drink first. There's a few scabby donkeys out there that were nearly on the plate.'

'Wonderful,' I say, almost meaning it.

***

Terry finishes off his curry and naturally a few bottles of beer to wash it down. Not that I have room to talk. I polished off whatever form of chicken curry it was with a bourbon and coke. The coke added in the last days to soften my consumption. Or maybe moderate my mood or just maybe feel less of an alcoholic.

Terry burps and I assume he is ready to talk.

'Tell me,' I say.

He passes me some photocopies. A whole set of company accounts by the look of it and then a few newspaper articles.

'You have been busy.' I say.

'Impressed?'

'Yes,' I say, flicking through the papers looking for the highlights. I am a little impressed. I sent him out for something to do but actually wasn't expecting much.

'To be fair, I had help.' He says.

'Ah.'

'Cam you see me flicking through books and papers. I'm as clumsy as fuck. I'd probably knock the cabinet over. I 'ad a word with one of the girls at the desk. Helpful she was. Told her what I was looking forward and she spent loads of time finding bits for me.'

'Ok, do you have a clue what she found? Did you read any of this?'

'I didn't exactly read it, but...'

I laugh. He is so predictable.

'And what did the lovely black lady tell you she found.'

'Don't start with that racist crap? Wind up merchant. If you're going to be smart, you can go do your own digging. I can go crack on with a Jack Ryan series on my lonesome.'

'Get on with it. There's some tissues in the kitchen if you need them. I know how much you like these men with guns,' I say.

He turns his head and stares back at me.

'Bring it on,' Terry replies.

'I can't resist winding you up sometimes is all. Too easy.'

'Good job, I liked your dad because if I was doing this for you...'

'You'd what?'

'You really are a.... fuck, you going to let me tell you about it or what?'

I smile flatly and let him continue. Banter is boring me now anyway.

He leans forward and wipes his mouth. I try not to imagine the left over curry on the back of his hand.

'In there's company accounts for ITA and the subsidiary companies. Fucking loads of companies it owns or got shares in. Nadia, that's her name. She knew a bit about them, apparently there have been a few court cases, she was studying at the university. They've got the fingers in a lot of pies. For example. People's bank... ha, it is nothing of the sort. Might as well call it bent for rent bank. Honestly talk about creaming off the top and the bottom. They owned a delivery company, supermarket chain, farms.'

'Owned out right?' I ask.

'I think she said they had shares, but she called it owning. I didn't look too far, never understand all that. Point is, they had it all ways. They was controlling the supply chain, the cash operation and the sales end. And they was doing it in all the countries all around as well.'

I nod along, listening but thinking why I am surprised. Of course they bought control like this. Typical of so many big companies coming into Africa with deep pockets and pretend scruples.

'Thing is, she said that was how it was then, twenty years ago. But she was talking about it all changing now. Some kind of scandals, don't know what. Most of it went over me head but's it's in those papers. She says that they had to split it all up. Drove it all underground. Auditors, tax people, courts and everything so they had to get a bit smarter. There was a lot of arrests. Money laundering.

'Wow,' I say. I flick through the papers as he's talking trying to find something to anchor my thoughts at the same time as listening.

'Then even worse. She gave me some stuff on the government ministers who were convicted. Taking bribes, favours. There were judges, everyone taking knock backs. Couldn't believe it. How the fuck did they get away with it? Are our lot doing all of this back home? Seriously? Or they just lah di dah shaking your hand and robbing your wallet with the other. At least every fucker knows what they are up to here.'

It's a fair rant. Nothing he says is wrong. But the point is, how they get away with it. Most people would abhor what they do, but corruption is a clever beast. It gets to the state where corruption is so prevalent that the only way to get anything done is to bribe. It becomes a way of life. Cost of doing business.

'Did you find Davies or Dad?' I ask.

'Yeah, well Davies was the boss in the 90's. MD or something. He was the controller. But he was nowhere near that court stuff. She did mention your Dad, but only coz he was on the business reports. He was the Finance guy. She said, he would have been the guy who knew all the ins and outs. Made out he might have been shifty but when asked for more about him, she said she didn't know for sure. But they signed the cheques so they must know right? Makes sense to me but what do I know? She said I could look through any of the court statements to find him but she was a bit bored by then. Said she had to go and no point me trying to read them. I can just about manage The Sun.'

I won't say the obvious. Far too much of an open goal. 'So I need to read through all this?'

'I suppose so. She left me a phone number if I wanted to go back.'

'Oh good, I can thank her for all her hard work.'

He opens his arm out in expectation of reward.

'No mention of my hard work then?'

'Looks like she provided all the paperwork and all thinking, you just brought it back. Taxi driver could have done that.'

I'm laughing as I explain. His face going puce is worth every word.

'You cheeky fucking…' he says and then stops short, knowing I'm winding him up. 'Anyway, I'm knackered now, going to down a few shandies and watch my stuff. Happy reading.'

'Yeah, sure,' I say, 'and I am grateful. I do appreciate the information. And to prove I am not a total cow, we can have a treat tomorrow. We're going on safari? Are you up for it?'

'Safari, wow! Serious? Lions, elephants?' Terry asks.

Good to see genuine excitement in his eyes.

'It's not a petting zoo. This is Africa in case you hadn't noticed. These animals do exist outside a David Attenborough documentary,' I say. I will have to resist winding him up one day, but it's too easy. 'Go get some sleep. Early start tomorrow.'

He goes off to his room with a chunter and I am alone again. The safari idea came to me out of nowhere. It's easy to do and I need to think all this through. The corruption, the women, where it all fits in.

I top up my glass and pick up the papers. A long night ahead.

***

I takes me an hour to find Dad.

It is an article from 1994. I would have been twenty, already at university in London. We were already back in the UK so I wonder if that's why. Dad had to leave because he must have known the news would break at some point. The article talked about a corruption scandal at ITA. An accusation of fraud laid at Dad.

The article is in the business news of the Nairobi Telegraph. His actual name is buried deep in the article but the inference was clear. Spencer McCann had been taking money for himself. He'd done it by using the cover of a local charity. The statement explains that ITA provided support for a number of local charities as part of their ethical contribution to the countries they were working in. However Dad was paying money into an

Orphan charity for girls that didn't exist. After investigation the charity was a front for a number of illegal payments to overseas banks. It didn't say anything about these accounts, the inference being that he was keeping the money for himself.

This must be the money sitting in my company accounts in Panama. Is it that simple? Few minutes of searching articles and it drops out. If I can find this, so can all the other people investigating Dad's history, including Police and Courts in the UK.

Did he really skim money for his own benefit? But that doesn't make any sense as he never lavished money on me or Ruby. I was at University and had my debts. Dad bunged me cash but I paid my own rent and worked in a bar to keep in food and booze. He didn't even pay it out for himself so what was he up to?

I looked through the bank history when I was in the apartment and since it had been in the name of PMC, the only money that had gone out of the account was paying the fees for the apartment and Bea's salary and taxes. So it must have been set up after all the fraudulent transactions were ended. The money was hidden from investigators once it was offshore so would have been hard to trace or retrieve.

The time period would be why it has grown, with high interest rates, no fees to pay, it was effectively doubling the balance every five years.

So Davies would have had no choice but to fire Dad from Kenya. But he kept his job because he worked for ITA well into the 2000s until he got an early retirement pay off in a reorganisation. That doesn't make sense if was accused of fraud in Kenya.

I did another search on the death of the girl back then and looked at the timeline. 1992. There are a few articles on the death of Bernadette being discovered and the investigation. Apparently she was found in street ditch out of sight from the road. She had been raped and beaten but had died from strangulation. The street was out of town and police believe she was dumped there rather than where she was murdered. It was the days before CCTV being in regular use and no witnesses. So probably little to go on.

Nothing about a trial or a conclusion which means there was no trial so no arrests. Is that telling as well?

I wonder if the connections start from the murder. Davies mixed up with a dead girl? He had an apparent fetish for young ones? Did Dad know? Well I suspect Johanna knew so Dad knew as well.

Dad had something on him. That's why he kept his job, but it must have been more than what he or others around him knew. Hard evidence would have been needed. I haven't found any sign of that either in his papers or in the house. But there must be something somewhere. It might need another search of the house or the apartment. Maybe Bea knows more and she has it somewhere. She had free run of the house. That will have to be solved back in the UK. For now I need to get more information here. It is clear Davies is well known and people know his reputation. I wonder if I can find out more about him. Dad had evidence. Did anyone else?

# CHAPTER 17

∞ § ∞

Thirty minutes' drive from the city and we arrive at Nairobi Wildlife Park. Hardly a moment taken to find ourselves in the African bush. It's the compact nature of the city that it doesn't take long to be free of the urban environment. Though the highway flyover running over the park means it is less a wilderness but more a country park.

Terry is in awe.

He clambers out of the car just staring at the view. He is wearing a beach shirt and heavy jeans. Like he doesn't have any decent clothes. But then he probably doesn't. With a plastic arm and a leg missing below the knee, I imagine his first choice of clothes are those he can get on rather than what they look like.

We go to the gate and pay for the guided tour. I have been here before and been to a few further out as well, those where you stay for a few days and get a much more immersive experience. This is a lot different from a zoo which is usually an artificial environment and the animals not native. This is a managed natural environment for the animals and a massive protected area.

We join the mini bus, glad of the air con. Definitely Terry needs it, as he uses his hat constantly to waft the heat and flies away. Poor guy, his body shape and lack of fitness were not designed for this heat.

I've paid for a private tour so we can spread out a little. After yesterday's tension I can breathe again. So glad to get away from the city and think about something else for the day. It is becoming oppressive and stressful. I didn't sleep much with the worries about what Dad might or might not have done.

The minibus winds its way along the trails. The bus doesn't come with a suspension it seems, as every bump rattles the van. Terry curses with each rut and stone hit. We get the compulsory commentary about the history of the park and the animals. I'm not listening much, not because I've heard it before or know better, it just doesn't concern me. I'm happy for my mind to drift and enjoy the landscape.

'Over there,' Terry points and I can see the elephants at a water hole. We drive closer and the view of the lake leading from the trees gets bigger. We pause and Terry reaches forward through the open window to take photographs with his phone. Probably needs a better camera to take decent shots and if I'd thought about it earlier, could have bought one. But I didn't so he will have to make do.

'There'll be crocs and hippos in there.' I tell Terry.

'Amazing, don't suppose we can get out.'

'There are places but not out here in the wild areas. Though can you imagine how disappointed a croc is when he comes for you and grabs the wrong leg? He'll get a chunk of metal for lunch.'

'Good one, very good,' he laughs. 'And I'll give him a right hook with this arm. Get that on the noggin and it won't know what hit it.'

'Yeah, good job as you're not going to out run a tortoise.'

'Even funnier.' He says with an exaggerated snigger. 'Where's the lions? Do they have wildebeests?'

'You've been watching too much TV again haven't you?' Feels like I'm in the car with a child but then when was the last time I got to think like a child. And Terry. He is soaking up every view. Phone snapping everything.

Seeing the animals in this place is awe inspiring. Whilst this is a sanctuary and poachers are kept away, the animals live and die via the nature's rules. The guide tells us some of the rhinos were killed last year for the price of their horns. This sickest thing ever is killing an animal for one redundant part of it, not for food but for pure luxury indulgence. Fortunately they've come up with a plan to remove the tusks humanely before the poachers can. It's kind of sad to see a Rhino without its horn but it's better than the tragedy of wiping the whole species out for a cynically stupid reason.

As always when I see the lions they are lying under a tree. We stop for a while but nothing seems to be happening. Perhaps when it's cooler in the evening, we could see them hunt. But then the guides would keep their distance. Whilst it is a spectacle to see a hunt, it's dangerous to interfere or get caught in a stampede.

Terry continues with his camera shots and I rest back in the seat and close my eyes.

The plains, the lakes and the mountains around are vast. Especially if you take the view away from the city skyline. The open spaces, the scope of the landscape is hard to comprehend, setting off from here to the west it feels like the open spaces go on forever. Taking the right line there would be nothing except the land until the Atlantic appears in the Nigerian delta hundreds of miles away. The continent is not just about its people but the incredible environment. Like the rainforests of Brazil and wild mountains in Borneo I love the idea of undiscovered places untouched by the outside world. Whilst there are less of them in the vast expanse of Africa, they do still exist. Probably, like the outback in Australia, there really isn't much to see. I will still go with the fantasy of a space where civilisation could have taken a different road. An alternate world where people grew up equal and collaborative rather than seeing life as a competition.

The dream or the fantasy. Whatever it is, I do get a sense for all the disasters of war and corruption and even ancient tribal migrations that forced inevitable hardship, people like me coming from another continent; westerners, colonists, and missionaries, brought something worse.

They may have lacked structure but they survived before we came with guns and money and look what a legacy we left behind. And so the debate will go on.

A question I often asked Dad about working for a tobacco company, was his opinion on smoking. He and mum smoked and many of the people around us did. They gave up when we were kids but they were still heavily involved with the promotion and business of selling products they knew would make people ill or even kill them.

I don't recall the exact answer. It was fairly glib, probably something about it being good business and making a lot of money in taxes for the countries. And if they didn't do it, someone else would. There were plenty of other companies doing the same. Thinking about it, I am reminded once when Dad tried to tell me that ITA were more ethical than other companies, making safer products and doing lots of research on less harmful tobacco. Yeah dad. Right on.

One of my more rebellious actions as a daughter of the company itself was to hate smoking. Though, Walter more than made up for my abstention, sniffing and snorting and probably injecting any substance available.

Not many get to be more ethically superior. It's a bit like the doctrinal line of Jesus about those without sin should cast the first stone. We all sin environmentally as it's almost impossible to be a westerner without air travel, oil consumption, mass produced food, roads and building. Tobacco, alcohol and meat have major ethical issues but producing and eating non-meat products from all parts of the world brings problems. So even clean living vegetarians carry some guilt. Unless we effectively live off the environment purely within immediate vicinity we are none of us innocent of the rough practices of those that produce the goods we consume. This was kind of Dad's point, we can strive to work for better conditions and impacts of the products we make. But that ignores that we delude ourselves, turning a blind eye to the corruptive and exploitative nature of mass production to pretend that we are slightly more pure in our ethics.

The day passes quickly and thankfully Terry's excitement and crass commentary saves me from self-examination. I am pleased to get back to the visitor centre and grab a late lunch.

I am so glad we came. Definitely the right thing. Just the release of tension between Terry and I is worth it, but then seeing the absolute joy on his face was a worth the whole trip to Kenya. Despite me ribbing him, I see someone changing every day and that cannot ever be a bad thing. What about me? Am I changing as well?

After Terry empties the visitor shop of model giraffes, elephants, monkey, books, cards and a few scary masks, we head to the car.

'You know something. These masks had some horrible rituals.' He tells me as we walk to the car. I knew this was one of his areas of fascination. I don't get to hear the details as someone is by my car.

Getting closer he becomes familiar. The tall figure, the white hair. Last seen only 3 days ago in Cape Town.

'Henrik,' I say.

'Pearl, Pearl, Pearl,' he says. 'And who's your friend here? Looks like he's had a bad time of it.'

I stand looking at him as he leans on the car, arms crossed. Pleased with himself. His height has more impact in the open air away from the rain of Cape Town. His stature is imposing even leaning lazily as he is.

'Should I be surprised to see you or perhaps pleased?' I ask.

'I don't care what you think?' he says, 'but if you keep hanging around Nairobi and sniffing round the past then I guess you will see a lot more of me. Believe me I don't want to look at your ugly face any more than you want to see mine.'

And the accent is still horrid, it grates like finger nails on a blackboard. Adding the know-all smugness, he's baiting me for a reaction that I don't want to give him. I want to keep cool.

'Who's this joker?' Terry asks.

'Go home Pearl,' he says, 'pay the man his money and life will be very much better for all of us.'

'And if I don't?' I ask.

'Then life will be worse.' He gets up off the car and walks to his own land rover. There is a driver in the car but I can't see who it is. In a moment, he's gone.

I look at Terry and he's staring back at the car.

'You going to tell me who the fuck that was?'

'Henrik Dahl. I told you about him in South Africa. But what and who he is, I really don't know. Whatever, he's bad for us,' I reply.

***

The drive back doesn't take long which is good as I'm in no mood to talk. I explain the conversation we had in Cape Town and how he is connected to Nigel Davies in some kind of business way, but there's little more to add. The practicality of the business arrangements is academic and not something that bothers me. It is their joint intent to get me to pay back this money and to stop looking for whatever secrets there are from the past.

Back at the house, Terry decides to go to his room, maybe realising I need to be alone.

I pick up my phone and see I have a new WhatsApp message. It's a local number.

Sis, don't fuck around with Henrik. He's bad news. Get out of Kenya. Dean.

How come everyone seems to know where I am all of a sudden? I told no-one, except Terry of course and Ruby. I didn't really think too much about who would know but I'm pissed off that they do. And it seems, they know more about my business than I do. That is even more irritating. Basically I'm being warned off. Go home feeble girl, don't mess with the big boys.

Well guess what big boys, I am not going anywhere until I know what's happening.

I go back to my digging, once again inspired by the threats. Something to hide boys means something to find. They are worried about me which gives me a little hope. With the stuff Terry already uncovered from a few hours in the library I can connect a few more dots. Now that Dean/Walt is out of South Africa I can assume my one million rand has been wasted. Does that mean he can't go back there again without getting locked up or can they get him over the South African border easily? Does he even have another identity that I don't know about? I am so naïve.

Henrik Dahl. I did all the digging on him yesterday and his company does show up on the list of those partly owned by ITA. So that's how they are linked corporately. As I read the company records it all feels too legitimate and above board. Having met Henrik Dahl I believe he is not a corporate animal, suits and handshakes type. He is a doer and a networker. He knows all the people locally who can give him what he wants. Whatever that might be.

The more I think about these businesses I start to wonder if anyone does anything legitimately anymore. Is everything a front for something else?

I should ring the number that I got the text from and see if Walt or Dean as he says he is will tell me more. But I don't know if it's even him and then I can't trust a word he says. A faked death is a pretty large blot on the timeline of trust and stitching me up with the dodgy Operations Director of ALC seems another low trick.  These people. My brother running rings around me, fake businesses, stealing cash, drugs, prostitutes and how much corruption going on all around.

Unbelievable. I swear to myself. Tomorrow, the fight back starts.

# CHAPTER 18

$$\infty \ \S \ \infty$$

Another Nairobi morning comes round. We are at the breakfast table on the garden patio. The chattering of birds competes with the hum of the city streets. Sitting on the patio with the warm sun and lovely green garden, it feels like the suburbs of any normal city. Which is right. Nairobi is the same as any modern city with its wealthy and middle classes. The problem is the lower classes of the city have little or nothing. The lifestyle of the poor is not remotely close to those of the regular educated population.

We are dining on eggs, ham and bread I got from the supermarket on the first day. The sun is warm already as is Terry. He's sweating as he downs the fresh orange juice like a pint of beer.

'This Nadia you met at the Library?' I say.

'Yep,' Terry replies.

He wipes his mouth again with the back of his hand and I want to slap him. I pass him a serviette to make the point. He picks it up and manages to hold it against his false arm, but it drops to the floor. I pick it up in silence and place it back on the table. I know, I know...I need to stop obsessing about his clumsiness. He can't help it.

'Can we go see her today?' I ask, trying to talk about something else. 'Should be ok right?'

'I can call her if you like. She was friendly and all that.'

'No don't do that. Not that I am suggesting anything but I don't want to telegraph what we are doing in advance.'

'You getting paranoid, Pearl?' He says, 'next you'll be suggesting we get some burner phones and go all spook like.'

'You joke, but the burner phones is not a bad idea.'

'Probably for the best. But really, should we be that scared? I mean the South African was just a lanky streak of piss. Kick him in the bollocks and he's nobody. He was just some pretty boy smart arse.'

He picks up the dirty serviette and wipes the sweat from his brow. I avoid looking if the remnants of the egg and orange juice are now adorning his forehead.

'Seriously Terry, is this you saying you could have him? Are we in the playground now? Twat him with your stick. Honestly.'

'I'm just saying he isn't that scary. Now if he was wearing one of them masks I picked up at the shop and had all that body paint, I'd have been calling in the cavalry.'

'You never stop do you?' I seriously don't know why I bother having these discussions. Where's the wall? I need to go bang my head against it for a while. 'Anyway, back to adult conversation. I think Henrik Dahl is scary, not because he's bigger than me but because it's quite feasible he could murder someone and get away with it. He got my brother out of South Africa with a drugs conviction pending. He's got access to money, maybe courts. He knows his way round even better than I do. They faked a death and got away with it. Yeah, I think he's worthy of some concern, don't you?'

'Different type of enemy than I'm used to.' He says, followed by a loud burp. 'I'm more used to those you can point a gun at.'

And there is another great example of stating the fucking obvious. But I deploy suitable restraint and keep my sarcasm to myself. He's too exhausting to argue with.

'I think I have two advantages that I need to exploit. Get your army head on and help me. What would you do?'

'What advantages do you 'think you have first?'

'One they want something from me. Probably the money but also my silence. Obviously they could murder me, arrange an accident but I think I already brought too much attention to them, so that would seem to be a strong advantage. Second is, they might know their way round the corruption circles and the courts, but I also know as much about local people and the way they think and act. I am used to dealing the different mind-sets and cultures. I talk to them all the time so maybe they might trust me. If in doubt money helps right? I've got plenty of that to use.'

'How much money we talking Pearl, you keep saying you have money but old Spencer didn't seem to have much. If he ferreted some away it can't have been that much.'

'Sorry,' I say, 'but I may as well tell you now. I told you before that there was some money the bailiffs wanted but didn't tell you exactly. I wasn't sure how much to tell you before, I didn't want to scare you or... well I don't know.'

'It's ok, not sure I'd trust me after first meeting me either.'

I laugh but only for a second.

'Fifty six million dollars,' I say. 'About forty million pounds.'

His jaw almost to the floor.

'Fuck me, girl. That's a serious wedge. Spencer was a busy boy.'

He is laughing but it's like most people's reaction when you say such a large amount of money. Everyone laughs because none of us know how to deal with it. I've known for a week and I still haven't worked out what to do.

'Much of it is interest, been sat there a while. But still it's a lot of money.'

'I see why you kept that one quiet. I thought you said the bailiffs only wanted 100k. Anyway, it's all numbers to me. But Pearl, those people are not going to roll over for that money, they are going to want it back. And yes, if that lanky twat knows about that money, he is a scary fucker because that's enough to kill for.'

At least, I now feel I have his proper attention. He reaches this time for a clean serviette and I'm somewhat more relieved that he uses this to wipe his brow.

'Tell me about it. But Dad took the money for a reason and kept it because… I'm not sure but he obviously had something in mind.'

'No idea and he didn't give me a sodding penny. Maybe I need to think about old Spencer differently. Secretive old boy. Seriously sly one.' He pauses. 'Shouldn't you be forgetting all this Pearl? I mean you could pay them off and still have some decent coin left for a nice life. You don't need all this crap do you?'

'I could,' I pause and take a deep breath. 'But I don't think I can. Dad left me a message saying he wanted me to do the right thing. So I'm here, doing the right thing.'

'Yeah I get you. Telling you now though, most folk would have had a party and then gone off to Bermuda or Barbados. Wouldn't have seen them again.'

'Yeah, that's never been me.'

I'm feeling hot and now it's me reaching for a serviette to dry my face. I do it demonstratively slowly hoping he takes note. He's not even looking at me. He's looking up into the sky at plane flying over.

So tell me Army man. If you were in your Afghan village and you wanted to turn native, what would you do? Who would help you?'

'Ah now you're talking.' He says, 'The women, especially them with kids. They were clever, all ears to what was going on and the men completely underestimated them. The beaten wives, the most vulnerable. They listened to everything because they needed to keep safe. React to a pin drop. Plus, they had nothing to lose. They were permanently scared of their husbands and their families. And us of course.'

'Not the men?' I ask. 'Surely the men had the better intelligence.'

'Couldn't be trusted. I mean most of the time the women couldn't be either but you had a better chance with them. The men were professional liars if I can say it. Often the friendly ones turned out up to be spies. So we went to the women folk.'

'The women with kids, thought we could offer them something. We gave them small bits of cash, some bread or anything electrical. They could trade these for cash. Often they would suggest we took their eldest to UK or America or anywhere. They were desperate but if I lived like them I would be too. But yeah, when you find someone who's only hope for survival is whatever you got to offer, that's when you get information.'

'Ok,' I say. 'Not sure that helps me in this.'

'Yeah it does Pearl. You just said yourself, you know these people, and you know how they think and what they need. You keep rattling on about your projects and how much of hero you are. That means get in the gutter with them. Find a way.'

'Am I that bad?' I ask.

'Pearl, it's like the fucking 9 o'clock news when you're going on. What's that women on the BBC with the miserable voice? You're like her…. Droning on when all we want to know is the footie results.'

'At least I'm not going on about the boys and my time in Afghanistan.'

We laugh but then it's time to move on.

'So Nadia then.' I say, 'then the burner phones.'

He's right though. My line of attack is finding the victims and getting them to talk. The refuge is also interesting but unless I can get them outside there is little I can do. It's too controlled an environment. Plenty to think about.

***

The Macmillan Library is a typical colonial building with grand colonnades over the entrance. It is impressive and daunting but as a library it feels right. Books are awe inspiring so the buildings that house them should also draw people in.

Terry directs me to the newspaper room.

There is no sign of Nadia which is a bit disappointing but doesn't mean I can't do my own searches. I think back to my school days when a visit here was an occasional outing. Oh for the innocence of those days searching out the stories of the great

British explorers and how they brought religion and civilisation. Even in the midst of a large black population, much of our historic education seems to ignore the bulk of the people in the streets around us. Why let a bit of white supremacy get in the way of a good education?

'Should I text her?' Terry says. He's taken to the chair and is flicking through his phone. I should have left him in a pub with an Arsenal match to watch. Or maybe I'll find a caveman museum and he would really be in his element.

'Leave it. We're here now and can do our own digging.'

Come on Pearl, where to start with all this, I say to myself. What 'would I do if it was work?

Then I realise I have been so obsessed with the logistics of the tobacco industry I have forgotten about my relationship with the country and numerous projects in this region. Some of those people must still be around.

I dig around the Oxfam website and look for contacts and then MSF, Water Aid. Then Red Cross. Bingo. Charles Newell. Swiss guy. I've worked with him. Last time I saw him he was in Ethiopia but these people move around constantly as the priorities shift.

I ping him on WhatsApp and see if he replies. It's not his local number but he should still pick it up.

A few minutes later. Success. He gives me a number to call locally.

'Charles, how are you?'

It takes a few minutes of explaining I am in Kenya and fortunately he is in Mombasa and therefore I am not obliged to go see him. Besides I am not sure what he would make of Terry.

'Quick question?' I ask.

'Sure go ahead.'

'I am looking for someone in the Kenyan government health department. Senior person. Someone you think is good and honest.'

'There are a couple of people I deal with,' he says. Let me think. 'What's the brief? You looking for a desk job?'

'Ha-ha, no some family business to deal with. It is tobacco related. Anybody involved in any of the anti-tobacco campaigns?

He thinks for a minute.

'I will send you a name on WhatsApp. He's a bit difficult to get hold of. Made quite a name for himself with his campaigns against the industry in East Africa. But if he picks up, he's definitely your man. For a change, he's not corruptible. Or at least he seems that way. It's more than I can say for some of his department.

We finish the conversation and in a few moments, get a text with the name I need.

Aashir Kaul. Phone number and email alongside the message.

I google him and start reading about his record.

***

The library is boring and can't help feeling a little exposed.

After the scare at the park yesterday I am beginning to feel that I am being watched.

Every time I catch someone's eye, I wonder if they are spying on me. And I have to be realistic, Dahl and whoever he has around seem to have a good idea of my movements and probably my motivation, which means they know a lot more than I do and are scared that if I am left to my own devices that I will find out whatever secrets they have. Not knowing is exhausting.

Most of the people around me are young university kids, occasionally older. All black, locals as far as I can tell. Terry and I stand out like virgins at a Satanist's ball. We must be the easiest targets for supervision ever.

Whilst I am not afraid to rock anyone's boat I do feel like a kid poking a snake with a stick thinking I can tame it. It's going to bite me quite a few times before I get to learn what I need to know and by that time... who knows. But Henrik clearly has the means to do what he wants.

Every time I think about it or look at another journal or do a newspaper search, I sigh. My energy drops and I'm not sure I'm getting anywhere. Maybe Terry is right and I'm not built for research.

So we have to be more strategic. Make a plan. Actually talk to people.

Information is important but more than that I need hard evidence. Something that I can use to turn the guns back on them.

I send an email to Aashir because that's a good place to start. But it might be a while before he replies. I decide to give up on the library and go get some coffee outside.

'Coming?' I ask Terry, 'or is Angry Birds keeping you too busy?'

'Ha-ha,' he replies.

We walk along the road, keeping with Terry's pace. Someone comes right up close to me.  I turn and jump a little.  It's Jamila'

'Keep walking,' she says, 'I don't want to be seen talking to you.'

'Who's this?' Terry says stopping.

'Terry, I'll tell you in a moment.'

Jamila is walking swiftly and I speed up to catch up with her. Behind me, Terry is lagging and I decide it's more important to keep up with Jamila.

'Thought you tore up my number.' I say to her.

'I have to, told you the rules.' She says. We cross the road and walk past the coffee shop, 'you took your time in there, been waiting outside for ages.'

She drags me into an alleyway.

'Why didn't you come in?'

'Because I don't want to be seen with you. People will be watching you.'

'So how did you find me?' I ask.

'Same way you found me.' She's smiles like she's looking at a five year old who's just discovered how to count to ten. 'Anyway, I need to be quick. Someone came to our place. Asking questions. I told you, we don't want attention and you need to keep these people away from us. It's dangerous, it's literally life or death for those girls that no-one finds them. You got it?'

'Yes, of course,' I say. I am looking up and down the alley as she speaks. If I wasn't nervous before, I am now. 'But I need something to go on. If I can going to steer them away from you, there must be someone who can help me.'

She shoves a piece of paper in my hand.

'This place,' she says, 'go there. But don't go in. Watch it from outside, you can decide what to do after that.

'But what is it the place?'

'You're a clever girl, you'll work it out.'

She then walks away. I see Terry at the top of the alley waiting for me. Jamila rushes past him and I guess by the time I get to the street entrance, she will have gone.

'Jesus,' Terry says. He has sweat all over him. The rushing around obviously hasn't done him any good. 'She was a bit swift. You ok girl?'

'Yeah, I'm fine. But we got somewhere to go now. Lets' go get that coffee and dig out the map.'

# CHAPTER 19

$$\infty \; \S \; \infty$$

I fear coming to this part of town. Kibera.

It's renowned slum area. The scale of the place only becomes apparent once you are in it. Streets, alley ways and homes hidden behind others. The towers of the city are still visible in the distance but they may as well be on the moon for these people. This is their reality and the extent of their ambition. The smell of animals, sewage, discarded food, oil and every other smell imaginable invade my nostrils and I know I will reek of it for days afterwards. The memory of these places lives long in the mind.

The iron roofs give rudimentary shelter, there is water running in various places and even power in some parts. There are schools and community councils running in the settlement provided by tribal and cultural groups hence there is a social order to things. But it is also close knit with a mistrust of anyone in authority, especially foreigners. Other than targets for stealing or carjacking, foreigners are portrayed as the historic cause of the problems for these people though the truth is far more complicated. There have been a numerous local disputes, lack of cooperation and tribal conflicts. Colonialists didn't help but it is not always easy to work out equitable social solutions for these groups when each see themselves as more important than the others.

I don't fear the place as I've been going into townships and settlements like this for years but I'm more wary than usual. Terry is watchful yet he must have seen the same kinds of places in Kabul.

'Just be glad it's the middle of the day,' he says.

We stop at the entrance to the district. A dirt track off the road. I park at the side and pay some kids to mind the car. There's no guarantee it will still be here when I come back but if we are in the car we will attract too much attention. I've given Terry a scarf to wear to cover his face, partly to make us less obvious but stops breathing in the smell to a certain extent.

Even so as we enter the first street every face watches us. The kids run around. Chickens, cats and dogs nose around unconcerned with our presence. I feel so self-conscious. Women are washing clothes in bowls, cleaning or cooking. The men are in groups chewing khat and smoking cigarettes. Khat is horrible stuff. Chewing the stems and the leaves acts as some kind of stimulant and so it goes, also causes mental issues in the population. Probably like cannabis and other drugs. It doesn't do any good.

I hear a metallic clang behind me and turn quickly. It's just a bowl being dropped by a kid. Why am I so nervous? Because, like Jamila says, we are easily found.

I check Jamila's instructions. Two more streets.

I'm still not sure what I expect to find or how I'll be able to observe what's going on and still stay a safe distance. But she says it will be obvious, so obvious it must be.

'Don't like this,' Terry says.

He's been pretty quiet and I wonder if it was right to bring him. He's not agile and if we have to run, he just can't. But I feel better with him here and he insisted on coming anyway.

'It will be ok,' I say, for the sake of saying it, not because I feel it.

I am distracted by a group of kittens in the corner. The mother watches me with a 'don't come any closer' look. Yeah I know how she feels.

A kid runs in front of us and I get my mind back to what we are looking for.

We come to a cross roads and an open space. Multiple streets veer off from this point. Across the way I see a minibus and a few young girls are stepping inside. They are made up, short skirts and strappy tops. They appear from a larger slum building which I assume must be where they stay.

I nudge Terry and point him to what I am looking at.

'Prossies,' he says.

'Yep.' I say. 'Jamila, was right. It's obvious what this place is.'

'Where they going to then?'

'Your guess is as good as mine.'

I hear a bell and shouting behind us in Swahili. I realise we are standing blocking the way so step to the side. A few kids run past, the bell is metal buckets being banged together. Must be going to the water tap.

'How do we find out where they are going? Who's managing them? Should we go inside?'

'I don't think we should do that,' I say, 'there is likely to be man around, handling them. Some kind of pimp. He will be armed or have dogs. These girls are assets whether he owns them or someone else does. We won't be welcome and the girls won't talk.'

'Then all we got is load of whores. There's the same down the high street back home. It doesn't mean anything.'

'Don't call them whores Terry. These girls didn't apply for a job here.'

'What else do I call them? Pearl. What's the right word? I'm not saying they are bad people, but Prossies, whores? It's the only word I know.'

'Let's just call them girls for now.' I say, 'that's more than enough to describe them. But remember they are victims not ladies of the night or sex workers or whores as you said it.'

'Yeah I get it. Still doesn't answer my question.'

'They must leave the estate, the same way we came in right?' I'm thinking out loud.

'If you say so?'

'Then we follow them. There might be another lot coming later. If we wait we can find out where they are going?'

'That's a bit risky,' Terry says, 'what if we get seen? Can you not just get one of the girls on their own, talk to them?'

'Round here,' I wonder, 'maybe. Maybe if we come back. But I will have to wait and see if I can get one of them alone. Could take some time.'

'Ok, we can go get the car. We'll feel safer in there anyway. But we got to be careful even in the car, Pearl. Once it gets dark and they see us in that 4by4, we could get turned over so easy.'

He's right, but I haven't got a better plan at the moment. This feels a world away from Nigel Davies and Studenham Hall. But the distance between the two is getting shorter by the minute. I see you Nigel Davies and your type.

***

We wait an hour.

It's getting late in the afternoon and I know Terry doesn't want to be out past dark. My nice big Toyota is a prime target for a gang and it would be an easy take. Apart from the unrestrained violence of some of the gangs, there is no way to predict whether they will leave us alone and just take the car. I shiver to think of what else they might do.

I've talked myself out of such situations before. Not a hijack but more confrontations. Villages and ruling houses are dominated by male groups. Education and reason are not features of their decision making. It's more about protecting their positions and ensuring they can keep control over what's happening. I learnt a few words of Swahili and other dialects on advice. Also it's easy to pick up words and phrases when working in local groups. It's not about being fluent but understanding what is being said or being able to be understood.

Just before all this started I had to manage a group of men in Dar Es Salaam. They were pissed off that I was suggesting their meeting house be moved from the edge of the river because I was proposing they build a dyke there. They didn't have a problem with the dyke but with their inconvenience. We met three times to discuss it and there was no moving on it. Despite the village houses being constantly under water they had put stilts on the elder's place so they didn't see the urgency. After the last meeting we were surrounded and persuaded to leave. I always end up being at the front of these confrontation. Most of the men, the translators and the glory boys who are the vocation volunteers stay back as if it's not their business to decide on what's right and wrong. If we know in advance there's going to be trouble we will bring some security but that's expensive so we only use it by exception.

The young men surrounded four of us and there was some pushing. I needed to find an in. The key is making them believe you are giving them something they want or an idea to improve their glorification within the village.

'New Palace,' I shouted in Swahili, pointing to a high spot on the hill at the other side of the village. Why they hadn't put it there in the first place and moved more of the village to the hillier side, seemed mad to me, but the pier for the fish was here as well as the main traders and they liked to be close to what's going on.

I picked the biggest member of the group and whisper in his ear. Pointing once more. I also added the key bit of information in that we will promise to build it for him. He nodded, then pushed me out of the way like discarded rubbish and walked to the hill, the rest of the men following behind as well as much of the village. He stood upon a small hill, with a panoramic view of the area and declared this as the new palace. We were allowed to get on with preparing the dyke and the strong flood gates restricting the river foreshore for when it breaches again.

Not all problems are solved so easily but the technique is useful. I'm not sure the same applies to aggressive gangs.

A minibus appears.

'Go,' Terry says as it pulls onto the main road. I pull out from the layby and follow the minibus back in to the city. The sun is setting behind us. I can see the glow over the horizon in the rear view mirror.

Terry is watching behind but in the busy traffic and poor light it's impossible to pick out if we are being followed. We reach a major intersection and follow the bus off to the left. It's heading north past the greenbelt areas. It's the opposite part of town to where we are staying and I don't know it at all. Cars easily pass between us and the bus as traffic comes and goes but we are able to follow without much issue.

Another junction and the cars between us go the same way. I start to wonder. They are two saloon cars and I can't see the badges. Difficult to see how many people are in the cars.

Could be coincidence. Next junction the minibus goes right, so do the cars and so do we.

'I think we should turn back,' Terry says.

'Hmmm,' I say. I'm not sure but I am worried.

'We can try again tomorrow Pearl, we don't have to solve this now. If we get stuck out here with them gangs we're toast.'

'Yeah ok,' I hear the panic in his voice. Don't want to say anything about him being the military man and supposed to be the cooler of us, but I guess if he is nervous, I should be.

I pull onto the side of the road and wait for the vehicles ahead to disappear into the distance. When a gap in the traffic allows I do a U-Turn and start to head back to the main road.

Terry relaxes and lets go of the arm rest.

'It's the right thing,' he says. 'These folk know the streets better than we do and we have no idea where we are going or where we'll end up.'

'Yeah, agreed,' I say. I don't agree but I am happy to retreat for the day. Been a big day already.

As we reach the main freeway, two cars pull in front of us.

'Fuck,' Terry says. 'That's them same cars. They've come back for us.'

'How do you know?' I ask, 'they look like any two cars. All the same to me.'

'Because you see that sticker on the back. It's the name Alamo Park. It's white on the dark car. I can see it again. I made a note of it, just the name stuck in me head. When you get close up you can see it.'

I don't try to get close up. I trust him.

'What do we do now?' I say.

'It's a case of if they know where we are going or not? But if there are cars in front, there is probably some behind who can follow us.'

I look in the mirror. There are headlights but who is to say what they are.

'Can we lose them?'

'Don't drive home would be my first instinct. Maybe if we drive into the city, it'll be easier to lose them.'

I regret renting a big car now, easy to spot.

I pull out into the fast lane and overtake the cars in front. I try to keep a good pace so at least they will struggle to get in front again.

'If I do something unpredictable,' I say, 'they might not be able to follow.'

As we approach the next junction, I veer off at the last minute. A few horns sound but I manage to navigate the off ramp just in time.

As I take the next turning, there are cars behind us but I have no idea if they followed us or not.

I see a petrol garage and well lit up store. I decide to pull in and wait a moment. I pull the car around and watch the street.

There are no obvious cars waiting or looking for us. I wonder if the moment has passed or not.

'What was that about then?' I ask.

'A warning I 'think.'

We look at each other. I don't have anything to say.

I wait a five minutes watching for any movement and then decide it's time to drive off. If I was ever in doubt we were being watched, that doubt has gone.

***

Thirty minutes later and we are back to the house. I check the gate is locked as Terry makes his way inside.

I hear a shout from the house as he opens the door.

I run over to see him looking down. I reach down to pick up the brick attached to a piece of stone. I am careful to mind the broken glass around it. Inspecting the door frame it seems they threw the stone from fairly close by.

Opening the piece of paper, I see it's a print out of the newspaper article I already had with Dad named as the indicted criminal. I show it Terry.

Neither of us say anything. I clear up the glass whilst he is in the kitchen with a rapidly retrieved beer.

'I poured you a rum,' he says. I guess there is little more to say. We know we are vulnerable and people know where we are. But neither of us are sure what else to do.

'Thanks.' I take a sip and pick up my phone.

WhatsApp messages.

First is predictable.

'Sis, I can't hold back the tide any longer. Go home and pay them. It's getting dangerous for all of us.'

I flick on and a few messages from friends. Usual stuff.

At the bottom is a message from Ruby.

'The bailiffs have been back. Call me!'

I move to the other room and call her.

She answers in one ring.

'They came to me this time?' she says. Without pausing to take a breath she keeps going. 'They scared me. Fortunately Jake was home and he managed to get rid of them. But it's like what they said to you. They are looking for money. They reckon Dad has defrauded all this money but there is nothing in his accounts. I checked with Rebecca. I'm scared they'll take the house Pearl.'

'Don't worry Ruby,' I say, 'they are bluffing.'

'How can you say that Pearl?' Her voice is raised so I hold her a little way from my ears. I don't need the screeching. 'You know something don't you. Dad always favoured you. Has he given you something, told you? You know something. I swear if I lose this house, Pearl, I will come for you to pay the bills.'

I let her rant a little more before I speak.

'I've found out a few things here,' I say, 'look I don't know the facts but somehow Dad was mixed up in a financial scandal here in Kenya.'

'But why now. Why are they coming after us now, they could have done this anytime. And where is the money anyway.'

I daren't tell her that I know exactly where the money is or she will insist I pay them off and we all go back to our quiet lives. But I'm not going to do that.

'I think Dad knew something that kept Davies from pursuing him. But I don't know what it is. Now he's gone, they probably feel they can get away with it.'

'But how can we give them money, we don't have. This is horrible.'

'I know, I know.' There is not much I can say. I finish the call reassuring her that I will make sure she doesn't lose her home, whatever happens. She doesn't believe me but hangs up anyway. It's not hard to imagine that Ruby will be stressing for days to come expecting the bailiffs to come back. It hardens my resolve to sort this.

Checking further down the phone there is an email response from Aashir Kaul?

He's given me a number to call, saying he is happy to see me as soon as possible. Is this another step closer? I hope so as I'm beginning to wonder if we are even safe in this house any more.

# CHAPTER 20

## ∞ § ∞

After yesterday's sweating, we eat breakfast this morning inside under the air-conditioning fan.

I've made a decision.

'I think you should go home.' I say to Terry.

'No way, Pearl. You can't just dump me.'

'It's not safe Terry and I can't protect you. It's my family and my battle to fight.'

'No way.'

'Your flight home is tomorrow. I think you should take it.'

'You want rid of me?'

He stares at me. He  knows I don't want rid of him but wants me to say it so I feel like the hard faced bitch I am and he can feel better about himself.'

'No, actually I don't.' I reply, surprising myself. It would have easy to send him off with a row and admonishment but he doesn't deserve that. For all his problems having him here has helped.

'I am used to being on my own,' I say, 'I hate looking out for other people. You already know I can be a bitch.'

'Yeah you can,' he says, too easily. 'But I'm still not going even if I have to pay for my own hotel and plane. And beer,' he adds.

I laugh at his joke.

'I'm sorry, I hate this. If anything happened to you, I would feel guilty forever. I brought you into this and it's just not fair to ask you to stay. What if one of them shoots you?'

'And what if one of them shoots you?' The smile has gone now. 'What would I feel like if I left you here and you got shot or they killed you? Fuck girl, it's not all about you, you know. Besides I've been in the army and yes it was scary but I know how it feels for a gun to be pointed at you, but I also know how to react and keep calm.'

'You were the one panicking last night?' I say. The words feel curt and I'm not sure why I'm attacking him. Is that just me?

'I was worried for good reason. We were taking chances for no good outcome. We know where those prossies… sorry girls were going. They were going to service some rich folk but that's nothing. It's the oldest profession in the world and proving that rich men like to pay for a shag gets us nowhere. You were being reckless and you know it. Go see that guy today. I will wait here and watch the house. He will give you far more information than them girls. Leave them alone. Can you imagine what would happen if you spoke to one of them and they saw you. That girl would be dead in a ditch and it would be your fault. You are putting them at risk with your snooping.'

'You thought about this haven't you?'

'What do you think?'

I shrug, not much point in replying. He is right though and I should have worked out the same. I walk to the French doors, staring out over the colourful plants and trees in the garden. As if they were going to give me some inspiration.

I turn back to him.

'Ok,' I say, 'you're right. Stay here today and keep an eye on things. Don't get pissed as it's no good if you are passed out and the baddies come by.'

'Give me a break,' he says, shaking his head. 'One day, I'm seriously going to tell you to fuck right off.'

'Pleased that I can still wind you up.' I laugh.

'If your brother comes anywhere near this place I'm going to slap his drug filled face so hard. He is a fucking stooge, a fool. An embarrassment of a man and he needs a good kicking. And what about the government guy? You can't trust any of them politicians. They lie for a living, just remember that. You are too soft, believe any old shit if it sounds good.'

I know he means it. But information is information and I need a lot more than I have.

***

I take a taxi as parking might be difficult

The address is an anonymous office block, not too old. As long as the air con works then I will be happy as it's another baking day outside.

I'm wearing the same trousers and blouse I wore for the funeral, at least smarter than my usual hippy pants and t-shirt. Feel I need to be at least presentable in one of these places.

After a few minutes of ID checks and passport being copied I am shown up to the top floor and the rather dull office of the Health Secretary. A large olive coloured display is above the door, a distinct coat of arms of two green lions. Feels very colonial still. Better something to contrast the brown décor which gives the impression that nothing exciting ever happens here.

I wait dutifully in the reception area. Briefly glancing at the view, I can see the safari park from two days ago. Feels already another lifetime. My life has accelerated so quickly, I've aged ten years in two weeks.

The lady behind the desk informs me I can go in.

Aashir Kaul is a in a light suit. Smart and bespectacled. Not unlike his picture on LinkedIn. But then I'm not sure why this is a surprise.

The office is full of photographs of the minister out in villages and communities. I can see instantly that he sees his job in those terms. I guess if I'd seem him photographed with politicians or business men that would have presented a view of a very different person. I'm quietly pleased with his choice.

'Please Miss McCann, sit down.'

'Thank you for seeing me.' I say, taking the seat offered

'I will be frank,' he says, 'I only agreed to see you because you mentioned your father and I have to admit to looking you up. I guess you would expect me to. Your vocation does you credit and as minister of health I am grateful for the work you have done in our communities and I'm sure the ministers in our neighbouring countries would share the same sentiments.'

'Thank you,' I say, genuinely humbled. It's not often that I get any credit or thanks especially from politicians. Often we rather diminish their efforts and they don't appreciate it.

'Tell me again, how I can help?'

I explain about finding the articles on Dad's trial and his subsequent exile from Kenya. And mention that I have heard that he has been involved with the anti-tobacco corruption campaign for some time and might know more about it.'

'Hmmm,' he says. 'It's true, I have long been a campaigner against the tobacco firms. Though let me start by saying I knew your father and thought him a good man. Don't see this as a single thing. As you will know from your work, most people see these things as black and white. Tobacco farming and the whole industry provides significant revenue for the country much as coffee, minerals, farming does. We could go on. None of these industries come with a clean health certificate. We need them as much as they need us.'

'But I have always insisted, they must pay a price. They are not free to turn our wonderful country into a cash cow for their shareholders. They are not free to exploit our people for their profit and they are not free to commit crimes at will and then get away with them because they have better lawyers.'

The passion from the man is obvious and I could hug him. I won't but listening to leaders such as him speak makes such a difference. I have heard many an African leader use similar powerful words, Mugabe being the best example of an impassioned speaker. But you could see his lies fall out of his mouth just as everyone could see the contempt he had for the people who put him in power. Aashir Kaul speaks far less eloquently but I believe him far more.

'But you are a man alone with the fight, or there are not many of you?'

'Oh no, there are many of us in this government who will fight with our last breath for what is right. Don't underestimate that.'

Now I know he is being political. This government will be as full of charlatans and dodgy movers as every other. But I let it pass.

'But it is not easy. The lobbies are full of persuasive men with their promise of ethics and charity. Always good intentions. And often we have to take them at their word. Of course they break their word and we are back to the courts and penalties and even criminal acts. We threaten and convict but before long we are back to the same place. Promises of good intentions and investment and the circle is closed.'

The passiveness of his voice tells me his weariness of the fight.

'Only a few weeks ago, the northern state regional government were prosecuting a case over illegal crop spraying damaging a whole water system poisoning villages and killing some pregnant mothers and infant children. In the dock were officials from the local company claiming that the products were labelled incorrectly and they were given assurances by the chemicals giant selling them that they were safe to use. When the judge ordered the chemical company to be indicted as suspects under investigation, he suddenly fell ill. He had a heart attack according to official reports. Classic natural causes lie when in fact he was stabbed in broad daylight in his own office. I know this and so do many in the government but it took weeks of asking questions before anyone in the regional office would admit to it. By that time the trial had gone ahead with a new judge and the local officials were convicted. The company paid a fine whilst the local officials were imprisoned or probably, if they were expats they were expelled from Kenya. You see the problem is not just wanting to fight but that often the weapons by which justice is upheld are vulnerable to such acts. We have been left with a situation to prove that local officials turned a blind eye to a murder presumably for money and that the replacement judge was suitably well disposed to the management to turn over the dead judge's rulings. It is quite exhausting but we never give up.'

I am surprised but then not surprised. I wonder why it is still happening in 2019.' And just as Aashir says, despite the best efforts of good people, they do not have all the power they seek.

The clock has moved on and I realise my allotted time is running out. Best get back to why I'm here.

'And you say you knew my father?'

'I did,' he says, quietly. 'I'm afraid your father was a casualty of such an arrangement, fortunately no-one was murdered but it was a case I think of him falling victim to lack of executive oversight or let's say sharp practice. He was rather hung out to dry by his colleagues but in this case he didn't help his own cause as he used the lack of oversight for his apparent own purposes. The accounts were audited and we discovered one of the charities they were claiming tax relief for simply didn't exist. He was taking money from the company and laundering it out of the country. We investigated and for once it was a relatively easy conclusion. The hardest battles are the class action smoking cases where we take years proving the links to cancer. Or even such as the negligence case with the crop spraying. Even with the use of proxy local companies for corruption it is messy and takes a degree of whistle-blower exposure to succeed. Here was rather an open goal.'

My feet and hands are like lead. I am frozen in my chair listening to him explain how my father undertook such a crime. A crime that was easily provable. But only in an environment perhaps as Aashir said, that in normal circumstances where corporate oversight is slack, this crime is easy to get away with it. But if he had a falling out with someone or some part of the chain of command and they chose to expose his scheme then it would all have fallen into place. What a messy outcome.

'Did you speak to him about it?' I ask.

'Yes I did actually when the initial investigation started. I was a negotiator in those days in the Trade Department and had been dealing with him in setting up funding deals for a number of other charity projects. As I said before. I know the value of their money and I've been a civil servant here for a long time before I was in government. We were always plugging schemes to these executives and they saw it as good for business.'

'Ok.' Nothing new to learn there.

'But your father was astute and I suspect there was far more to his scheme than he let on to me.'

'Go on,' I say.

'This is a little delicate, given your profession, but I trust you came here with good intentions and I am sharing this on the basis you wish to find good in what your father did. Look, corruption does not end with the people flashing the money as such. Do you understand that?'

I nod, feels like a rather obvious point.

'Those who receive the money often take it eagerly. Of course that is the case. But it's not just the back office, brown paper bag corruption I'm referring too. Do you get what I mean?'

'Not sure I do.'

'If you are a charity and you're getting major exposure and donations from a significant source. If that is keeping you in business to do all of the virtuous things you are doing then surely you will be happy not to fight back too much.'

'So you're saying that the charities are complicit?'

'Yes, I am. I not saying it is overt and obvious. The game is played more subtly than that. But by consequence, this is what can happen.'

I pause for a moment, taking in what he is saying. Relating it to my own experience. My own naivety.

'But these days there are so many ethics boards, it wouldn't happen.'

'Yes, of course. Twenty, thirty years ago it was a far darker world. And remember it was a long time ago when your father was convicted. These days, a health or community charity would never touch a donation made directly from a tobacco company. But there are other mechanisms even now where it happens. More under the radar, I suppose.'

'I'm still struggling with complicit element of charities doing this. Unless coercion is involved. Blackmail perhaps?'

He pauses for a moment.

'It certainly is a factor but it is mostly much more simple corruption. How much do you understand money laundering? I feel this will help you imagine how the process works.'

'I understand that it is a way of taking cash generated from crime and turning it into legitimate money in a bank,' I reply.

'It is exactly that. And tobacco suffers from two major issues with this kind of crime. Firstly it generates a large amount of cash from sales which means that it is a ripe environment for laundering money. But also it makes it harder because it means that even more cash than normal has to be managed once it is in the hands of the company.'

'I see.' I get what he is saying but hard to see the point.

'Crime and tobacco quite often go together. In manufacturing, it's very easy to overestimate crops to hide cash. For example if I make one million cigarettes, I can report that I actually made two million which helps me to increase the amount going into sales circulation and means that any cash received from sales can be cleansed easily. So cash from other illegal activity, drugs, theft, fraud and prostitution can all be put through the company and paid back through banks to wealthy recipients.'

'So you can see how massive amounts of cash can be generated. Now comes the mechanism for giving it back. First they have to give it all back to those criminal networks that put the cash in. Plus the tobacco company needs its cut of the profits. No-one sets up this complex an operation for fun. Finally, large profits equal large tax and that also needs to be avoided. Hence there are numerous investments programs run by affiliate companies. Taxi businesses, schools being built, property investments, banking even. Imagine if the company washing money buys an apartment block then charges an excessive rent which is compensated through the payroll, then money is successfully cleansed. But the final scam is charity funding. Firstly it avoids taxes and secondly a friendly charity can easily move the money into its wider accounting framework and even out of the country.

'Friendly charity?'

'We all enjoy the nice things in life, Miss McCann, even executives in charities. You will know of many such corruption scandals at all levels of charities. Exploitation just like in businesses. Many are just as vulnerable to cash as much as the next man. Twenty/Thirty years of hard graft might ease your conscience but it doesn't provide a comfortable retirement. Cash can be king.'

I nod. I can't deny any of this.

'And my father.'

'He understood this as I suspect he was quite an expert in the above arrangements. No-one gets to be a senior finance director in a company like ITA without knowing this and many other scams. I do however believe he wanted to use the money under this fake charity name for his own purpose. Something he could do outside the radar of scrutiny from those on the take. I might be naïve but I felt he had good intentions.'

'But he got caught?'

'He did and if he'd stayed in Kenya, he would have been convicted. Of course he left before the trial so he was rather convicted in his absence but he was convicted just the same.'

I sigh deeply. No arguing with the facts. Mother must have been horrified with the ordeal. She would have been ashamed of what was happening. Her name being brought through the mud because of Dad's dodgy dealings. But he must have a reason, I am stuck with that question in my mind.

'What was the name of the fake charity?' I ask.

'It was set up as an Orphans charity. I don't recall the name exactly. When I say it didn't exist. It did. But the names of the trustees were not real. There was an address, official documentation and a bank account. But all it did was take money and move it out. There was no-one running it. It was a front for money to be laundered. Let me get the case details.'

He rattles around in his cabinet for a moment and then moves to his laptop.

'Here it is,' he says. 'I thought for a moment I had the case file still but it's probably gone to an archive.

He turns the screen around and shows me the charity details.

The Angels. A charity for abandoned children.

The details look official and I scan the screen for something that means something. The name sticks in my mind as well. Reminds me of... It was so dad to be religious or Christian in approach.

Then I get to the bottom of the screen. Executive officer: Beatrice Lovane.

I am stunned. Frozen. How the hell? Should I ask? Should I say something?

'Beatrice Lovane?' I ask, 'she is listed as being the executive officer? Did you find her or was she important to the case?'

'I told you,' he says, 'she didn't exist. We looked into her. There is no Beatrice Lovane. It was a fake name. No-one in Kenya with that name or at least anything to do with this charity.'

The more I learn about what this is all about the less I seem to understand. But the next memory hits me. The Angels. The painting of the whisky barrel back in his bedroom. The Angels' Share. This was Dad all over and only he would have known the significance of the name. Like a teaser. He was farming off the profits from the company to give to the Angels. Wow. I shake my head in both respect and horror. Unbelievable.

He was still laundering money but there is some hope hidden in his motives. I will cling onto that.

# CHAPTER 21

∞ § ∞

The taxi winds its way through the city. I am lost in a whirlwind of thoughts. Apart from The Angel's share which will stay with me forever, I'm still trying to decide whether Bea mugged me or she's some kind of hero. She's obviously been connected with Dad for years and Beatrice Lovane is also not her real name. There is a reason she didn't show up in any searches. But then I hardly checked her passport when I met her.

But she didn't rob me and she didn't exactly lie to me, just left out a whole load of shit and let me go through a degree of pain to find it out. Am I being put through some kind of test? One day there will be a big reveal and the whole family will appear and shout surprise.

I don't think, I've been played, but I am being left to flounder.

The car pulls into my street and I immediately see something is wrong. The gate is open. Terry wouldn't have left it open.

I pay the taxi and rush inside.

The car is on the drive but the tires are slashed and the windows smashed.

The door is not just open it's hanging off its hinges. It's been battered down. Whoever came here meant business.

'Terry,' I shout. 'Terry.'

I walk through every room but he's not there. Then up the stairs, in the bathroom. In every room, I'm expecting to see him lying in a pool of blood. Please be ok, please be ok, I say to myself. The last room is my bedroom and it's empty. I lean against the door and take a breath.

I return down the stairs at least sure he's not here, no-one is here. I wonder if he somehow managed to escape but it's doubtful. He can't run, he would have no chance.

In the back room, I go to my rucksack and my laptop's not there. I guessed even before I got to it. Fortunately I have my money and purse with me as well as my passport.

Apart from trashing the place and smashing the front door there seems to be no other damage. I walk back to the hall and all hope that Terry escaped flitters away. His stick is on the floor and there is no chance he would go anywhere without that.

I should have known they'd come. In fact I did know it. That's why I told Terry to go home. And now what do I do?

Before I get to answer my own question my phone rings. It's the local number that Walt has been using to text me.

'I told you that there would be trouble sis.' He says. He sounds agitated which I assume means he's high.

'Where's Terry?' I ask.

'Seriously sis, I thought you could do better than this cripple.'

'Don't call him that!' I shout. 'And before you start assuming he's my boyfriend and using that against him, he's not, he's a friend.' I don't know why I'm doing this but I don't want him using relationships to either wind me up or Terry.

I am marching up and down the hall.

'Don't give a shit, to be honest. Anyway, you can have him back tomorrow. He's a bit worse for wear tonight. Henrik will pay you a visit in the morning. You might want to be open to his offer.

'What do you want from me, Walt?' I use his old name to get under his skin. I don't want him to forget who he is.

'Me. I want fuck all. But you are messing with the wrong people Pearl. They want their money back.'

'Let me talk to Terry.'

'He's a bit fucked, to be fair. He's sleeping on the sofa, but he'll be back in the morning. Bit of a bang on the head. But to be honest, you might not want him back. Wouldn't take much to finish him off, maybe another bang on the head. I can sell those prosthetics for good money round here and dump the rest in the swamp. Not hard to dump a body in Kenya as you well know.'

I put the phone down on him. I can't listen to him mocking me anymore. Whatever Walter was or is, he's no longer my brother.

Dealing with him is one thing. What will I do with Henrik tomorrow?

***

I wake up in the chair, still dressed. It's just coming light and I can hear sounds from the road.

I must have fallen asleep watching the door, expecting something at any moment. I closed the gate and barricaded the door but with no idea how long it would last.

There is no point calling the police, not until Terry is back. I can't risk anything else going wrong. So instead I rehearse the moment when Henrik arrives. What I'm going to say to him and how will I get out of it.

Looking out over the garden, it seems so peaceful. The morning light with the spectrum of red promising so much hope and all I feel is despair. They are winning, I know they are because I am only scraping the surface, underestimating how they operate, how hard they have worked to keep their lifestyle and power. And perhaps, they see exposure not just as an end to their lifestyle but with it will come some kind of retribution.

Is that what I want? Retribution? At this time, it's too early to tell. I only know of some of what they have done and if my father was somehow facilitating this, then how I can seek retribution?

I'm clear what my task is. First I refuse to be intimidated. Clearly I worry them or they wouldn't be following me around Nairobi. I need to keep that in mind. Second is not to hand over a penny to them. Yes, they'll keep coming after me, but they can't do anything to me. I thought this through last night. Without me, they don't get the money and it's enough to be important.

One more thing struck me as well. I'm not the only threat to them. The elusive Beatrice. She's disappeared but whoever she is or was, she was on Dad's side. And, I reason with perhaps more hope than logic, that if anything happened to me, she would come out of hibernation. The very fact that her name is on that document is proof that she knows far more about them than she told me.

I make some tea whilst I wait. I rinse my face, forcing myself awake. Though at least I don't have the fog of rum or bourbon dulling my senses, just lack of sleep. I didn't touch a drop last night, needing to stay focussed on what I needed to do.

The gate opens. I'm ready. I wonder how they broke the code for the door but I'm past working out the various security gadgets. That's number 99 on a list of a hundred worries.

I see Terry first. He is standing and trying to walk. Henrik Dahl is behind him, arms folded. He is wearing a blue smart shirt, tucked in white chinos. Sunglasses hide his eyes.

I rush out with Terry's stick, passing the smashed up car and hug him briefly.

'Fucking glad to see you,' he says. 'Don't give him a fucking penny.'

His head is wounded and blood on his good hand. His shirt is torn and his trousers half down.

'You ok?' I ask, handing him his stick.

He grabs it and keeps walking to the house.

'Are you going to invite me in?' Henrik asks.

'What's the point, I know what you want?'

He laughs. Even the sound of his laughter seems visceral. Deliberately nasty. Sharp and aggressive.

'Then why are you still here?'

'Because, whatever it is you do… and I still don't understand, it seems to involve me and my family. It's hard to ignore.'

He walks closer until he's directly in front of me. I move towards to him. We are a foot apart. I refuse to feel meek. Up close I can smell after shave. Abundant, floral, odd. With the sweet smell of the flowers in the garden it's sickly.

'Pay your debts and it will all be over.' He speaks slowly, engineering additional menace.

'Give me my laptop back?' I say, 'can't do anything without it.'

'Get a new one,' he says, 'yours is proving useful.'

I hate to think what they will find on it. I never imagined it being stolen and read. My whole life exposed plus all my contacts and correspondence. But that's not the issue now.

'Twenty four hours,' he says. 'Next time, I will be bring the plastic bits of your friend for a souvenir. The hyenas can have the soft bits.'

'Oh, such a big man.' I say, 'so smart.'

He grabs me by the throat.

'Next it will be your drug addict brother who will have an overdose. I've been wanting to do it for years but occasionally he has his uses, like flushing you out. Then it'll be your sweet sister. I will do a video montage.' He tightens his grip and lifts me. 'And by that time my patience will have run out and you'll have a nasty little accident.'

'Why do you want the money?' I ask. 'Surely you can get it back other ways. Your business must be flooded with cash.'

I get the words out, in between breaths. He lets go and I relax a little. Glad at least I didn't squeak.

He steps back, wanting to leave.

'Your father committed a serious crime and a lot of people were severely hampered by his errors. Those mistakes need to be paid for. Now he is dead, you have to pay.'

'But you are threatening me now. Why didn't you threaten him?'

He is walking away and I seize my moment and follow him to the car.

'Because he had you? Didn't he? You couldn't touch him. No matter what you tried, he never gave you and your friends a penny and that seriously pisses you off.'

He lashes out and catches me full in the face. My lip busts but I manage to stand my ground. He stars and then turns away. Not that I think he has a problem with hitting women but I think if I was a man he may have gone further. I can hearing him cursing in Afrikaans and he returns to the car. He doesn't look back. Once inside, the tyres screech as his driver speeds away.

Shaking, I head back to the house. I go to the mirror in the hall and see the fat lip forming. I grab some toilet paper and then go to see Terry. He's sat slumped in the chair.

'Hey, wake up' I say, shaking him. 'Look, sorry to do this to you but you got to go. Two hours until we need you to be at the airport. So get a shower get changed and get a cab. It's not safe.'

'Fuck off, Pearl,' he says, his voice sluggish. 'I need to sleep.'

'No, Terry,' I say, 'I need to disappear for a while. Whilst you're here I can't. I'll be fine. I know what to do now. Go get a shower and I'll fix your wounds when you come back down.'

He gets up but doesn't speak. I feel like I'm pushing him away but I can't afford the liability anymore.

# CHAPTER 22

$$\infty \, \S \, \infty$$

It's an hour before Terry is back down. He doesn't look good. His face is swollen and his right eye is not fully open. But he has got clean clothes on and looks better than he did.

We sit down at the table and I make some tea.

'It's for the best.' I say

He grumbles and I get the sense the fight has gone out of him.

'What did they do to you Terry?

'Gave me something, I think.' He is barely coherent and I wonder if it's wise to put him on a plane. But if I don't get him out of here now, today, I lose my window to get away. I daren't leave him here alone, he is too easy a target. Even moving him to a hotel will leave him isolated and I won't be able to do anything.

'They hit me. Fucking hard,' he rubs his head, 'tried to smack him one but bastard got out the way. I'll get the little fucker when I see him.'

I fear that chance will pass us by and I am more than happy not to see my brother again. Walt wouldn't dare come to UK of that I am quite sure, fake passport or not. I also don't want to be responsible for an assault conviction for Terry. His bravado for once is understood and welcome. I know he wants to protect me but he can't and he knows it too.

'What you going to do?' he asks.

'Once you are gone, I will clear off for a while. I know where to go. I need to get out from their immediate attention whilst I find the evidence I need. It's the only way to turn this around.'

'How you going to do that? Come back with me. We can sort it out back in home.'

'Not yet, Terry. There is something here they don't want me to find. Once I know what that is then I'll come home.'

He shakes his head and I understand his defeatism. Apart from whatever they slipped him to shut him up last night, having such a debilitating condition, confidence is easily knocked. Perhaps I am shutting him out for my own convenience but I am sure it's best for both of us.

'You can keep an eye on the house and keep those bailiffs away. And help Ruby.'

'She don't like me,' he says.

It's probably true and in the same position I might have been suspicious of Terry. In fact, the first time I met him I wanted to disregard him. But now I know him, I know why he is what he is. And he is learning. I won't change him and don't really want to. And his heart is as big as anyone. His passion for right and wrong is not misplaced, just misunderstood, perhaps, even by himself.

I call a taxi for him and we sit in silence for a few minutes. By the time the car arrives, I am stood waiting.

I hug him, feeling his left arm hold me tight. I think about how once I would have flinched from such contact but now it shows how far we've come together.

'Don't give them a penny,' he says as he heads for the taxi.

'I won't.'

I wave him goodbye, wiping a tear from my eye.

No time to dwell. Things to do.

***

I finish packing my rucksack. I've rung the owner and the hire car company. Spent quite some time apologising and saying I would call the police and then left them a credit card with which I have no doubt they will be swiping repeatedly until they get the necessary compensation.

Usually I would be fighting over every penny but PMC will no doubt have earned more interest in the last day than the value of at least the car and quite possibly the house as well.

I send a text to Ruby and Terry telling them this phone will be out of use in the next few days. Finally I call a taxi before taking the sim out and turning it off.

I stand in the broken doorway to wait. There is a body slumped against the gate. I walk over to investigate and see that it's Walt. He's slumped against the railings, out cold. He's wearing a white shirt and blue shorts, both stained. The shirt with dribble dripping from his open mouth, the shorts from... His cap is pushed to the side. There's no doubt he's dosed up and I suspect Henrik has dumped him here. I think Walt has served whatever purpose he was intended for and no longer has a use.

The taxi pulls up and I wonder what to do with Walt.

It only takes a moment for me to decide. Time to leave him. He made his decision long ago about how important we are to him, so I will return the same intent. I get in the back of the car and ask the driver to take me to mall. I don't look back. Walter can take his chances with his addiction and his conscience without mine troubling me.

# CHAPTER 23

∞ § ∞

By late afternoon. I have a new laptop and a local phone. The next taxi drops me at Muthurwa Market and I walk the familiar street and back round the alley. Once again eyes are on me as I approach the doorway. I wait for the door to open hoping my gamble is going to work.

The door opens and I enter.

In the reception area the same lady, Mary, is waiting at the desk. Today she is wearing bright green.

Before she can speak I start with my prepared speech.

'I need a place to stay,' I say, 'I am being threatened by a man, he's been following me round Nairobi and I don't feel safe. I would like to stay for a few days.

'Why don't you just leave the country?' she says. 'You have money, passport. You can go.'

'That's true,' I say, 'but as you know with some of the women here, these men don't give up and even back home, they will find me.'

'And in a few days. Surely they'll find you.'

Her voice is passive. She doesn't care if I'm in danger or not or that's how it feels. Or maybe she is immune to the stories that women tell each time they come. I hope not. Someone less determined might turn back and think this isn't the place for them.

'You are right. I'll be honest with you,' I say, 'I need to do some research and I'm hoping to prove this man and his colleagues are guilty of some horrendous crimes. Once I do that, I can return directly to the UK.'

'You know none of the women here can help you or we will ask them to leave.'

'I know.'

She looks at me for a few moments and then returns to the back office again. I wait patiently thinking that there is a chance they will ask me to leave but I'm hopeful my plea is a valid. After all it's a refuge.

She comes back after a few minutes.

'You can stay a week.' She says, 'any sign of trouble, upsetting the other girls then you have to leave. Phones?' She holds her hand out.

I give her my old phone without the SIM and also one of the new ones. I keep my new SIM in my purse and another new phone buried at the bottom of my bag.

'No phones allowed. If you need to make a call at some point you can ask for your phone and we will decide if we will allow you to use it. There is a Wi-Fi network here and you can use the internet however there is a built in VPN which distorts the location so that you will show as being in Dubai. This is for obvious reasons so this place remains hidden. You understand?'

I nod.

'Fill out this form and I need your passport.'

'You can't do that?' I say.

'Those are the rules,' she says, 'we need to protect ourselves. What's to stop you stealing from us or exposing us?'

I dig into my bag and pick out one of my two passports. One advantage of my job is that I have permission for a second passport. This is to cover for travelling to sanctioned countries where a stamp might preclude me from entry to others. It does mean if I need to run, I still have the capability to get home. Hopefully it won't come to that.

'One last thing,' she says, the keys dangling in her hands.

I look at her waiting for her to give me a clue and then I realise what she wants.

'A donation perhaps?' I ask.

She smiles back.

I give her some notes. 'If I'm allowed out, I will get some more cash. Is that ok?'

She gives me the keys and a print out of rules and instructions. The key says flat 200.

'You cannot go outside with the key. You must leave it here. There is someone at this desk night and day. Read the instructions, it will tell you more of the rules. You will find the flat well stocked for food for a few days do you should have no need to go out.'

'Do you do room service?' I say, with a smile. I can't resist at least a small joke to lighten the mood.

'Not funny,' she says.

Yeah, not funny. I know. I take the keys from her.  A young girl, in her teens, appears from the office.

'Patricia will show you to your room.'

'Thanks' I say. I grab my bag and follow Patricia down the corridor.

***

It's a flat. An apartment. Bedroom, bathroom, open plan kitchen and living space. It's sparsely furnished like any rental and I have a view through small warehouse style windows. There is no balcony but I guess outside space was not a prerequisite. I can see down to the warehouse below. From the street this place is hardly observable and it's so much of a concrete dinosaur, people probably take no notice of it.

They chose the location well.

I take out a bottle from my bag and search the fridge for some ice. The light is fading and I won't go out again today.

Opening my laptop, I will spend the evening reading and researching. The agenda is pretty much as follows:

International Tobacco Wikipedia and anything related to their operations in Kenya.

Legal cases involving International Tobacco.

Henrik Dahl and his logistics company.

After that, moving onto other organisations with bases here in this country. Oil, gas, diamonds, minerals and mining. Then widen the loop looking for organisations like UNICEF, WHO. They all have officials who are part of the expatriate scene.

And then the big charities.

It's clear from the conversation with Aashir that these groups live and mixed together. Yes, their organisations have very different goals but these communities of middle class whites and non-locals, mainly men, mix in the same circles. There are women and families just like mine but the lead employee, the reason the family is there is largely down to the men.

I've worked with a fair amount of the misogynist types in health organisations. I think about one prime example. Samuel Lopez, Regional head of a kids' charity for East Africa. He was Spanish, loud and talked about nothing other than his ethical work. I'd seen him speak at numerous conferences but he messed up one time getting caught for raping the wrong woman. He got himself hooked up with an undercover journalist, working among the women recording conversations and following up to see who was exploiting them. She found herself on the wrong side of Lopez and he beat her. She got away and next day, she was at the police headquarters with her editor and recording of the whole thing. Lopez didn't stand a chance.

Couldn't happen to a more horrible person. One of those who'd greased his way round every person to get to the top and he was universally hated by anyone who watched him work. Slimy, creepy and a convicted rapist rotting in prison. As a woman the conviction of shits like him gives a universal sense of pleasure and satisfaction that for all the times the arseholes get away with it, there is that one time when we win. Like a football team that hasn't scored all season, they will celebrate one lucky goal like they won the bloody cup.

Thinking about Lopez, gets me back to what this is about. I need a win like that. Dahl or his like. It won't be easy as ultimately, even with all this corruption I bet I don't find a single record of any transaction with Nigel Davies's name on it. The hard graft of doing deals and processing the money will be done by others.

But he likes young black girls and that is his weakness. And people knew it then and know it now. Dad knew it and presumably Dahl does, maybe even Walt knows it too. He murdered or had a girl murdered and dumped in the street. And there will be history. Like Lopez, Davies didn't decide one day he liked these women and got caught out the one time. He will have developed his tastes over time. Who is to say he still doesn't sit down in his mansion, lock his office door and put on videos for old times' sake and bang one out, if he still can at his age?

A video.

Of course. Why have I not even considered this? The 90's camcorder world. I remember we had one. Filmed everything. The opening of an envelope was recorded like a one-time celebration. We had loads of tapes. By the pool, parties. Mum hiding from the camera. But these dirty fuckers must have filmed their little adventures. How to get one over on the boss. Next time you want a pay rise and he refuses, play a little video of him and his favourite toy and cash is duly delivered. Probably not as simple as that but blackmail is not a complicated process. But it works both ways. Davies no doubt knew a lot about the other men's fetishes. It's just as likely some of the men were secretly keeping each other company whilst their wives were home alone. The more I think, the more I realise the potential for corruption is vast and the onset of easy recording capability was a bit like a credit card. Easy money at an affordable price.

I wonder if Dad had a video. Was that what kept Davies at bay? If he did, why didn't he leave it for me to find or give it to Beatrice? I searched the house and didn't find anything? But then I wasn't looking for a video, especially old camcorder stuff. Even then, it might have been converted to digital and put on a hard drive. I always thought dad was a technophobe but Beatrice might not have been. She told me she didn't know anything but she knows far more. Even down to her name being on that fake charity.

Worries for another day.

For now, I have to assume they don't have it. Or if they do, it's hidden or no-one wants to give it to me. So if I want some evidence then I will have to find my own. Or create my own. I can't imagine there aren't more of these videos around. There is a good possibility that at least one of these men went rogue when someone didn't pay their blackmail fee. Or that some of the women, like with Lopez, have got their own recordings.

This is crazy, I feel like I'm sat outside the sweet store and I have a bunch of keys but none of them fit the damn door.

I take more of the bourbon and start the searches. If I can tick a few boxes then I might have some stuff I can use. But actually, and this comes to really why I came back to the refuge. Despite my protestations at the door, I have every intention of mixing with the women here and asking discrete questions. Jamila, was a mine of useful information and if I can get her alone she will have more to say.

Research first. Find some names and faces. Do my homework. The information is out there, I just need it hard and incontrovertible. Once I have that, Davies can be put back in place. But then what do I do? I feel I am still on the first mile of a thousand mile journey.

# CHAPTER 24

∞ § ∞

Morning comes after a quiet night's sleep and at least a feeling of safety.

I pour some juice and sit at the table and take out the new phone and SIM. I send a text to Terry asking if he is home.

A beep follows soon after.

Knackered, sleeping. Where are you?

I text back, tell him I'm safe and to go back to sleep.

One worry less. Next is Ruby.

Two mins of chat and I tell her I have to go. She is also ok, no news. Still paranoid but nothing odd or out of the ordinary has occurred. Except this is all out of ordinary... It's bonkers.

I've still got $50million dollars sat in a bank account I seriously don't know what to do with the money. Apart from spending it on bouncing round the world chasing these corrupt fuckers, I have nothing to spend it on. I could give it away and probably will in the end but that's an exercise in priorities and choices I've not even thought about.

Then even more bonkers I'm hiding in a secret refuge in the middle of Nairobi, dodging ... dodging who? People I don't know. Even my brother. I'm at a firing squad and either I'm blindfolded or those shooting me are, so they don't see each other or me. I don't know, I'm confusing myself now.

Last night, I wrote down more names. People who turned up in different places. Some were connected to ITA, some with other

225

organisations but they were sponsors or names at corporate events or charity affairs. Whether they were the guilty ones or not, isn't clear. Maybe if I email the list to Aashir, he can tell me. I wonder if he will see me again. He did tell me he was happy to help and I suppose if I landed a few metaphorical punches on some of these names, he wouldn't be disappointed.

There's a knock.

I go to the door, tentatively. Someone knows I'm here. That didn't take long.

'Jamila,' I say as I open the door.

She doesn't wait for invite and walks directly past me.

'I see you found I was here then.'

'There are no secrets in this place,' she says. She's goes to the fridge and takes one of my beers. It's not even ten. I would have offered but even I don't at this time. It's like having Terry back.

'Why did you come back?' She asks. 'You are putting me in danger. All of us.'

This pisses me off. She's been playing the victim all along but she also gave me the information on the place in Kibera. She dangled a carrot for me to go after so she wanted me to find it and put me at risk to the subsequent consequences.

'Don't get smart with me.' I say, 'you knew I would go to Kibera and you knew I might get seen and that would get some questions asked, if not some unwelcome attention. If you can come here to hide, then why the hell shouldn't I?'

She takes a big glug of beer and walks to the window. She's obviously anxious. But why?

'Do you always drink so much?' I ask. 'Bit early for it.'

'I do what I want,' she shouts. Her pitch loud, more like a squeal.

'Ok no judgement,' I reply. Hands raised, waving my innocent flag.

'We don't want trouble here. I told you.' She walks and talks. 'It's peaceful here. Safe. Yes there is gossip and arguments between us but it's the safest place I've ever been in my life and I don't want to lose it. The other's too. You are trouble. You can go back to England, go back to your family or your charity. You can do that. We can't.'

'Ok,' I nod. I scratch my head and take stock. I'm unsure whether to go for a full scale rant or restrain myself. I go for the latter. Patience. I do not like being called out for my bit of privilege. I know very well that I pick and choose my life and it's on fairly safe terms but I also do not wear my background like a badge of honour nor do I use my get out of jail for free card often. I stay and fight for the people I work with.

But I don't want to justify myself here. Arrogance is like skin, we all have it and there are many different shades. She's wears the victim shade, with a chip on her shoulder as large as a king Edward potato. I've got my own arrogance and will decide when I will use it. But here and now, she's the tetchy prick and I need to rise above it.

I decide on a question to deflect the anger.

'Why did you send me to Kibera? You could have just left me not knowing anything but you let me go there, see what was going on. I could have been seen or something else happen. But ultimately you wanted me to see it and use it. Why do that if you want me to go home?'

'I want you to do something, Pearl. I want these people caught. It is one place, but there are others. Everywhere this is happening and I thought if I gave you information on one of these gangs you might find them. I don't know, I want to help alright but I can't do it myself.'

Then this is the nub of the issue. I get it. I calm down.

'Sit down,' I say. 'Let's talk.'

She does, wiping her eyes at the same time.

'I'm stuck Jamila. I couldn't go into that house where the women were as I knew I would put them at risk. Coming here, I also know I'm putting you at risk but this place at least is well guarded. But ultimately, I can't do anything about these men until someone gives me the means to do it. Someone who can speak in public, on record.'

'I am not the one.' She says, 'don't think about asking.'

'I'm not, I'm not.' I say. Defensive again. 'But someone's got to. Otherwise, what happens?'

'Nothing,' she says, her breath barely audible.

'Are there other victims here?' I ask.

'A few, yes. But they will say the same.' Jamila says. 'They are all scared. Plus this place, it takes the fight out of them. Once they are safe, they lose the anger.'

'But you haven't.'

She smiles. For the first time I see inside her heart. In one moment, she's revealed herself to me.

And then she begins to talk.

***

'I wasn't a virgin before I was brought to the capital.'

She pauses before speaking again. I've set myself not to comment or question and let her tell her story in her own time.

'There were six of us in the family, my mum was even pregnant again by the time I was being farmed out.' My father worked on the tobacco plantations to the north from here. The village was built for the purpose of servicing the farm and the fields. I had two brothers. One older, one younger. They were working in the fields as well. Only the youngest was sick continuously and was a poor worker. My older brother was stronger and they rewarded him with a gun and a job in security which meant beating the others. His initiation was to beat the younger one. These were the rules. Show how tough you are, let the weak die.'

'I was the compensation for my younger brother's weakness. We had too many girls and not enough men and boys working. I wanted to be in school but instead my mother dressed me up nice and sent me to the militia leader's tent. I was naive at the time. I didn't know what it was about. I was to ask if there was any work I could do for them. Cooking, cleaning. That's when it started. I was fourteen, well developed as I said before, but I was young and fresh and there on a plate for them.'

She is crying as she talks. The fan in the ceiling rattles as it spins, a weird contrast to the silent tension and the occasional sniffles.

'I was so scared. Before I went there I knew the men were bad. The guns, the bullying, the brutality for anyone who doesn't do as they say. I was scared before I went there but I didn't understand about the sex. What they wanted from me. It was sick. Horrible.'

'The worse thing was, Father wouldn't have me in the house after that. Like I was the dirty one, I was the trash. He gave me to them and washed his hands of any consequences. His part of the deal was done.'

'That's horrible,' I say. 'How did you get to here then?'

'For a while, I was kept in the hut of one of the militia guards. Apart from the fact that he took his pleasures from me, he used me to cook and clean. He also kept the other men away mostly. I still hated every minute of the day he was around, but it was better than being passed round like a parcel.'

'The reason I got away from them, was basically fresh meat. I was no longer the novelty so when the traffickers came round looking for girls for the city, I was put on the bus. I'd never been out of the village before, well no more than walking to other neighbourhood ones. It was a completely new adventure. At first I was excited to get away but then it was same horror, just a different routine and different people.'

'We were kept in the township, just like in Kibera. There was twenty girls kept in three rooms. The only difference was there was a more professional element to it. A working shower and a mirror. We were also given some nice clothes and some make-up. The older girls told us how to put it on, how to look good for the men. I sometimes look back and wonder why we made ourselves more attractive. I mean it would have been better to look ugly right, they'd leave us alone then. But we did. There was a little bit of pride in looking as good as we could. Maybe it helped with the psychology, like we were a bit more in control. Am I explaining myself well?'

'Yes, sure go ahead. It's fine.'

I am listening and taking in every word. Not because of what she is saying, I have heard similar before or could even guess if I gave it a moment's consideration. But my thoughts are really about how we let this happen. By we, I mean the world, the rulers, the legislators, the institutions we all rely on for normal life. Yet here we are. Not just happening then but looking at the girls in Kibera I saw, it's still happening now. Here and probably numerous others. Enraging and utterly tragic.

'It was like a job,' Jamila continues, her voice is more regular now. Less emotional and angry. 'We did our days' work and came back.'

'What if you got pregnant?'

'They sent you to a doctor and he would deal with it. That was another disgusting experience, but having your body abused was so normal, you began to feel nothing. Just numb. And then if you refused to go, they just kicked you out on the street. So we went along with it.'

'How long before you got away?'

'I was eighteen when I came here,' she says. 'I was so happy. I cried for years for myself and for the other girls.'

'And what about the other girls?'

'I guess some came here, others found their own way. You're a girl right, you know we can be bitches to each other. Even in a situation like in those hostels, sharing the rooms, there were those who thought they were better than the others. Who was in favour with the pimps, mainly because they were prepared to do... you know I mean, do what was necessary. So we looked out for each other. Others, well I can't care too much for, if you know what I mean. They made their choices.'

The failings of sisterhood right there.

'What happened here? How did they look after you?'

'You seen it right?' There are rules. We are not supposed to go to each other's flats, only meet in the communal areas, but as I am a long termer, I can get away with a certain amount. You get a place to stay and you get to stay safe. We are a collective.

Some are teachers, some are counsellors, and some even know the law. Others will cook for parties, keep the place clean. No money changes hands inside except through the front desk. Mary handles that and I pay the bills, like I told you. We all have an allowance for extras, so if we go out we can get clothes, luxuries. But if you break any rules, they can stop the allowance.'

'Feels like half a prison.'

She laughs.

'That's the truth,' she says, 'Like I said it saved my life and I am giving back to it every day. But you are right. And that's what keeps us safe. Rules and security.'

'Sure.' I say, getting up. 'Drink?'

'Thought I was getting judged before.'

'Ha-ha, sorry about that. I didn't mean it.' I say. She looks at me, her head leant to the side. 'Ok I was. Guilty, and I have no room to talk either.'

'It's just boring round here.'

'You talk to the others don't you?'

I use the bottle opener to take the top off a beer and hand it to her. I do the same with another bottle then sit back at the table.

'Cheers,' we both say as we clink bottles.

'We do talk, of course. But most of it's the same. Some of the girls get itchy feet. Want to go meet guys, party etc. So they gossip. Complain about Mary and some of the other bosses you haven't met yet.'

'But guys are a no no, right?' I ask.

'Definitely can't bring a guy in here, that's for sure, and we are not allowed to tell them where we live, anything like that. If any girl breaks the rules on that, they can be banned. It happens.'

I see the point but I also think it must be hard to enforce as well.

We've built a reasonable rapport and I wonder if I'm ready to test the water with her. Will she let me move the conversation on? She's told me so much, fascinating but it gives me nothing to work with.

'Do you trust me?' I ask, dipping a toe in the water. Will the water be warm enough to venture deeper?

She thinks for a moment, walks around and doesn't speak.

'Will you be offended if I say no?''

'Err no, I guess. What else can I say?'

'It's not that I don't like you and I don't get what you are trying to do. Well actually I'm not sure I fully understand why you are here in this place at all. But the reason I don't trust you is, I know you want more from me than I can give you. And at some point you're going to ask me and I don't know how I will respond. But that's the bit I don't trust, even though you are looking at me like a puppy with soft eyes and giving me beer, at some point you going to ask me. You going to push me to do something I don't want to.'

'OK, I get it. And maybe you are right. But you are still here, so there's hope.'

Jamila laughs. 'You really know your game, I give you that.'

She moves to the sofa and sprawls out. Looks like she's here for the afternoon. Looks like my plans for going doing more digging around have changed too.

I go sit on the chair opposite her.

'I was thinking last night about the way you get people to fund this place. You told me there were ways they could influence or make people pay. Does that mean you have videos, recordings, photographs?'

'I can't answer that. I would get thrown out of here in a second. I told you, you would ask me to do something I don't want to.'

'I haven't asked you to do anything,' I say.

'But you are going to, am I wrong?'

'I don't know what I am asking, Jamila. I'm just wanting to find stuff out. But yes ultimately, from everything you told me I would like something I can take from it. Something I can use to stop these bastards. Otherwise, you are right. I should get the next plane home and leave you all to it.'

'I need to think.' She says, leaning forward. 'There is stuff. When the girls come first here, sometimes they still have evidence on them. We use rape kits, hair samples and we get a friendly doctor at the hospital to run them. Police and prosecutors won't do anything even with a DNA sample but they still will provide information through the right channels. That's one way we find them. We have our databases, the faces are usually the same, so we know who's in the frame. And yes, if needs be we will set up videos and bugs. Your friend who told me about this place. She was one we could ask. She would go into a house unobserved. Discreet and efficient we make use of what we can get.'

'And you never think of taking it to the police or courts to shame them at least?'

'It doesn't work. Unless it's convenient for an enemy of a politician or business deal gone wrong and they want to expose someone, or humiliate them for whatever advantage. We don't care about that, we only care about getting enough money to keep this place going and keep us safe. It's just easier this way.'

I sigh.

'But surely this just lets it all continue, more women, more girls, more tragedies.'

'We can't solve every problem.'

The fan rattles away and it's getting annoying so I get up and switch it off. 'How do you sort the aircon in here?' I ask. 'Fan is so noisy.'

'You don't,' she says. 'You can ring maintenance and they'll come check. But not today. Not until I've gone anyway.'

'Ok cards on the table.' I say. 'What would it take for me to get my hands on that evidence and find something I could use? I promise I won't bring anyone's name into it, just need something to work with.'

'Woah Pearl,' she says, 'I am out of here if that's where we are going to go. I'm not even allowed to go in that office. Lock and key. Lord almighty is not allowed in there, so especially not the likes of you and me.'

'But you are thinking about it, aren't you?'

She grabs the beer and drinks.

'We could just ask,' I say.

The look of horror on her face is worth it even if she might be tempted to run away.

# CHAPTER 25

∞ § ∞

The fun doesn't last long and Jamila says she will think about it.

There's a text.

'Call me if you can.'

From Ruby.

I was kind of expecting something to happen. Henrik Dahl threatened it. There isn't even time to start to dial before Ruby is calling me. She must have seen I'd read the message.

'The police are here. Searching the house. They've extended their warrant to me. I'm going crazy Pearl, the kids are crying. Jake is looking at me like I robbed a bank and ready to take the kids to his mothers.'

'Might not be a bad idea,' I say.

'Pearl, you're not helping,' she screams. 'When are you coming home? You need to fix this.'

'Soon, Ruby. Few more days. Look Dad's solicitor is ok. Call him, he might be able to help you.'

'It's ok, Jake has got one he knows.'

At least she sounds calmer now. I feel bad for her and I can already imagine Jake blaming me for everything and that won't help.

'Seriously, what's happening Pearl. What was Dad involved in? You must have found out by now.'

I wonder how to put it.

'The short answer is yes. The long answer is more complicated. He was prosecuted in Kenya for stealing money from his company. It was swept under the carpet so he could come back to UK.'

'Really?' she asks, 'And is this money they want now? Who has it Pearl? Do you know where this money is?'

I am not going to answer it.

'I'm looking into it,' I say, 'I think Dad did it for a reason and there was a reason he was able to keep it from them until now.'

'Jesus, Pearl, this sounds dodgy. Can we not just go to the police and say we don't know anything about it?'

I stare out the window at the early evening darkness setting in wondering why we didn't do exactly that.

'Because Ruby, someone thinks we do know about it and there is evidence to support it. Until we can prove otherwise, it is better we say as little as possible.'

We end the call no further forward. I daren't tell her about the money as she will just tell me to pay it back and I'm not going to do that.

I reflect on the day and wonder what to do next. I need to give Jamila some time to work out a plan as she thinks asking to see those files will get us both thrown out. I'm less worried about me but I can see Jamila's concern. This is her life not mine.

So I will go back to today's plan tomorrow and return to the ministry of Health and see what I can garner from there.

I give myself two days. If I haven't got any further by that time I will go back to the UK. I can't keep running away and letting other people suffer the consequences. Two days is all.

In the meantime, I need to sleep.

***

I make my way out the same way as last time. At least this time I don't have to be escorted. I can return the same way before the market closes. A thumb print is required on the touch pad and the door will open. Very high tech. But I have to be back in daylight otherwise it's the same entrance as usual with people watching me as I wait for Mary to let me in.

From the market I take a cab to the Ministry of Health. I had no reply from my email but decide to take my chances. Maybe someone from his office will see me instead.

Once I reach the building, I sign in again using my second passport. After a few minutes, I'm informed that the minister is out, but I can have a few minutes with one his team.

Disappointing. I liked Kaur, he was a decent person and offered some good insight into how this could have worked.

At the top of the lift, I am back in the office and I announce my presence. After few seconds, I am invited into an office by a young professional looking lady. She is in a light business suit and ultra-smart. Career girl I decide.

Her name tag says as Lilia Munyani.

We sit in a small glass booth.

'Miss McCann.'

'Call me Pearl please. And you are Lilia?'

'Yes I am. How is it I can help you?'

Her smile is broad and worn well. It's natural without being fake so I take it her intention is to be helpful and not obstructive. Let's see.

'I came to see the Minister earlier in the week and have a few follow up questions.'

'Yes, I'm aware. Fire away. I don't have the minister's knowledge and experience but I can look them up.'

I start with the boss man.

'Nigel Davies.'

She taps away on her laptop and returns a profile screen. It is the same Nigel Davies I have seen in younger days. It give his time in employment. Names him as managing direct of ITA Kenya. All stuff I already knew.

'Is there any more sensitive information about him?'

'Oh I wouldn't know that and I would have to discuss with the Minister first.' She plays with her hands a little nervously.

A disappointing start to the conversation. That's the problem without Aashir. I am kicking myself for not asking when I was here last time.

'Henrik Dahl,' I say next.

Against she taps away and reveals the screen.

Several posts listed.

'He has been a key opponent of Tobacco reforms and been involved in media campaigns challenging the personal freedom to choose. Even I have heard of him.'

Interesting that she has heard of him. Especially as Lilia was quite possibly not even born when we were in Kenya. It seems Henrik Dahl is not a shy retiring figure.

I list out further names from my research but most of it confirms what I already know. After a few minutes Lilia discreetly attempts to check her watch and I realise that I am outstaying my welcome.

Lilia tried her best to be fair but I suspect with the best will in the world she wasn't going to have any insight, so I leave it at that. Of course I thank her politely. She's a sweet person and I'm hoping after years of working here she has developed far more cynicism for the world and starts charting the destruction of some of these people on my list and those that might follow on. I can wish.

Outside the building I head over to the taxi rank. As I walk along the square, two large men appear beside me. I look at each of them in turn and realise they are here for me. Moving quickly I turn and start to run, but I find the large hands of one of them on my arm. I think about screaming.

'Don't scream,' one says. 'Someone wants to offer a ride to you is all. Don't panic.'

They hold onto my arms firmly and encourage me along. Within seconds I am in the back seat of Dahl's Land Rover. I don't know why I'm surprised.

'Nice to see you Pearl.' He says from the front.

One of the men gets in the front seat. The other stays in the back with me. The engine starts and we pull into the traffic.

'I wish I could say the same to you.'

'Save your energy, Pearl. Don't get angry at me. Your father and for that matter your brother have delinquent tendencies. Your father has rather given you a very poor inheritance. As for your brother, I think we both share the same opinion of him.'

'Where is Walter?' I ask.

'I would rather ask you, last time, I saw him he was propping up your gate post. Did you really just leave him there? Tut tut. And I thought you were all about charity.'

I don't respond to his windups. We are travelling through the city but I'm not sure where we are going?

'Before you ask, I'm taking you back to the refuge. Your nice little hidey hole.'

I try not to react. I wasn't expecting this. Do I validate his knowledge or do I play dumb. Once again he is ahead of me.

'You think no-one knows about that place. We tolerate it. As long as they keep away from us we'll keep away from them. It's a cosy arrangement isn't it?'

Again I keep quiet. I don't want to give him any information or a way of trapping me into something.

'We are very quiet today. That's fine, don't need any of your outbursts. I do however have an offer to make you. We are little tired of the sanctuary. Over the years, it's become an expensive luxury and some of my colleagues and friends would rather they leave their precious money to their children or their whores. I really don't know. But they would rather not have their memory upset by these lying and manipulative women so it's time is over.'

I won't rise to his attempts to bait me. I just hold my tongue whilst he carries on. The sooner I can get out of this car the better.

'Here's the deal. I got a couple of contacts with a neat line in explosives. You know what I mean. It would be a shame for the building to collapse. All those poor innocent women, screaming for their lives.'

'What do you want?'

'You can keep your dirty little inheritance from Pops. If you get those women to hand over their records. All the stuff they faked and mocked up on various perfectly decent citizens to use as blackmail.'

'You're not even real.'

'Hey, I'm entitled to my opinion, you can have yours. I think they are lying bitches you think somehow they are heroines. I really don't care. The deal is clear. You get them off my back and those of my friends and I'll leave you alone and them. If you don't, then I will set fire to the place.'

The car pulls up at the market.

'24 hours Pearl. I have the explosives ready. It will be a tragic terrorist incident. You know the drill. Call me on this number when you are ready.' He hands me a card.

I get out the car and run into the market. In the crowd I easily disappear. I check behind me and they didn't follow me. I decide to use the market entrance as I can't be on the street any longer. A few seconds later I am inside and run through the underpass into the main building. I am still looking over my shoulder and relieved to get back to the reception. As I enter, I see Mary is not alone.

Jamila sits in one chair with five other women who are staring at me. I look at Jamila but she can't look me in the eye.

My bag is packed and sitting in front of the desk. She's told the Mary and the refuge managers what I want.

# CHAPTER 26

## ∞ § ∞

'Look, I know what you are thinking.' I say.

'I warned you not to interfere with the girls here or cause trouble.' Mary, the receptionist says. 'But you did, so you have to leave.'

'We've spent too long building this place up to risk anything. You must leave.' This time it's a women I haven't met before. I assume she is the elusive management, Jamila talked about.

'Your bag and belongings are there. We've returned your donation so we are square. Neither owes each other anything.' Mary continues.

'Look ladies. I need to tell you something. It's really important. I know you think I am trouble and maybe you are right. But I have to tell you something. I've just been dropped off by Henrik Dahl. He knows all about this place.'

The women look at each other.

'People know about us. The tall lady in a bright gold dress and headscarf at the back says. . 'There is nothing they can do to stop us. Henrik Dahl has been trying for years to close us down. But we're still here.'

'Look, I am sure he has. He's just told me he is planning to blow the place up. Arrange a terrorist attack. Tomorrow at this time. He wants all your information or it's the end. He's says that many of those who pay you want rid of your threat. They think you have benefited well beyond your importance.'

'We won't give in to his threats. He's tried many things on us but like I say, we are still here. Now I think you should leave.'

I'm running out of things to say or do. Henrik looked serious to me but they are absolutely not budging an inch.

'OK,' I say, 'Is it me you don't believe or him? Just to check because I believed him even if you don't believe me. So, even if you kick me out, I think you are going to have to do something.'

They look at each other. I think there are doubts.

'I believe her,' Jamila says. 'We all know Henrik Dahl hates us. He might be using the opportunity of having Pearl here to exploit us.'

'Ok If I'm wrong and we do something to stop Henrik Dahl, then that's fine. It's only him and no-one else. If I'm right, then doing something has to be the answer. We either try to stop him or you are putting everyone's lives at risk.'

'And what are we supposed to do? The tall lady asks.

'I am guessing you have a file on Henrik Dahl.'

None of them speak as they each look at the other. I take silence as yes.

'Then I know what to do. If you let me help I will be gone by this time tomorrow and you won't see me again. If you kick me out, then there is nothing I can do.'

Again no-one is ready to speak. I don't think any of them want to be seen to let me win. So I take the initiative for them.

'Here's what I think we should do.'

***

'You better come through here.'

I follow the tall lady into the back office. There are no windows
and a security monitor shows pictures from the front door. A TV
Screen shows some rolling local news. There are four desks with
desktop computers. There is another room in the corner with a
glass screen.

I am then chaperoned to small office.

'Sit down please. I'm Rose, the manager of the residence.'

'Nice to meet you.' I say. I realise I've still got Dahl's business
card in my hand and put it on the desk. 'If you don't believe me,
you can call him on this number.'

'Oh I believe you,' she says, 'it's just that he has threatened us
before and I have no idea if he means it or not.'

'And what happened the last time?'

She looks at me, her height is imposing giving me the sense she
is looking down at me, but I ignore it.

'Nothing. Absolutely nothing. He threatened to torch us, shoot
the women and even launch a few rocket from out of town.'

I don't know what to say. Admittedly, I haven't been here
before and she has.

'I suppose he looked like he meant it.'

She turns to a cabinet behind and produces a large file. Most of
it is online now, but here is his old file. I flick through it. Articles.
Photographs. Other white men, black girls.  There are long
telephoto shots as well as close up intimate ones. It all shows his
links with others and with the girls. Numerous and extensive.
Looking at more of the men's faces I see a younger picture of
Dad and in the same shot, Nigel Davies. They are all together.

I hand her the file back.

'Why don't you take these photographs to the justice ministry? He would be off your back with all this evidence.'

She sighs. I'm not impressing this lady.

'It's how we survive. He will get angry and shout. As will others of his type, but they know hurting us is the nuclear option. Any pain he inflicts on our ladies will mean publishing his record. Social media, law suits, private prosecutions. He will never work again. He would be untouchable.'

'Isn't that good thing?' I ask.

'Not if we lose this place.'

I think for a moment. She might be right about Dahl and I am losing the argument. But having seen the file on Henrik Dahl, there is probably a file in there on Nigel Davies, maybe even one on Dad. I want to see those files so want to keep the conversation going.

'With the greatest respect.' What a crap phrase that is. 'Why would you lose it? I'm sure this plenty of women with the same or new problems.'

'So even more important that we are here.'

'Yes, but you are here because these men continue to get away with their behaviour. By taking their money you give them carte blanche to do what they want. Do you not struggle with that?'

I am getting impatient, but try to keep a calm tone.

'I think this conversation is over.' She says.

'Look, I've got a suggestion. Please hear me out. And it might bring you out of the shadows a little. I'm not changing your philosophy or probably not going to remove your customers but let's say, you could have a clear out of some of these long term repeat abusers. Surely it would feel good to get some of these men.'

The same look of suspicion. I'm clinging on, hoping she will listen.

'You've got a filing cabinet full of people who have been doing this for years. Every one of those files is a court case, a tale of violence and abuse which will never be punished.'

She says nothing.

'It's a waste right? It keeps this place going but all the work and effort you put in to exploiting the cash situation, that's nothing compared with the potential ruin they have caused.' I keep treading the thin line of blame and my own arrogance. 'I think we can humiliate and get a few of them off the streets and I can promise to replace any monies lost from their exposure.'

Her eyebrows are raised. At least I am getting her attention now.

'Do you know how much money that is? It takes hundreds of thousands of dollars a year to feed and keep this place going. Your charity salary won't even pay the bill for the air con.'

'Oh I have the money and I can prove it, if that helps. But you need to listen to my plan.'

'Go on.'

The more I think about it, the more this feels right. I get the evidence, I need. I get to shame these bastards and I get to find a place for the money dad stole.

'How many women are currently here?'

'About 200,' she says. 'Please keep in mind some of them are vulnerable.'

'That's ok, those that you don't want to go out in public don't have to. The rest will be fine.'

'We need the women, face scarves and as many billboards we can put together. Oh and we need the news media and TV crews.'

'What are you planning?' She asks.

'We're going on a march, Rose. All the way to the Parliament building. We are going to make as much noise as possible so that everyone can see the faces of the abusers. We will tell our stories to anyone who asks. Not one of them can touch us or you. Because we've done nothing wrong. You've been hiding from the public for so long, you've forgotten your own power as women.'

She is listening but will she agree?

'It's time to stand up as women and say these people's names. Let's put Henrik Dahl to shame. He daren't sue, because that will only mean more women, more stories.'

'But they really will come for us then.'

'You said yourself, the nuclear option for them is equally disastrous. Honestly Rose, stand tall and be proud of what you've done here. It's a new start.'

# CHAPTER 27

∞ § ∞

It doesn't work.

I tried. My heart is heavy as I return to reception. I walk past Jamila who barely lifts her head in my direction. Mary supervises me collecting my bag. She hands me my passport and the cash I gave her in an envelope.

'Keep it,' I say. What's the point in fighting over the cash when there are such bigger issues at stake?

I lift my bag onto my shoulder, feeling it to make sure my laptop is packed. I assume they give me everything back that I asked for. As I head for the exit corridor, Jamila rushes up to me and gives me a hug, so I drop the bag to hug her back. I'm not sure it adds value to either of us but it's best to part on good terms. I guess I am like a tornado coming and destroying the neighbourhood, and whilst some people might like new windows and their houses rebuilt, the consequences of destroying what they had is too much.

As has been said too many times, I can just get on a plane and go home. And now, I'm going to have to.

As for Henrik Dahl, I just don't know. He used me to bully these women as he probably has used every other opportunity in life to get them off his back. And perhaps rather selfishly I was hoping to get the file on Nigel Davies so I could close my own convenient loop.

I exit into the market, exhausted, find a cab and take myself to the Intercontinental Hotel. May as well be somewhere posh for my last night here. Though the first thing on my mind is a bed

250

for the night and sleep, I may as well do it in comfort. I will check out the flights for the morning and go back and fight whatever battle I can in London.

Will Henrik Dahl do his thing tomorrow? I actually don't know. He seemed serious to me but Rose was adamant that he wouldn't. I guess I've done all I can and Rose will have to take responsibility.

There is no queue at the rank so I take the first cab and I'm on my way.

I feel a failure yet I've learnt so much. I know now how they did what they did; how corruption breeds corruption; how it was easier to facilitate more corruption than it was to fight it and finally how it easy was to get away with it, even when caught.

The cab journey doesn't take long.

I don't even consider the room price as I hand over the credit card. It's almost as if nothing else matters. The weight on my shoulders is heavy as I head to my room. The crisp white sheets welcoming as I drop my bag, slip off my shoes and trousers and climb into the bed. I don't remember falling asleep.

***

I wake with the phone ringing beside me. The bedside clock says ten already.

Sitting up, I pick up the phone and see it's a local number.

'Where are you Pearl? You need to come? You did it.'

It's Jamila. Excitement in her voice.

'Slow down, sorry I've been in asleep. Tell me again.'

'We are going to do what you said. We are going to protest.'

Her voice is loud and excitable.

'Really?' I had honestly given up on the whole enterprise.

'You should have been here. After you went there was a big argument. Like nothing ever seen in this place. Word got around and girls came out of nowhere saying they wanted to protest. Nearly everyone wants to tell their story. We've been working on it all night. Placards, flags from old sheets, spray paint and making sure we can cover our faces. We're going to be in Parliament Square in two hours.'

I look at the clock again. Plenty of time for me to get sorted. I leap out of bed, my mind racing ahead to what I need to do.

'What did Rose say?' I ask.

'She caved. It was so funny to see it. She is such a stern woman but she realised she had a mutiny. We all promised we would do the protest and by the end of the day we would all be back tucked in as normal. She arranged extra security. Got everything sorted. The likes of Henrik Dahl can't touch us Pearl.'

It was 2:00 pm yesterday when he threatened to blow up the refuge. Would he still do it? Maybe that would be my role to play. Maybe once the march starts, I can distract him.

'And the media?'

'We have rung every station, every newspaper. We are going to meet at the Freedom Corner in Uhuru Park and then onto Kenyatta Avenue and turn towards Parliament and the Tower There will be at least a hundred of us. You're going to come aren't you?'

'I wouldn't miss it for the world.' I reply. I look out the window. Uhuru Park is just by the hotel so shouldn't take too long to get there. For once my choice of bed for the night is convenient.

'What are you expecting the Government to do?'

'We've prepared a document with a list of names and evidence. We will hand the same to the media and we will be demanding justice.'

'Brilliant,' I say. I can't quite believe what was a whim of convenience is coming true and then I wonder why it hadn't been done years ago.

# CHAPTER 28

## ∞ § ∞

I arrive at the Freedom Corner. I haven't been here before but a minute spent with the simple monument brings back the haunting memory of Colonial Britain. It shows a trader and peasant lady swapping goods but without looking at each other's faces to avoid giving each other away for fear they would be tortured. It's a remarkable image of defiance but even spending a moment to consider the evil of torture and the renowned brutality of the colonial leaders here is sickening. It's amazing and inspiring at the same time to realise how far Kenya and its people have come from those days. Yet here I am readying to prepare for a protest over decades of post-colonial abuse. This time not perpetrated by absolute rule, but the quiet systemic influence of money and power over populations. A power which allows rulers to get away with just about anything. If I didn't feel I was doing the right thing now, Freedom Corner has reminded me that justice doesn't come from hiding away but only when people stand together and fight for what is right.

It's just before Noon and I am looking out for the women. I'm excited and worried. And hot. The middle of the day is probably not the best time to do a march but it has to be done.

I don't see much sign of anything abnormal until I hear a noise. They are entering the park from the street. I assume they must have got a couple of minibuses to transport them all.

I walk over to where they are gathering in the clearing. They are chatting excitedly and rehearsing with the loudhailer and whistles. A drum forms a rhythm.

As they come together, and organise themselves, I'm astonished at what they have done. I am smiling with pride and can't remember the last time I felt so uplifted.

They organise themselves in rows of five dressed head to foot in white with patterned scarves covering all but their eyes. There are placards and at the back some mock-up banners.

I try to take in all the messages.

I can just make out words like rapist, violence and corruption. There are photographs on some of the placards and I can see they took me just as I advised and put the names on each one.

They chant the names in order followed by the accusation, rapist, murderer and paedophile. It's hard to make out the names but what is not in doubt is the image and impact they are creating.

People around the park are beginning to notice. I see phone cameras while others are watching.

As I get closer I look for Jamila. It's hard to see her given that all the faces are covered with the scarves. I study the variable size and proportions of all the women, to take a guess.

They walk passed me as the march begins, it's only then I hear my name.

'Pearl.'

I can't see who is shouting me. Then I see the ladies at the back break ranks and I can see one of them is Jamila. She passes me an extra banner. The photo is Nigel Davies and the heading in bold red on the card is Murderer.

I embrace her.

'You could have told me there was a uniform.' I say.

'Just glad you are still here.' She shouts to make herself heard.

I move alongside them and walk into street, causing the traffic to stop as we cross. Horns sound and we attract more attention.

The noise level rises. I am looking all around to see whether people understand what it's all about. The shouts from the women change to 'stop the corruption, stop the violence.'

People are clapping so it feels like it's going well.

But this is only the start and the attention might get a little more challenging. The police might not be so welcoming.

We turn the corner and into the quieter streets near the hotels. There are businesses, hotels and political buildings all around. As we pass each one, more people check us out. I spot a TV crew by a small monument with some photographers standing on top to get a better view. I hope they are getting the names on every placard.

The cheering continues.

I look behind and some people are beginning to follow.

Exactly as I hoped this morning. I didn't want the protest to be like a tin can rattling in a bin, noisy for a few minutes but quickly forgotten once the bin was put down. I wanted the noise to get louder and louder. It's a small protest but the noise has to go on long after everyone has run for cover.

We round the next corner and are back towards the hotel where I set off a short while ago.

Then the street was empty. Now there is a line of police waiting for us. Every one of them in full riot protective gear. Shields and helmets.

We all look at each other.

'Did anyone inform the police?' I ask Jamila.

'We discussed it,' she says, as loudly as she can over the noise. 'But we didn't in the end. We are not that many and honestly we weren't sure we'd attract that much attention. We just concentrated on the media. Look we didn't even hold the traffic up when we crossed the road. How can the police get involved? Full riot gear as well?'

'Because we are having an impact already.'

I run to the front. The girls fall out of line the closer they get to the police. I wonder whether it's just show of strength or if there is intent on taking us on. The media presence is stronger around us. People are coming out of the hotels. Surely the police will not pick a fight against unarmed women.

'Shout louder,' I scream. 'Make more noise. Don't let them intimidate you.'

They women turn to each other. Nervous exchanges. The masks hide their expressions but I can sense the tension as they shuffle slowly. Photographers get closer and take photographs of the placards. I run towards one of them and lift mine into the shot of the camera lens.

Seeing my energy the girls shout again and the drum is louder.

The police line holds firm as we get closer. I still don't know what we are going to do.

We are metres away. The police line covers the whole street. I look behind us and see that police have gathered on the other side. We are trapped. They are going to kettle us. A small group of unarmed women forced into an ever tightening huddle unable to move. The sort of treatment given to violent protestors.

We are now right in front of the police line. They are unmoved as we continue to shout. But the voices are waning as we look for support in each other. Nervous. Scared. What if they turn violent?  They look at me for confidence and then each other.

I shout as loud as I can, 'Girls, Sit down!' Hands out motioning everyone down. Don't move. Let them be the ones to come forward.

They duly take to the road surface. Everyone is quiet as we form a circle. The police haven't yet moved.

I run to Rose who is supposed to be the leader.

'You get any of these girls hurt, you are responsible,' she says.

Tell me something I don't know. I don't need reminding of the danger we are in.

'Have you got that petition?' I ask.

She pulls it from her bag and hands me the sheets of paper plus a USB stick.

I run towards a TV camera, unsure who is behind it.

'Can I speak? 'I ask the reporter nearby.

The reporter moves a boom microphone towards me.

'Introduce yourself,' the journalist says.

'My name is Pearl McCann and I am here with these women to protest about their treatment at the hands of privileged businessmen, charity leaders and government officials.'

'We are peaceful, unarmed. All of these women are innocent victims and you can see the Police won't let us proceed to the parliament.'

All around me, photographers and cameramen appear. Phones are recording and microphones are in my face. I don't want to stop talking.

I hold the papers high in the air.

'The names are here. All of them. They have been getting away with rape, murder, solicitation and assault. Every one of them, their crimes are here. Please, tell their stories.' I start to distribute the papers, wondering if I give them all to one person they will get removed. So I split them.

I keep the USB in my pocket. I daren't give that up. I will find an outlet on social media as soon as I get out of here.

There's a shout from behind. The police move forward.

Questions are coming fast from the reporters but as the police get closer, I decide to return to girls. There is a scrum as the watching crowd get out of the way. I am back among them as the police surround us.

I grab the loud hailer. I don't really know what to do but my instincts tell me not to shy away. Let it be seen that we are innocent.

I stand while the women sit around me.

'We are unarmed. We are women only. We just want to get our message to the people. Look at these women, all in white. They are innocent. The men we protest about are the evil ones. Nigel Davies, Henrik Dahl…' at each name a placard goes up.

A policeman reaches forward, grabs the loud hailer and pulls me out. I duck and sit down so he has to come further into the group. He steps away at that point, probably does not want to be seen as grabbing any of the others.

What happens now?

Do they arrest us? Drag us out? Do we put our hands up and surrender?

They stand over us, menacing. Batons in hand. They could beat us easily but they know they can't. It will look so bad.

It's time. We can't hold the line forever and I can't let the girls get hurt.

'Girls, stand up, put your placards down. Hands in the air.'

They tentatively follow. I move to the front.  We hold our hands high.

Like all of them, I can't see their faces. But I try to speak.

'We have stopped our protest. We will disperse peacefully if you let us. The girls have their hands high up. Please let us through.'

The officers look at each other. They don't move.

'Speak,' I say, 'what do you want us to do?'

The officer pushes me back and I fall on the floor. There is noise behind me I and I think they are about to charge us. The noise from the crowd and the horns is intense.

The police look at each other again.

The line opens and the police start to grab those at the front and push them out. We squeeze through one by one onto the open road. Hassled and prodded as we progress but ultimately we get away. As I approach the end of the line, the girls are disbursing randomly. I turn to the hotel.

'To the hotel,' I shout. It must be safe over there. I start to run. As I look round I can see others follow. I trip over on the pavement and scream. Women run around and leap over me as I lie on the floor. The momentum of the crowd is scary. As I get to my feet, I am pushed again from behind. My knee bangs hard on the edge of the concrete. My hands burn from grazes. Taking a deep breath, I try to stand again. Someone grabs my hair and yanks hard. Ignoring the pain, I turn to see who has hold of me.

Henrik Dahl is above me.  He pulls my hair again and kicks me. Prone on the ground, my side sore, I feel very vulnerable.  I squeal but he seems able to shove others away. There are no cameras, just people and police moving around me. Now, he grabs my arm and pulls me into his face, which is flush red with anger.

His fist slams into my stomach, winding me. I manage to lash out, kicking him. I look down and he has a small knife in his hand. He looks around and steps closer. He wants to kill me but it's the middle of the street. He can't'

'I will kill you,' he screams into my face and then looks to the knife. 'You will always be looking over your shoulder. One day I will get you.'

He's always had menace in his accent but it's nothing to the bitter shredded words that are forced from his mouth.

A movement comes from the right.

Someone starts kicking and beating him.  He lets go of me, falls to the ground.  I manage to stand up and see his assailant is Walter.

'Go,' Walter shouts, 'go!

'Dahl manages to turn around. Now Walter is on the ground as well. They kick and scream at each other. Dahl shifts his body. His arm moves.  I look at Walter and see his white shirt turn red. Where are the police?  Someone screams.  The police arrive and grab Dahl before he can run.  He is forced to the ground and held. He is wrestled to the floor and held. He looks over towards me, eyes bulging with the weight of the officer on him. Pure hate is directed my way.  Medics surround Walter and I am pushed out of the way. Some of the girls grab me and drag me towards the hotel. I want to go back and help Walter but I feel numb, like it's beyond me to intervene. He's just saved my life but I wouldn't be in this place if wasn't for his drug habit. I walk away sure that his fate is not mine to manage and Walter probably knows that.

Chaos is still around.  Reporters and camera crews film every movement, I wonder how they missed what just happened. But I am glad to run into the hotel foyer.

I find some of the others there, the scarves removed. They are hugging. Jamila is there as well.

I hug her.

'Thank God you got away,' she says, 'that was scary.'

'Look you need to get back to the refuge now. Let's get you into taxis. You are too exposed all in white.'

'Yes we will get back.' She says. 'But what about you?'

'I will be at the airport in a few hours on my way home.'

We look at the news screen and see the pictures with a breaking news banner. I am being interviewed and am screaming at the camera. I grab the chair beside me to steady myself, horrified and scared seeing my face on the screen, hearing the fear and panic in my voice.

'Oh wow,' Jamila says, 'that is brilliant. Look at you.'

I can't get to feeling pride about that but looking at the pictures of all the girls in white holding firm under pressure to scatter by the Police makes me glow with pride.

I grab Jamila's hand. My knee is screaming with pain and I need to steady myself.

'We did it,' I say, 'we did it together. Please go now and get safe. I will message you later once I am on my way.'

She hugs me once more.

'Some of the others won't say it but I will. We would never had done anything like this without you. In twenty four hours, whatever happens, we are different people. We should not be hiding anymore. We shouldn't be scared of these men.'

As we go to the foyer, the crowds have dissipated. The police are present but only to keep order. Apart from a few scuffles, there is not really anyone to arrest.

I am relieved to see them leave as I head back to my room. My knee stings but I won't let that stop my sense of achievement. I push the sight of Walter bleeding on the floor to the back of my mind. I have to leave now.

The USB stick is firmly stored in my pocket and I am excited to see what I have to take back home. But that will have to wait until I am safely in the airport lounge. Nigel Davies, whoever you are and whatever you did. You can't touch me anymore or my family.

# CHAPTER 29

∞ § ∞

ENGLAND

The stewardess wakes me from my hard slumber. I must have slept for all the ten hours of the flight as I don't even remember moving or going to sleep. This business class bed definitely works. Either that or maybe the last week has wiped me out completely.

I move and my bruises come to life. My knee, my head, my hands. I don't want to see a mirror.

I grab something to eat from the tray and do my best to get ready to land. I have to take a deep breath. I know the police will be waiting. I have to brace myself for what's going to happen next.

All the last weeks' efforts have been leading up to now. It's either a reckoning for me or for one posh, so far impenetrable Member of Parliament with a taste for under age African girls.

I make a point of going to the bathroom before facing the passport queue. I try to clean my face and the graze on my hand again. My hair is pulled back into a pony tail. As good as I'm going to be.

The mirror doesn't lie though. I'm not sure that long haul flights do much for the complexion but I look like I've been through a desert marathon with pock marks and tired lines round the eyes. If hadn't just lathered my face in cream I think my skin would be coming off in pieces. Not quite the dead eyes of my brother but not far off.

Thinking of Walter, I have to assume he didn't survive the stabbing. Whilst I will have to live with my conscience that he died saving my life, he had already burnt any bridges of rehabilitation with us. Whether Henrik Dahl would have stabbed me there and then in the street, I don't know. The way he threatened me but didn't actually push the knife in makes me think the moment passed. Maybe he was not as tough as I gave him credit for. Used to other people doing his dirty work perhaps. But Walter did what he did and I can't turn the clock back.

The mirror offers me no more reassurance so I leave it to the others in the bathroom. Maybe they will see more joy in their return to Blighty.  I need to get through the next ordeal and bring my life back to stability whatever that looks back.

The passport queue is now long. Even with e-gates it rarely moves quickly, but I am happy to make slow progress. Through the gap in the gates I see the police desk and imagine they are checking the cameras with me in the spotlight. I should take a bow.

Maybe not.

I place my passport on the reader and inevitably it pops up with a go to desk message. Here goes.

The office swipes my passport without comment and returns it. However I can already see two plain clothed police officers waiting; a bearded Asian man and smart younger olive skinned woman. My escort awaits.

'Pearl McCann?' The woman asks.

'Yes.' I reply, softly. My right arm begins to shake and I want to cry.

'Please come with us.'

I wipe my eyes and sniffle a little as I am escorted to a featureless room. I didn't expect that burst of emotion so try to stiffen myself to push it away. I don't need waterworks now. I've got the rest of my days to work out how I feel about things.

They leave me alone for a while, taking my passport and boarding card. I assume that tells them something they don't already know.

A few minutes later they both return.

The Asian officer introduces himself and then she does. I don't register the names, it really isn't important.

'I'm arresting you on suspicion of conspiracy to defraud International Tobacco Associates and associated companies.' The reading of my rights continues and I wait patiently for the conclusion. Fortunately I've had a few hours to prepare for this so got in my mind as to how I will approach it.

'Anything to say in response?' he asks.

'Nothing at this time.' I reply.

'Ok we will be taking you to a police station to be formally interviewed. Do you have a suitcase?'

I describe it for them as they go through the formalities and handcuffs are placed on me. They are heavy and I catch the graze on my wrist. Neither officer comments on my injuries.

I am escorted out to a police car, my suitcase being dragged by a uniformed officer. Who knew Police Officers could provide free porter services. A car door is open and I get the pleasure of blues and twos for the twenty minute journey down the M4. The officers don't speak so I stare out of the window, preparing myself for the inevitable interrogation. Saves on a taxi fare. I continue trying to find some humour what is probably going to be a difficult few hours. I still need to remind myself that I haven't done anything wrong.

***

I'm given time to get a solicitor. I use the duty one for now because I didn't think too much about arranging a proper lawyer.  Once the formalities are dealt with I will get some information on a decent legal defence.

The solicitor appointed is a twenty something Asian girl. She wears a blue dress suit but the dress stretches over her largish thighs. She is polite and apart from some initial small talk proceeds to ask me what I know of the charges. I don't think she is familiar with complicated finance cases and I have to explain three times about my father's business and how there is an accusation about his monetary theft from the accounts in Kenya. I am unsure whether they know about PMC or not, so I keep quiet. I need to hear the case against me before I know what kind of defence I need to make.

Eventually I am in front of the two officers again.

'What were you doing in Kenya?'

It's the first of no doubt many prying questions.

'I went there to take some time out after my father's death. I have some friends in Nairobi and thought it would be good for me before I go back to work.' I wonder if they have seen the TV pictures and my twenty-four hour media stardom.

They ask a little about my work and the countries I have worked in but it seems that this is just background and not the crucial element of the conversation. Whilst my travel and work history is unusual, it's not controversial. They don't mention the stuff on the TV so I wonder if they missed it. Surely not.

'You went to South Africa before going to Kenya.'

'My brother needed help.' I say.

'Your dead brother?' The woman asks. I figure it's easy to answer this as I have nothing to hide on this front. I knew as little as the next man about what my brother was doing and why he faked his death. It was certainly nothing I can be accused of being contributory to.

I explain about the call and the shock from hearing from him. And that he wanted help with the courts.

'And you paid the bail?'

'Yes,' I reply.

'With your own money.'

'Yes.' I keep my responses simple. I don't want to get drawn into explanations that might elongate this process.

'Your salary from the charities won't be that much. Wonder where you got that kind of money.' She prods but she's giving me easy replies.

'I'm a good saver. And to be honest in the swamps of Tanzania there isn't much call for sports cars and large TVs.'

That closes that loop but they are still curious about Walter's fake death. Again I give the answers I know about him being involved with some business people who I have no dealings with who arranged it.

'Doesn't it seem rather odd?' She asks. 'That's a highly criminal activity and you don't seem concerned about it.'

'I am concerned. And you can imagine, myself and my sister were deeply worried. But it has nothing to do with me. I can't answer much more than I have. It was a complete surprise to me as well.'

She looks at her colleague and picks up another sheet of paper. Thankfully she gives up on the Walter line. I suspect if I am interviewed again they will be many more questions on that, plus whether I saw him in Nairobi or not. That becomes more complicated.

'Your father was convicted of fraud in Kenya. Were you aware of that?'

How should I reply? I decide on half the truth.

'I became aware of it after the bailiffs visited my father's house. I googled some of my father's history and found a newspaper article. Before that I wasn't even aware if he'd been done for speeding.'

'Are you saying you have no prior knowledge of your father's financial history?'

'No.'

'Are you aware that your father created a company in your name?  PMC?'

'No.' My first full lie and it's a gamble. I don't believe they can prove I knew about this in the last week and it's a private bank. They would not be able to get access to the accounts in short order, especially from Panama.

'You are not aware?' She tries again.

'This is literally the first time I am hearing about it.'

'You can see how that might not feel very convincing from this side of the table.'

'I can see how it looks, but I did not know about this arrangement. I haven't even been in the UK for the last few years. Perhaps you can tell me all about it as I am not aware.'

I look at the solicitor who carries on making notes and apart from lifting her eyes to me, she shows no emotion.

Was this going the way they expected? I wonder what the complaint is. Should I try a bit of an attack?

'Can I ask?' I say, 'what's this about? You have asked me about my brother, my father and a company I've never heard of, but you haven't accused me of anything. Where is the connection to me?'

They look at each other and the Asian officer speaks.

'We have reason to believe that your father used the proceeds from the theft of company funds in Kenya to facilitate this business in your name to avoid detection. We have reason to believe as the owner of that company that you were complicit in those actions and therefore are now fully liable for the monies in the accounts and for conspiracy to defraud.'

I look at my solicitor and she doesn't respond. I figure, I will have to do my own work here.

'I've said I don't have knowledge of the company. You say it's in my name but I don't know about it, so how can I be complicit?'

She pushes forward a record of the company and the owner clearly stated as me. I've seen this before so I shrug.

'Ok,' I reply. 'But I am not aware of it.'

I pause and try another line.

'Even if I was, which I'm not, how does this prove my complicity in my father's actions? If he stole money back in the nineties, how come the company allowed him to continue working for them after that? The company must have known and didn't pursue it. He was even given a decent pension. I was at university when all this happened so I don't see how I am even close to be a co-conspirator. Finally, I've been living and working for twenty years in Africa and various other parts of the world. I am hardly the product of an international banking scam, am I?'

They look at each other again and I think I've provided a decent counter to their points. They don't have any evidence of my complicity because there is none. This is a pure fishing exercise.

'Do you know a woman named Beatrice Lovane?' She asks. I suppose this question was to be expected.

'I do. She looked after my father.'

'What was the relationship between her and your father?'

'I have no idea? Does it matter? I never met her with my father but I was aware of her.'

'She was an employee of your company?'

'Was she?' I reply, shrugging my shoulders. They are trying but they don't have any facts. And to be honest with myself, this all must look really dodgy. I can't blame them for looking at me even if they are looking in the wrong place.

'Do you know the name, Laila Dreidame?'

'No.' I don't.

'You've met a Laila Dreidame?'

'No,' I say firmly.

She shows me a photograph, which I glance at. The surprise must show on my face as I reply.

'That's Beatrice Lovane,' I reply.

'The lady you also never met?'

'Right, I've never met her but there are photographs at my father's house. Are they the same person?'

'You tell me,' she responds.

'I'm lost now,' I say.

'Doesn't matter. Miss Dreidame is helping us with our enquiries. We will see.'

'Are you familiar with a Nigel Davies?' She asks.

'Yes, since my father's funeral. I became aware he and my father worked together before he became an M.P. From what I read, he is the one alleging my father's financial impropriety.'

'Oh don't be shy,' she says. She passes me a photograph of me holding up a placard with his name on. 'It seems in Nairobi you had quite a lot to say about Mr Davies.'

So they were holding this back.

I pause waiting for her to push again. Not sure what I should say about this. Play safe I think, let them do the accusing.'

'I heard some things about Mr Davies from my friends in Nairobi. I just tagged along with the protests they were making. It's not for me to say much more.'

She mutters a response.

'Fortunately for you, I can't ask you much more about why you were making such an accusation as it is not my jurisdiction unless you want to give me a statement now.'

'No,' I say. She's tempting me to go on record because that will give her cause to ask me more but I've not even decided what to do next about Nigel Davies.

'You might want to be careful what you say now you're back in the UK. You are already quite the celebrity on the news.'

'Oh,' I say. I hadn't quite bargained on that.

They get up together. 'You can go now. Please leave your contact details with the front desk.'

And that's it. They dropped a nice bombshell at the end but I am relieved they have nothing on me so far. What Beatrice has to say or her current persona as Laila will be up to her. But for now I need to dodge media interest before I decide what happens next with Nigel Davies.

# CHAPTER 30

∞ § ∞

I am back in Greenwich in my apartment and sitting up in bed with the TV on. At least, I've had chance to shower and eat something.

The news is on and I haven't been able to take my eyes of it.

The new agencies are publishing the names and faces we had on our placards. Though I can sense the legal caveats being used to protect any defamation challenges.

But social media carries far less the legal subtleties as people share and comment on numerous articles. There are American, French, Dutch, Spanish as well as British names forming a complex framework of elites who were actively involved in the sex scandal. A name has popped up for it. The Smoke Ring, centring on the tobacco links.

Front and centre for British News is Nigel Davies. So far he has simply refuted any allegations but media pressure is growing. Studenham hall is closed. Media are encamped outside, though there is a good chance he isn't actually there. Makes me wonder how much the current Lady Studenham knows of her husband's past. Well if she didn't know before, she certainly does now. He can deny it all he likes but I imagine Lady Studenham will provide a grimmer level of scrutiny when her family name is dragged into the mud.

I avoided turning on my phone until I got back to the flat. I wanted the time to breathe first. But having dealt with the Police, I need to face the wrath of the rest of the world.

Taking a deep breath, I put my old SIM back in. Twenty voice mails. First few are media asking for comments so I start deleting them. They will keep coming I guess and before long they will know I am back in the UK and come knocking on Dad's door. Being a little sly, I didn't give this as my contact address.

I need the time.

Nairobi was a whirlwind crashing from one drama to another and resulting in the emotion of the march. I never planned it and never expected that this trip would lead to such a place. But what a feeling it was to be able to scream for those women, so abused and so neglected by those around them.

They won't welcome the attention and I am sure Rose will have locked them down for days now to avoid any further intrusion into their lives.

At least they can take pleasure in watching the multiple arrests of men all around the country. I wonder how many were stopped at airports and borders, in a desperate attempt to get away from legal jurisdiction People like Davies can escape that for some time, maybe forever as the case of extradition takes it's time but they can't ignore the debate in the media that rages on.

The power of the smoke ring envelopes not only those named but their families and associates.

And then there is me. My face where I never wanted it. Screaming into a camera like a banshee. Apparently I'm in hiding. Which is true and they will track me down. But for these last few hours, despite the interview from the police, it has been nice to have time process what I've learnt and work out what to do next.

I open the laptop and review the folder on the USB with the evidence of Nigel Davies' sexual desires. There are numerous videos and sound recordings. Plus some documents.

The pictures are not good quality but the sound is better. His name is referred to and he is caught asking for and demanding young women. There is a scene of mass rape at a sports club. He is pictured at the door in sports gear, like he'd just been to a tennis match. A naked girl is placed on a table tennis table. Because of the poor quality the rape itself is not clear but the behaviour, the cheering and the sickening misogyny is unmistakable. They are queuing up to rape underage girls and they seem to enjoy every minute of it.

And then the murdered girl. Bernadette as she was called. The folder on the disk has her name on. There is no evidence of her murder or her rape, only the aftermath at the house where it happened. The men are shouting at each other to go after her. Davies voice is clear as is that of a much younger Henrik Dahl. It would not be provable in court that Davies ordered her to be murdered but the fact that he was at that party and she died soon after does not look good and will destroy any reputation he has.

And that is now what I need to decide. What to do with this information. I still need to decide, not because of Davies. I do believe if he could, he would try to punish me in some way but it would only incriminate him further. I could publish all of this and potentially get him in court but then every element of this story would become apparent.

Including that of my father.

Dad had a folder of his own. I didn't find any evidence of involvement in rape. But he was present in these groups. He was mixing and freely discussing activities with them. He was culpable.

So I can see why he hesitated to go after Davies. Because his own name would be dragged into it. He would have been a poor witness and the family would have been exposed.

I guess it comes back to Beatrice's comment to me about doing the right thing. Dad hadn't the courage and from the grave he is asking me if I do.

I still don't know the answer, though actually if he keeps encouraging the police to dig then inevitably I will have to hand over all I have in evidence because I can't keep denying it. I'm not going to jail for Davies or for Dad. I haven't done anything wrong.

Still, my bank account swells with money. I haven't worked out the full story behind Dad's actions but my current theory is that there was so much laundering of money for dodgy purposes he decided to create his own pot alongside Beatrice or Laila. What they intended to do under the guise of the Angels I don't know. It will be a question for her if I ever get to see her again. This time I will not let her get away with anything but the truth. I know enough to ask proper questions.

I'm seeing Dad as ultimately a nice guy. But his story is somewhat chequered and I think Beatrice knows him warts and all.

The one unmissable point, even if he wasn't directly guilty of the sex crimes of his associates, the police will conclude he was a common thief. And I am the beneficiary. A burden I'm less than comfortable with.

***

I can't deny, arriving back at Dad's house, I'm looking forward to see Terry and fortunately there is no media here.

He's waiting at the gate as I pull onto the drive in my new hire car. Good job the rental company didn't check for my previous rental reference in Nairobi. I smile at his white T-Shirt with a massive elephant motive.

I step out and wander round the car to hug him.

'Fucking hell, Pearl,' he says, 'go easy on the hugs, you'll have me on the floor.'

'How's your head?' I ask.

'Where there's no sense, there's no feeling. How's the knee?'

'Painful, but I don't think I need to lose the leg like some I know. Made of tough stuff us McCanns. 'I say with a laugh. I grab my bag and we walk into the house. Immediately Terry goes for the fridge. I don't mind.

'I ordered a delivery,' he says, 'knew you were coming so had to treble the usual.'

'Funny,' I say, looking round the kitchen once more.

The house feels emptier than ever. Dad's presence reducing with every day that passes. The dust of the old overtaken by that of the new. The Police have been round and searched the place. They've probably taken all the technology and the statements that I went through. But good luck if they want to find anything in there. I didn't.

'Cheers,' he says as we sit at the same spot as before, across the kitchen table. 'You won't want to know me now that you are famous. How does that work? You're not even pretty.'

'You're full of it today. Keep them coming. Is this pay back because I was taking the piss out of you?'

'Yeah,' he says, 'but must have been scary with that Dahl feller coming after you.'

'Petrified, though I didn't have much time to think about it. Adrenaline took over I suppose. I was more trying to understand what the police were doing. I think they had the impression from whoever organised them that we were armed or it was going to turn violent, hence they turned up in riot gear. When they realised we were just a small bunch of harmless women, they didn't know what to do. They were expecting to charge us and then they didn't dare. Not with cameras and media all around. It was only as we broke up that things kicked off a bit.'

'You looked good, though. With the chanting and cheering. In your element.'

'It was good, wasn't it?'

'What about your brother then? Have you heard anything?'

'I don't think he made it to be honest, but I can't find any news on him. After what happened and what he did to you, I can't get involved in it Terry. I know he saved me but I can't wipe out the last few years when I already thought he was dead. It's almost easier to think of him that way than it is to think about his addiction and complete lack of morality. Does that make sense?'

'Yeah course. But what you going to do now?'

'What do you think I should do,' I ask?

'Why you asking me? You're one with the brains and the ideas.'

I laugh. If only I did.

'Ok, let me put another way. You must get angry with what happened to you in the past. People who put you in harm's way. The politics of it. Don't you feel like protesting government corruption?'

'Never,' he says, 'never did, never will. Absolutely no point to question when you serve Queen and country. I don't watch the political shows. I signed up for the army, I went where they sent me. Conscience is for those guys to worry about. I got enough to worry about with the heebeegeebees in my head. I haven't got enough space for questioning whether I should have even been there.'

'Yeah, I get it.'

'But you're different. Nigel Davies is a pedo and shouldn't be a free man. It's that simple.'

'I know, I know. But it feels like I'm doing it more for revenge than for any great judicial cause. He's got better lawyers than I'll ever have, and there is no crime in the UK as far as we have proof of. It's up to Kenya if they demand his extradition or not. My guess, in a year's' time we'll all have moved on and he will be old news.'

'But we should at least shame him out of his seat. Get him to resign.'

'And how we going to do that?' I reply.

'Says the girl who turned a whole country on its head in five minutes. Two ways I see it, one is the nice way… just ask him.' He laughs. 'I've heard worse ideas. The other one, is by force. I don't mean by legal force, but the social media. Get the lefties on the cause, the libs, they love a good drum to bang. Tory rapist, give them some of those headlines you got tucked away on your file.'

I think for a minute,

'He won't see me, will he?'

'He will, but not where the press will be. But I promise you, you have him properly scared. My guess is this police thing will go away. The money forgotten. You have as much on him as he has on you. Like with Spencer he will be looking for a truce.'

'Like you say as well, he should be locked up. A truce feels unsatisfactory.'

'Too right.'

'Might be out of my hands though. Read this.' I open up the laptop and show him the folders we have. Lists of names, most of which I never even got round to opening. I show him Nigel Davies folder and let him watch.

'If the police get hold of this information, he might not make it to a prison cell but his reputation will be shredded.'

'You should put it out there. Anonymously or something.'

'It feels a low trick.' I say. 'I need to face him first. I need to see his reaction. Does it make sense?'

'Fucking throw away the key is what I think. But whatever you want Pearl.'

I smile. He's right. But how do I get to see him.

***

Before long, Terry is asleep. Almost used to him snoring the afternoon away. Not that it's something I wish to get used to.

I walk round the house for no other reason than boredom. With the cleaning Ruby's done I am beginning to lose the sense of him. Even then, the more I know of him, the less he feels like my Dad. In the bedroom, Ruby has stripped the bed and cleaned the carpet. The pictures from the wall are in the corner and sitting plum at the front is the whisky picture, The Angels Share.

It still makes me smile and gives me that tiny bit of hope that he wanted something good from that money. When he named that fake charity, The Angels Share, I would put money on that joke being in his mind.

As well as the pictures there is a box with all the paraphernalia from the dressing table. I pick it up and sort through it. Small reminders of the past. The blue Tagine is on the top and I remove the lid. All the contents have been discarded and probably binned. Ruby was never a hoarder. I hear the door and jump. Being clumsy, I drop the lid and it smashes on the floor. Cursing I go to the living room and see Ruby coming in.

'Oh hi,' I say, 'just be a second. I just dropped the lid of that old tagine. I will clear it up.

'Oh ok, Terry's here I see.' She looks down at him with a frown. She's more concerned with him than the Tagine. Definitely not sentimental.

'Leave him alone,' I say, 'he's not doing any harm.'

Ruby picks up his discarded bottles and takes them to the sink. I leave her to it as I go back to the bedroom with a dustpan and brush. I start to clean up and notice a bit of sellotape stuck to the floor with a piece of the lid. As I pull it off a tiny micro disk is stuck to it. I grab it and put it on the dressing table. I finish clearing up and then bring it out to the living room.

'Look what I found in the bedroom,' I say to Ruby.

She looks at the disk and back at me.

'I can see you are excited but I wish I could go back to knowing nothing about Dad. That doesn't mean I don't like having you around, Pearl, but please, no more. I'm not sure I can take any more revelations.'

And I still haven't told her that I've got the money sat in Panama.

'I will go through it first and vet it for you, is that ok?'

She shrugs and goes back to making a drink.

I go to the laptop but can't find a drive that will read the micro disc. I need a card reader. But it should fit in my Samsung phone. I get a pin to open the drive and then start finding my way through the directory.

The drive has some videos, photos and documents. Dad was not very tech competent so I wonder if he put this together. And then I wonder if Bea did it. Another thing she probably never told me. But by Dad leaving it in the tagine I suspect he intended me or Ruby to find it when we cleaned the house. It was well hidden from prying eyes.

The photographs are copies of many old print photos converted onto digital. Lots of family photos from various places. A bit of a shocker seeing me as freckled teenager. I was never pretty. Ruby was the good looking one even if she was smaller. Walter a young kid always hanging around the pool.

I have flicked through what feels like hundreds of pictures so I move to the videos. I click play on the first one and I'm transported back to a family barbecue at the house in Nairobi. This time I focus on the guests' faces. They are familiar but I don't recall names. The clothes so dated and predictable with plain chinos and flowery shirts. The quality is a little poor, especially when I press pause to see the group in one shot. I'm pretty sure that one of those faces is that of a younger Nigel Davies. I keep going through them and he pops up in a few. I also think I've found the tall skinny figure of Henrik Dahl. None of this is anything useful. I could have done with it two weeks ago but it still doesn't say much.

I check the dates of the videos and pick one of the later ones. As soon as I click play I recognise it. I've already seen this video in the refuge evidence folders. So Dad had it too. Even with the blurred stills and the confusing action as it's playing I can see the horror of it. In a court with a strong witness it is compelling. Enough for a scandal and for someone watching to be convinced it's real but maybe not sufficient to convict formally given how hard it is to get a rape conviction.

This is the evidence Dad had on Nigel Davies. This is what kept Davies from demanding that money back or even getting him locked up.

Ruby returns with a drink and sits beside me.

'It's all here, Ruby.' I say. 'I'm afraid Dad was present at some horrible assaults. He was part of it just as we talked about yesterday. I don't think he did anything but he saw it and did nothing.'

'But why would he do nothing? He recorded it and watched. How could he?'

'I wish I knew, I wish I knew.'

We hug. I don't show her the videos. I think she is happy to never see them and content herself with the father she remembers. I wish I could do the same.

'I best get off,' she says, 'Jake's got the kids and I don't want to leave him too long.'

I let her go without protest. I can read between the lines but that's her business to manage. I have mine to handle.

# CHAPTER 31

## ∞ § ∞

Later, I take the train back to London. With the house stripped I don't want to stay there. I'd rather go back to the new place. It's beginning to feel like mine.

It is very dark as I walk round to the entrance hall and I feel some of that paranoia from Nairobi. I am relieved when I get to the lights of the foyer. I open my mailbox and surprised to have mail. It's an envelope. Pearl McCann written on the front. No address so it's been hand delivered.

I take it up to the apartment, not wanting to hang around in the hall.

Once through the door I open it. It's handwritten.

'Miss McCann, a car will be waiting for you at 9:00 tomorrow. I believe we have some business to conclude.'

I look out the window and down to the street. Nothing stands out but in this glass bowl I feel a bit like a goldfish. Nigel Davies knows about this place. Perhaps I shouldn't be surprised. Perhaps he has known about it longer than I have. But I feel his eyes on me and for first time I close the blinds.

Will I go tomorrow? Will it be safe? I honestly don't know. But I can't miss the opportunity to conclude this. A meeting with Nigel Davies is what I wanted and now I have it.

***

The driver asks me for my phone as I get into the car. I comply as I guess this is going to be a discreet meeting. I've already sent Terry a link to all the documents and told him about the message. So I have my leverage in case the conversation goes darker than I hope. Other than that, I lean back in the comfortable leather seats of the Range Rover and wonder what he could possibly want to say to me.

We pull into a remote farmhouse somewhere along the A27 in Sussex. There is a short dirt track drive and the house is secluded by trees. A nowhere kind of place and probably useful to hide out in.

The driver opens a door at the back of the house and points me towards the conservatory. Inside, a small table is kitted out neatly with drinks. More interestingly already sitting there is Beatrice Lovane or should I call her Laila. She half smiles and I see she looks as uncomfortable as me. I sit at a seat in the bay window. Looking out through the window, I see a stone patio and a long manicured garden. In the distance I see the coastline and the sea. A room with a view. So Nigel Davies, the proceeds of a comfortable retirement.

The man himself appears a moment later, this time more casual in blue trousers and an open necked white shirt.

'Help yourself to drinks,' he says.

I pour some water and Bea takes the same.

He pours a gin and adds some tonic. It feels too civilised.

Now he is sits in an armchair and leans forwards, looking at both of us in turn.

'I've asked both of you to join me here as I feel we have a mutual interest in resolving some issues between us.'

'You're the one with the issues,' Bea says. 'Me and Pearl are all fine.'

I stare at Bea talking for me. She's in a flowery dress today with a large red scarf. It suits her better.  If she wants to be aggressive then fine. But let's see where it's going first.

'Oh really. Maybe we should discuss your numerous identities and please remember you are still a wanted convict in Nairobi. And Miss McCann here has already lied to the Police. Ladies we all have our problems to manage.'

'My problems don't involve raping teenage girls.' I say, taking the same line as Bea. I like making Davies nervous and it shows our power.

He holds his hands out flat in a calming motion.

'Be careful ladies. I fear we've got off on the wrong foot. Let's just say we can all make life a little difficult for each other. And we can make things a little easier as well.'

'What's the point of this,' I ask? 'We can't walk away and shake hands, pretend this never happened. Too much is out of our control, even if we wanted to.'

'Yes, you are right. The stunt you pulled in Nairobi has rather created a problem.' It's amazing how he is talking without anger. I recall his outburst when I met him two weeks ago, but today he is all civility and pretend charm. There must be a catch coming.

'I rather believe we all have something invested in a positive outcome. As I say we all have something to make life difficult for the others. So perhaps I propose we agree to suspend hostilities, we can all then go back to whatever normal life we desire and manage our affairs appropriately.'

'But you're a paedophile,' Beatrice says before I can, 'that doesn't come into the category of inconvenience. You raped friends of mine and you have sticky fingers all over a murder.'

'You see, there you go again,' he says. 'You're taking completely the wrong attitude to this conversation. I don't want us to get into a confrontation. It might not end well for me but nor for you ladies. It could be costly and as we have seen, there can be consequences outside of our control.'

I look out the window over the bay. The perfect English life contained in one view. Yet inside, a perfect English lie.

'My price is the truth,' I say. 'I want you to give me the truth about my Dad. And you Bea, I want the truth from both of you. If I get it, I'm happy to walk out of here and as long as you stay away from me and my family, you won't hear from me again.'

'You can't agree to that,' Bea says. 'I don't agree to it. That betrays those girls you marched with.'

'You do what you want,' I say, 'but you owe me a lot of explanations. And you already betrayed those girls by being here and lying to me.'

This is a nightmare.

'We all have to agree,' he says, 'otherwise there is no point. Pearl, if I can call you that, I remember you as a child growing up. You were always so sensible, so strong. I envied the passion in you. Your father was very proud of you.'

I feel sick him talking about me in such terms. He turns to Beatrice.

'Beatrice, I am sorry about what happened in my company. I am sorry about your friends. It was unacceptable and I apologise.'

He just apologised for rape. Like he was confessing to a bad night on the drink. I pour the whisky into a glass, I need something stronger to get through this.

'Say it,' Bea says, her voice wavering, 'say you raped me.'

I watch her. She is crying as she speaks but there is no missing the tension. Her history is far worse than I realise. Why didn't she tell me? Why didn't she save me all the heartache?

'Say it,' she says again. 'And whilst you are it, tell us both how you murdered Bernadette. How you let that poor innocent girl to die the street.'

She stands and grabs her bag ready to leave.

'Say it or am I out of this door. You raped me. You raped my friends. Say it now.' Bea is shaking and I think she's going to fall over. She moves to go round Davies's chair. He stands up blocking her.

'I'll give you both some time to think.' He says and leaves the room Beatrice sits again and pours a drink of water. She wipes her eyes.

'Bastard,' she says.

'Why Beatrice? Is that what I should call you?' I ask. 'Why didn't you tell me all this when I met you. I'm so sorry.'

'Call me Bea, I'm used to it now. I didn't tell you because you weren't ready to hear it. I would have told you in time, but I had to get away. I was upset when Spencer passed. And you needed to learn more about your father. You went a lot further than I ever expected. I guess you surprised me.'

'What you going to do about Davies?' I ask. 'You know you'll never get him in a court or you would have done it already.'

'I just wanted to hear it from his mouth. I wanted him to suffer for what he did. What the others did.'

I look to the hallway and wonder how long I have alone with her. I decide to take my chances.

'Seeing as we are in an honest speaking mode. Tell me about you and my Dad. What did you do?'

She pours vodka on top of her water and takes a big gulp.

'Spencer was a good man,' she says, 'don't read too much into him mixing with people like Davies. He was stuck with them in Kenya, but he wasn't one of them.'

'He was the first man I had sex with,' she says, 'but you see he was gentle with me. I was scared and he took his time. I was of age. Like the others you probably met, we came from the slums. Sex was money and I was told I was pretty. It wasn't all that bad as long as I did what the men wanted. So I did.'

I nurse the drink in my hand and try not to cringe at what she is saying. Prostitutes as well as money laundering. And she talks of him as a good man.

'Spencer looked out for me. He couldn't do anything you know that don't you? If he had intervened there would have been consequences. He felt terribly guilty most of the time. Gave me extra cash and gifts to try and get out of it. I don't think he went with any other girls after me. Maybe I was such a bad fuck or something,' she jokes.

'The others weren't kind,' she says as her smile fades.

'One day he suggested something. He said he could provide some money for me if I could run away. I told him he was crazy. He bought a house and said anytime we wanted we could go there. He would take care of all expenses. I was too scared to run. All of us were. Then Bernadette was killed and we saw our futures then. After that night I ran away. Went to the safe house. Spencer came to visit. Not for sex I will add. He never went near me after that. He just brought me what I needed.'

'How did you get involved with Angels charity?'

'I didn't know about that for a while. He got me a new name, Beatrice, so I could get away. Angels was some kind of cover name he used. It was all his idea.'

'Eventually we persuaded more women to join us and we had to set up a bigger place. He needed more money.'

'But they found out and you were in trouble?'

'That's where it all went wrong. Spencer had to leave. But I guess you know that already. But what I didn't know is that Spencer hadn't just been paying us money. He had taken millions of dollars over the years. I didn't find that out until later. We dispersed as a group. Some women went to the refuge that you found, others took money and ran like me. I got a new passport and moved around getting work and trying to live a life. When your dad became ill and your mum died, your dad paid for me to come to the UK. I looked after him and he provided me with a decent income. There is little more to know, to be honest.'

It all makes sense, I suppose. Dad was stealing money but it is unclear why because not all the money he used went to the girls. He kept some for his own use and then never used it. Maybe it was his bit of rebellion against the people he worked with. A way of taking something from them. I wonder if he felt trapped by his life. He was in too deep.

'I can't tell you what to do, Bea,' I say to her, 'But I think we both need to leave this all behind.'

I stop talking when Nigel Davies comes back in the room. He pours another drink.

'Hope you've had time to reconsider my proposal,' he says.

I look to Bea. She shakes her head.

'No or yes,' I ask her.

She nods. I think I understand. She doesn't want to speak to him.

'We need some guarantees,' I say.

'I would have thought nothing changes,' he says, 'you still have what you have. I have what I have, surely that closes the matter.'

I wonder. There is little now he can do to us without hurting himself.

'No more calls on my family. No more bailiffs. Whatever money my father took will be put to a charity, perhaps for the protection of these women you and your like abused.'

I look at Bea and she nods again.

'Seems a reasonable outcome.'

'Then our business is completed. Your driver will take us back?'

'Of course,' he replies. He is sullen, looks to have aged in the conversation. No longer the man who threatened me.

I get up and Bea follows my lead.

'How is your dear lady wife?' I ask. He stares back but doesn't reply to my windup. I guess that tells me everything.

The driver escorts us to the car and we head back.

Neither of us speak for a while. Our thoughts our own. The car drops me off first.

'Where will you go now?' I ask.

She shrugs. 'Home,' she says after a moment.

'And where's that?'

'Don't think you really want to know,' she says.

More than that, she doesn't want to tell me but I'm not going to press.

'If you want anything, you know where to find me.'

We hug. I don't think we will see each other again. As with Davies, our business is done.

# CHAPTER 32

∞ § ∞

A week later I take Terry to the Indian restaurant opposite the conservative club.

A last meal before I go back to Africa.

'So Bea was looking out for Spencer,' he says, between large mouthfuls of Lamb Madras.

'Yes. She didn't take any money because she didn't need to. What does it tell you about trusting black women?

'Yeah, whatever,' he says. 'But you got to see it from my point of view.'

I look back sternly and he gives up.

'What you going to do with all the money then?'

'What I said I would. I'm going to give it to the refuge and other places like it. It will take some time to manage because I will need to establish some ethical credentials and appoint some trustees to manage it.'

'You got to keep some for yourself though.'

'I don't need money. I've paid off all Ruby's debts. You'll never want for money will you with the money I gave you. I have enough for me.'

'Yeah thanks for the cheque. Keep me in beer and curry forever. But don't you fancy an Island for yourself. You've earned it Pearl. Queen Pearl and her empire. Would suit you. You can have your special school trips where you can give your racism lectures and how to be a hero to poor guys like me.'

'Funny boy.'

Thing is, I could do many things. But I don't see myself being different. I'm desperate to get back to something proper and purposeful like before. Things were so much simpler. And maybe once I am knackered then there is something left to enjoy. Plus I will keep my home in London.

'I see, Davies has resigned his seat.'

'And Lady Studenham has retired her marriage.' I reply.

'Cheers to that,' Terry says, raising his pint of beer. 'Still think he should be behind bars.'

'And so should Dad have been.'

'Yeah but the police told you they were not going to proceed with your case.'

'Doesn't mean that Dad was not guilty. But without Davies acting as a witness they didn't have a case against me.'

'Too right, honestly they should be giving you a medal.' He says.

'Not for me,' I say. 'If anyone should be given one it's those girls who overcame their fears to protest in Nairobi. They are the Angels.'

And that's it. They get the Angel's Share. That's where the money will go. I take a sip of bourbon and silently drink to Dad and the Angels.

THE END

# Acknowledgements

This story is inspired by Diane Moody. I first met Di in the early 1990s whilst we were both on a course for NHS Managers where she worked in health promotion. During the course she went to Bangladesh for a month working with communities out there on heart disease prevention. I knew then that her attitude to life ambitions were unlike anyone else I knew. This was the work she had always wanted to do. Diane sadly passed away in 2017 of natural causes in her home in Juba, South Sudan. She was the Country Manager for the Norwegian Red Cross.

Even before she passed away, I always imagined using her story as the basis of a character. I joked to her that she should write a book of her life. She had so many stories to tell. So from Di, I decided on Pearl. Di was a completely different personality and had nothing of the arrogance and self-righteousness of Pearl. She did, however, share Pearl's passion for what she was doing and a love for Africa and its people.

Two things struck me about her approach to life. One was whenever we met up, which was maybe once or twice in a year, if she was in London, we would talk as if it was only yesterday we had last been for dinner. And when she departed, it was always like it would be tomorrow when we would see each other again. She wasn't one for melancholy or drama.

The second significant trait was her attitude to the places and people she supported. She would talk about being in Harare, Windhoek and Johannesburg in the sense I would talk about a trip to the shops. She would go to remote events in Kenya, holiday on her own in Zanzibar or Goa for weeks at a time. It was routine, undramatic and a sense that people were the same everywhere. Like Pearl, she could list the inventory of Countries she had worked in like a dictionary. As part of her role at the Red Cross she was on the emergency disasters team going out to Pakistan after major floods, Haiti after the hurricane disaster and most recently to Nepal after an earthquake. Extraordinary commitment and fearless in going into these disaster zones.

She saved her first loves for her friends dotted in various corners of the world, Radio 4, (her companion in her lonely adventures), a good book, red wine, the sun and the beach. Her weekends in her Juba apartment were spent by the pool at the back of her complex in 35 degree sun.

In writing the book I needed Pearl to challenge the reader a little more. Di was humble, never complained for a second about her life, nor did she brag or seek reward. She just got on with it as it was what she wanted to do. She also realised that the choice of life style was hers alone and didn't impose any expectation on others. Pearl needed to more disruptive and angry for this story to succeed.

Naturally some of the locations in the book were inspired by Diane's stories, including her lovely apartment on Deptford High Street and hopefully I do them justice. My final hope is to inspire in the reader that whilst Pearl may not endearing to you personally with her bad habits and hang-ups, women like Pearl and Di exist. Not everyone fits into the neat square box of life and it's ok to want to do something different and still find happiness and satisfaction. Diane reminded me in conversation that Juba was her home not London, despite the wall of her Juba apartment having holes caused by gunshots. That told me everything.

Thanks as always to my writing friends determined to squeeze more books from me, to Nina for her picky editing and to those who have the patience to read and comment on my variable work. Without any of you I wouldn't be able to do this.

www.ingramcontent.com/pod-product-compliance
Lightning Source LLC
Chambersburg PA
CBHW070623100726
47907CB00007B/1836